Charlotte
Confederate
Cavalry
Soldier

ANGEL MATTHEWS

CONTENTS

ACKNOWLEDGMENTS

With the exception of historical figures,
all characters, letters, and conversations in this novel are of my own mind.
I have spent many hours researching, and I believe the conversations are true to the character of the historical figures.
I only hope I have done them justice.
As for the characters I have created, any resemblance to living people, present or past is coincidental.
With the exception of William Smith. He is based on my brother Steve (Pedro) Gauldin, a fair, honest, hardworking man that died at the age of 46 years and 2 months. I miss him every day.
I wish I could call him to say, I finished writing my book!
Jeremiah Turner is based on my husband. It would have been impossible to simply imagine the love Charlotte and Jeremiah share. I am blessed to know that kind of love.
I love you Grant Matthews!
I have tried to weave my characters around the real facts of history.
I must say, I haven't found any evidence to support the idea of a female amongst Mosby's Rangers. In the book, I have a story about General Grant having the Sheriff of Gibsonville removed. This also is fictitious.
The dates given for my fictitious characters are only there to help the reader understand what is going on in the lives of these characters.
The dates given for information concerning events in history are true and accurate to the best of my knowledge.

1 CHILDHOOD

February 24, 1843. Mama has been in labor for twenty-eight hours, she's having a hard time. She was a very small and frail woman. Aunt Polly was with her and tending her. Aunt Polly softly talked to her, calming and encouraging her. Mama called Aunt Polly, Sissy. Aunt Polly called Mama, Ms. Abby. Aunt Polly, being older, had been with Mama all of her life. She now feared she would be there at her death.

No doctor was coming. Aunt Polly was a midwife. When there was a neighbor woman nearby having a baby, they would send for her. She knew things like how to make us better when we're sick, feeling bad, and especially giving birth.

Aunt Polly was a year older than Mama. She wasn't tiny and frail, she was a large woman, a good deal taller than Mama, and a good deal heavier too.

The head of the bed was to the north, the feet to the south. It was situated like that because of the superstition, or "old wives tale", that you sleep better that way. In the northeast corner of the room was a cradle, with Aunt Polly's baby, Sara, quietly sleeping. Aunt Polly had been in the cradle in the room when my Mama was born, just like Sara was now, waiting on me.

The smell of oak wood, which was burning in the fireplace, hung in the air. Aunt Polly was opening jars of herbs and using a mortar and pestle to crush them, adding the smell of herbs to the scent of the burning wood. Willow bark crushed and mixed with water was given to Mama to help get her fever down. Black cohosh mixed with water was also given to her, to help the contractions push me out, and to help stop the bleeding.

It was snowing on the day I was born. Right before I arrived into the world, Aunt Polly heard thunder. She knew the thunder meant snow again within ten days. She also took the thunder snow as a sign that everything was going to be alright. She covered the mirror, she said mirrors attract lightning.

There was mistletoe already in the room for good luck. Now it would help protect us from the lightning also. She knew all the "old wives tales".

Daddy and Uncle Henry were in the parlor talking and waiting. Uncle Henry had brought a couple of their cigars. They smoked and waited.

These were cigars from last summer's tobacco crop. Daddy was impressed and commented to Uncle Henry that these were the best yet.

Finally, I arrived, big and loud! I cried so loud I woke Sara.

Aunt Polly cleaned me up, swaddled me and laid me in Mama's arms. She continued to tend to Mama. Poor Mama was so weak, she had lost a lot of blood, and now her fever had gotten worse.

Aunt Polly had told her to sleep, "I'll take care of this big girl."

Aunt Polly picked up Sara and sat in the rocking chair beside Mama. She unbuttoned her blouse, revealing her breasts. She held Sara to one and me to the other. Mama was too sick to feed me. Aunt Polly whispered, "I reckon y'all two will be sisters too, just like your Mamas."

After feeding us babies, Aunt Polly lay Sara in the cradle and took me into the parlor to meet my daddy and Uncle Henry.

Daddy was amazed at how big I was. He was worried for Mama.

Aunt Polly said to Uncle Henry, "Go get Lorett." Lorett was the wife of the blacksmith that worked for Daddy. "See if she can come tend the house, whilst I tend to Ms. Abby and the babies."

Two days after I was born, the doctor stopped by. He asked, "Aunt Polly, what are you giving her?"

Aunt Polly replied, "White willow bark for a fever, black cohosh and cinnamon to stop bleeding."

The doctor nodded and said, "Very good, she seems to be doing well, all we can do is wait. I'll be stopping by during my normal rounds in a week, send for me if you need me sooner." He looked over at Daddy and said, "As big, loud, and hungry as that baby is, I think she'll be just fine."

Mama, Aunt Polly, Sara, and me all shared that bedroom for the first month of my life. Aunt Polly took care of all of us.

Mama recovered slowly. Aunt Polly continued to tend to us and nurse me along with Sara. Mama never was well enough to nurse me. Aunt Polly had always said, it was a miracle that me and Mama lived.

From the moment I was born, I had two Mamas. I was born on a Friday. Aunt Polly always said, Friday's child is loving and giving. Sara was born on a Tuesday. Tuesday's child is full of grace.

As Mama got better, Lorett was sent home, and Aunt Polly tended the house with me and Sara always close by.

When Aunt Polly would take us outside with her to do the laundry, Sara was always content to just sit in the grass and play with her baby doll.

Me? I wanted to crawl away, I guess I wanted to see what was going on.

As I got older, Aunt Polly would sit me on Buttercup. Buttercup was an old palomino broodmare. She had given birth to ten or so babies. I reckon the mama in her just took over when Aunt Polly would sit me on her back. There wasn't a saddle or bridle when I was a baby. I would just sit on her and she would slowly walk around, keeping me happy. Aunt Polly always told me that many times she would look up and I would be lying down, sleeping on Buttercup's back as she walked around.

As I got older, I would get Buttercup to go further away than Aunt Polly thought I should. Aunt Polly would call and call for me to come back. I would act like I couldn't hear her, so she would call to Buttercup and she would bring me back to Aunt Polly. All of these things were told to me as I grew up.

I think my first memory was sharing an apple with Buttercup. I would take a bite, let Buttercup take a bite, and then I would take another bite, and so on.

Aunt Polly saw what I was doing, swatted me on the behind and said, "Don't be eating after that filthy animal. Now you get inside and get cleaned up, you smell like a horse."

I replied, "I like the way a horse smells, and Buttercup is not a filthy animal!"

Aunt Polly sternly looked at me and said, "Girl, don't you sass me!"

I replied, "Yes ma'am, I'm sorry Aunt Polly."

I still like the smell of a horse. I just never said that to Aunt Polly again. I still share apples, but now I take a bite, then give the horse the rest of the apple.

Aunt Polly was a proud woman.

She would tell me, "Your Uncle Henry likes a big woman."

She could cook better than anybody in the world. I learned to cook by being in the kitchen and helping her. She took care of all of us. She seemed to like to work and get things done. I rarely saw her sit and sew, like Mama did all of the time. She had fancy clothes, she just said they weren't practical for wearing every day while working. Aunt Polly wore an apron and she had her hair up in the back and covered all day.

When she sat down at the table for supper she was dressed as fine as everybody else. She was a kind, loving woman that liked to smile.

She would say things like, don't rock an empty rocking chair, it invites evil spirits. When you make your bed, make sure the open end of the pillow case is to the inside, so evil spirits can't come from under the bed and get into your pillowcase, and your dreams. Don't stand on a bridge and say goodbye to someone you want to see again, if you do, you won't ever see them again. Don't sweep under the bed of a sick person, they will die. Don't take an old broom to a new house. If the sunset is red, the weather will be clear, if it's yellow, it's gonna rain. If you tell a dream before breakfast, it will come true. If a girl leaves cobwebs on the kitchen door, her sweetheart won't come back. She had a saying for just about everything you could think of.

Don't cross her on it either, she didn't think it was funny and would swat your behind!

She wasn't the proper lady that Mama was, but she seemed really happy. Her smile was real. She taught me manners, she was quick to swat my behind and make me act like somebody, as she would say.

Many times I would hear her tell Mama, "I declare, I think those girls got mixed up as babies. I would swear that Charlotte is my daughter and Sara is yours."

Mama would laugh and say, "Sissy, I do believe you are right."

Aunt Polly always had something cooking, of course there was always coffee on the stove. Daddy and Uncle Henry would come in the kitchen for some coffee, and never left without eating something.

She would ask, "You men just want coffee or y'all want something to eat with that?"

Daddy always answered, "You don't get to be a fat man by turning down good grub, what do you have in here today?"

There might be stews, biscuits, ham, bacon, cobblers, cookies, cakes... you never knew what she felt like cooking, you did know that whatever it was, it would be good. She would make little hard candies, with white sugar, honey, cinnamon, and cloves. Daddy would always have a small bag of these with him, he said they were good for a cough. He mostly liked to take them with him when he and Uncle Henry would visit the farm workers. The children would come out and wait for him to get off of his horse and they would wait their turn as he handed out the candies.

They would giggle and say, "Thank you Uncle William." Daddy loved that.

On Aunt Polly's table there was always honey, molasses, preserves of all kinds, pickled peaches, and fresh churned butter. Most of the time, it was more fun to eat in the kitchen than the dining room, I reckon because it felt like it was full of love.

Mama wanted me to be a lady, this was torturous to me. She would have me and Sara dress like ladies and come down for tea, then there was study time. After a couple of hours of book learning, we would start sewing. Learning to cross-stitch, how to mend socks, how to make a dress, how to make a shirt. The entire time all I wanted to do was go to the stables with Daddy and Uncle Henry.

Mama would always correct me, saying, "You shouldn't say ain't, you should say isn't."

I would always say, "If I say "isn't", people will think I'm uppity, you and Sara are the only people I know that say isn't."

Aunt Polly would swat my behind and tell me to apologize to Mama.

"I'm sorry Mama." I would quickly say.

Mama was the only child of her parents to live to be an adult. She was about five feet tall, around one hundred pounds, had an hourglass figure, with a tiny waist. She always wore her hair up and always had on makeup. Only a little bit, so as to look naturally beautiful, as she would say. Mama was a beautiful woman.

Her daddy had inherited a large fortune and vast amounts of land from his wife's family. Mama was a lady in every sense of the word. She had been taught to be a proper wife. Keep your place, keep opinions to yourself, mind your manners, and please your husband in every way. She knew how to run a household, how to dance, how to entertain, and most importantly, how to be charming and graceful in every situation. She was the picture of a Victorian Lady of Society.

My daddy loved her dearly, in spite of all that!

Her parents were disappointed in her wanting to marry Daddy. He didn't have enough money to suit them. He wasn't in the same social class, however, he was honest and hardworking. They knew he loved her, so they finally agreed to the marriage. He wouldn't take anything from them. Grandfather offered money to help get them started, but Daddy refused.

My grandparents had moved to Paris, France, before I was born. It seemed as though they just didn't care for America. They thought people in Paris were more cultured. They would send me the most grand gifts. When I was younger it was mostly dolls and such, but as I got older they would send jewelry, furs, ball gowns, and fancy shoes, always the latest fashions from Paris.

When I was about five years old I realized they weren't sending these things to Sara. I refused to accept any more gifts unless they would send Sara the same things, which they did. It was wonderful to get packages from them, but I would have rather had grandparents.

Mama never stopped trying to make me into a lady.

I would always say, "I'm happy with who I am."

Once Aunt Polly said, "You ain't never gonna get a man if you don't start acting like a lady."

I told her, "I don't need a man!"

Aunt Polly said, "You're young and stupid, now shut that smart mouth of yours and mind your manners!"

Like always, I quickly replied, "Yes ma'am."

Sara was the exact opposite of me, she loved being a lady. She was small like Mama, and hung onto every word Mama said. She spent all of her time with Mama. Sara was like Mama's shadow, and Mama loved it too.

Thinking back, I don't ever remember Aunt Polly swatting Sara's behind. One time Sara was on the front porch with Mama, sewing something, like always. Aunt Polly came out and told Sara she needed her to come do a chore or something.

Sara rudely said, "I'm helping Aunt Abby!"

Aunt Polly was ready to skin her good.

Mama reached over, lightly patted Sara's hand, and said, "Sara, a lady always minds her manners. Now apologize to your mother."

Sara softly said, "I'm sorry Mama." She had tears in her eyes. She was so small and timid, she looked pitiful. I reckon she was worried she had disappointed both of them.

Mama asked Aunt Polly, "Sissy, isn't there anyone else you can get to help you? Sara is helping me right now."

Aunt Polly said, "Yes, Ms. Abby," and went on about her business.

Sara looked at Mama with those tears in her eyes. Mama wiped away the tears, smiled and said, "Don't fret, now let's get back to what we were doing."

I believe that was the only time Sara ever got into trouble.

Sara was one month older than me. She was quiet, but was always eager to listen and learn. She was too delicate for chores or riding horses, so she spent her days with Mama. I always looked out for her. She was older but it felt like she was the baby of the family. Her bedroom was right beside mine. Many nights we would both lay in my bed or hers talking and giggling.

Daddy would holler, "Y'all better hush up, don't make me come in there!"

We would quickly go to our own rooms and get to sleep.

Sara wanted to be a fine lady, just like Mama. She was always asking Mama questions. Whatever Mama was doing, Sara was doing it too. I reckon I was that way with Aunt Polly. Sara would giggle and squeal, she was so prissy. She too, had long hair, and always wore it up. She loved wearing the fancy dresses her and Mama would make. She loved lace. I don't think they made her one dress that didn't have lace on it. She would spend time every morning getting prim and proper before coming down to breakfast. I just wanted to get outside as quick as I could.

We did spend a lot of time together, playing, going to the stables. She always complained about the smell. She liked rubbing the horses, but she didn't care for riding them. I liked riding. Mama didn't know it, but I had become a decent horse rider. Mama liked making riding habits for me, I think she liked seeing me ride sidesaddle. I liked riding like Daddy. He made me promise not to tell Mama. When I was about ten years old, he let me start working out the race horses.

He had some fast horses, and the faster they ran, the more I liked it.

My daddy, William Smith, was a large man, a bit heavy. He had blond hair, brown eyes, and loved to smile and laugh. He was calm, patient, and kind. Daddy had a reputation for being fair and honest. If he told you something, believe it!

Mama and Daddy had been married about ten years before I was born. I was the only child they would have.

Daddy and Uncle Henry were a lot alike. You would think they were brothers instead of Uncle Henry being Aunt Polly's husband. Most of the time they were together in the fields, the garden, or riding off to the other parts of the farm to check on the workers. They both had always worked hard to make the farm profitable, now it was starting to pay off.

Daddy had acquired a lot of smaller farms. Some would call his place a plantation, but he never did. He said it sounded like putting on airs. He was just a farmer that happened to be doing well at the time.

A few years before, Daddy, Mama, Uncle Henry, and Aunt Polly went to a pig pickin' at the home of the Slade family in Caswell County. While they were there, Uncle Henry was told of a mistake made while curing tobacco. By adding a blast of heat after the curing had started, the tobacco turned a beautiful golden yellow, had a sweetness to it, and was mellow when smoked. Uncle Henry wasted no time in telling Daddy.

Daddy went to work buying up the small farms around his, borrowing money against his farm, with the faith that it would pay off. When he finished using all the money he could borrow, he had about fifteen hundred acres.

They then went to work building more tobacco barns to cure the tobacco, and packhouses to store it in before taking it to market.

They planted tobacco in every field. That year when he sold his tobacco it sold for four times the amount of the year before. The tobacco was called bright leaf. Before bright leaf, tobacco from North Carolina wasn't considered to be very good and never brought a good price.

Daddy and Uncle Henry used the little farms Daddy had bought, differently than most other farmers around us. They put the skilled workers in the main house of each farm. People like the blacksmith, wheelwright, saddle maker, cooper, and so on. At each farm the smaller houses were for the field workers. Each person in the main house kind of oversaw the field workers, directing them on the work for each day.

Daddy and Uncle Henry would ride the farm about twice a week to make sure things were going well. Of course it took a couple of days to complete each trip.

Aunt Polly said, "Them trips take so long because them men are so long-winded. They'll talk all day."

Daddy liked to work in the garden. He loved growing things. He always planted hot peppers, never ate any, he just liked growing them.

He would joke and say, "To get really hot peppers, plant them when you're real mad." and then he would laugh.

He also liked to race horses. He just had fun breeding, raising, training them, and then seeing what they could do in a race. It was fun for him.

Uncle Henry was serious about racing. He would get mad as a hornet if their horse lost.

Daddy would always laugh and say, "I'm here to have fun, win or lose."

I guess Daddy's biggest flaw was he liked to cuss, and he did it very well. Mama was the only person I never heard him cuss around. Yes, he would even cuss around the preacher.

He was just being himself. I reckon Mama had expressed her dissatisfaction of hearing such words, so he made sure she didn't have to.

Daddy and Uncle Henry rolled cigars. They cured some of the tobacco differently for the cigars. I remember everybody always wanted to buy some.

Daddy would just smile and say, "How 'bout you come over and we'll enjoy a cigar, a drink, and maybe share a story or two?"

Uncle Henry had made a fine cedar box for keeping the cigars in. They also made a bit of wine and sippin' whiskey. Not a lot, just enough to have when the gentlemen retired to smoke and drink after supper.

Sometimes on quiet summer evenings, Daddy and Uncle Henry would sit on the front porch, smoking a cigar, and tasting the wine, or sippin' the whiskey. They were always talking about what could be done to make things better. I still remember the smell of cedar and tobacco, a hint of whiskey or wine in the air, as me and Sara would run around catching lightning bugs. Sara would always squeal when she would catch one. In the distance most of the time we could hear a bobwhite quail. They'd sound like they are calling out, "bob...White!". I suppose that's how they got their name.

Once I heard Daddy telling Uncle Henry, "I've heard alcohol is a gift from God. Drunkenness is from the devil. I do believe God has blessed us with the know how to make this fine wine and whiskey. Let's pray the devil don't jump in here and mess it up, it surely would be a sad thing not to have the pleasure of sharing these things with you."

Uncle Henry just nodded his head and said, "Yes, Willie, that would be a sad thing."

Uncle Henry was a large man, I guess he was about as tall as Daddy, not quite as heavy.

He had dark hair, dark brown eyes, and he, like Daddy, laughed and smiled a lot. They were always together working, joking with each other, and having a good time. You could tell they respected each other.

Uncle Henry was a smart man. I'd bet there was nothing he couldn't do. If something was broke, he would fix it. Sometimes he would have to make a part so he could fix something. Many times he would go to the blacksmith shop and make a tool or a part to fix what he was working on.

One time Daddy brought home a brand new carriage. It was beautiful, white with blue seats. It was called a vis-à-vis. That's a carriage that has a seat up front for the driver, with two bench seats in the back facing each other, for the passengers. It had a top that could be put down.

Sara and I were so excited to get in it. We climbed up in the carriage, our skirts mashed up against each other. By this time the fashion was to wear large hoop skirts.

Daddy said, "I reckon the carriage makers can't keep up with the changing ladies styles, huh, Henry? If it was a bit longer they would like it better. I reckon we'll catch an earful about wrinkled skirts."

Uncle Henry walked around the carriage, looking at it and studying it, he stepped up and bounced on it. Walked around a little more, crawled under it. Then he stood up and said proudly, "Willie, I can make it longer!"

Daddy laughed real big and loud, then said, "This is a brand new carriage. How do you plan to make it longer, without destroying it?"

Uncle Henry said, "Well see, if I saw it in half right here..." but before he could say anything else.

Daddy said loudly, "Saw it in half! I can't afford to saw a new carriage in half!" laughing the whole time.

"Henry, this carriage cost me four hundred and fifty dollars."

Uncle Henry said, "Willie, listen to me for a minute, I know I can do it. Here's how."

They talked awhile, and soon Daddy stopped laughing and started asking questions.

The next thing we knew, they had the carriage in the barn and Uncle Henry was sawing it in half. For two days, the neighbor men came by to "gawk", as Daddy called it.

They would laugh, and one said, "William, I can't believe you let him tear up that new carriage."

Daddy puffed up, grinned and said, "Tear it up? Hell, he's making it better!"

On the third day they pulled the new, longer carriage out of the barn, two horses hitched up to it.

Daddy said, "We have to go into town." He leaned back on the rear seat with a cigar in his mouth, then he asked, "Henry, you ready?"

Uncle Henry was up in the driver's seat and said, "Yea Willie, I'm ready."

Daddy said, "No wait. We'll get a driver and you kick back in this other seat, enjoy a cigar with me, and ride in style."

Uncle Henry said, "That's the best idea I've heard all day!"

Daddy hollered for Sam. Sam was the driver that normally drove us when Daddy or Uncle Henry weren't available. Sam came over, jumped up in the driver's seat and off they went. Daddy wanted to show off the carriage, but I think mostly he wanted to brag on Uncle Henry. When they got to the store, the neighbor men agreed it was longer, but said it would break, right there in the middle, when it was loaded.

Daddy said, "Oh hell no it won't, all y'all get up in here." When the carriage was as full as Daddy could get it. He said, "Sam, drive us around the block."

They rode around and the carriage held. That convinced them. After that day people believed Uncle Henry could fix near about anything. People talked about that for years.

2 THE AWAKENING

Growing up, I was surrounded by a family that loved me. As a child I never once heard the word nigger or slave.

When I was around fourteen years old, my daddy's brother Lucas and his family came to visit.

Lucas told Uncle Henry, "Grab that bag boy!"

Uncle Henry said, "Yes sir," and picked up the bag.

Daddy told Uncle Henry, "Please put the bag down."

Uncle Henry did.

Daddy turned to Uncle Lucas and said, "Henry is not a boy. He is a man. A man that deserves respect, he is not to be given orders. If you want him to do something, all you have to do is ask in a respectful manner, just like you would be asking me, and he will be more than happy to do it for you. If you can't treat him and everybody else around here with respect, well, then just leave that bag where it is and y'all can leave."

Uncle Lucas said, "I'm sorry William. Henry, would you mind unloading my bags for me?"

Uncle Henry said, "I'd be happy to, Mr. Lucas."

Uncle Lucas' kids, my cousins Joshua and Abraham, were out back and I heard them talking about it and calling Uncle Henry and Aunt Polly niggers.

I asked, "What's a nigger?"

Joshua said smugly, "Well, you see, niggers are black people. Black people don't have souls, they are like animals and need white people to take care of them.

That's why we keep them as slaves. They work for us, and in return we take care of them, just like a dumb old horse or a cow." Then they both laughed.

Abraham then said, "Damn, you're stupid, I reckon you're as stupid as your daddy, treatin' niggers like they are somebody."

I was so mad! I jumped on both of them and starting beating them up pretty good. They began screaming and making an awful sounding ruckus. Aunt Polly came outside, yanked me off of them, whipped my butt, and sent me in the house. I never spoke to those cousins again.

What they said about Aunt Polly, Uncle Henry, Sara, and all of Daddy's workers wasn't true. Aunt Polly was Mama's sister. After all, Mama called her Sissy. Aunt Polly nursed me because Mama was too sick. She had a soul, a kind, loving soul. She loved me, and I loved her. I always thought her skin was darker than Mama's because Mama was sickly and hardly ever went outside. When she did go outside, she had a parasol with her, stayed on the porch, or in the shade of the trees. Aunt Polly was always outside, doing the laundry, tending Mama's flowers, and stuff like that. She never used a parasol.

I would go outside with Aunt Polly, Daddy, and Uncle Henry, and my skin started getting darker, I just thought it would get darker the more I was outside. Sara stayed with Mama most of the time and her skin wasn't as dark as Aunt Polly and Uncle Henry's. It wasn't as light as Mama's either, but I figured with enough time, it would be.

I didn't know that some people were born a different color and you stayed that way. I reckon I was quite ignorant. I had never heard such talk before, and I hated it!

As we got older, Sara and I spent less time playing, and more of our time together was spent walking along the flower gardens talking.

She liked the new blacksmith, George, and that seemed to be all she wanted to talk about. I hadn't seen any boy I cared to talk about. She was hoping to start courtin' George, but he would have to talk to Uncle Henry before that could happen. Oh, how she worried that her daddy would say no.

I said, "Why would Uncle Henry say no? He likes George."

She said, "Because George is five years older than me."

I asked, "When is George gonna talk to Uncle Henry?"

She said, "He's trying to figure out what to say. He's never asked a man if he could court his daughter."

I said, "Maybe George should talk to Daddy first, and Daddy could advise him on what he should say to Uncle Henry."

She pondered on it for a second, then said, "That's a good idea. I'll talk to George about it in the morning."

It was January, 1859, and I was fifteen years old. Me, Mama, Aunt Polly, and Sara went to Paris, France. We were to visit my grandparents. We rode on a train, and then, luxury passage on a steamship. It took only eleven days to cross the ocean.

I saw my grandparents for the first time in my life. They were elegant. I think they might have thought Mama had let me act too much like my daddy. I didn't really care, I liked being like my daddy!

We went to the Louvre Museum. Oh, the things we saw! Leonardo Da Vinci's, Mona Lisa! Michelangelo's, Dying Slave Sculpture! It was a muscular, naked man.

I asked Mama, "Why is he naked?"

She ignored me.

I asked, "What's a slave?"

Mama said in a hushed voice, "A slave is somebody that works for you."

I said, "Oh, like Daddy's workers back home?"

"Yes," she replied, "exactly like Daddy's workers back home."

Quizzically, I asked, "Well, why do people call them slaves here, and workers back home?"

She said, "They call them slaves at home too."

I said, in what Aunt Polly would call, a smart tone, "I've never heard Daddy or Uncle Henry call them slaves."

She then firmly said, "We don't like talking about slaves."

In that same tone, I said, "I hear Daddy and Uncle Henry talking about the workers all the time."

Mama took me aside, and quietly told me, "Don't be silly, you know the black people that work for us are slaves. We own them, this is embarrassing, and you need to stop it right now young lady!" Mama started to walk away.

I said, "Mama I don't know! What do you mean own? You can't own a person!"

She turned and said sternly, "Charlotte, I'm telling you to be quiet!"

I said, "Are you saying, black people are niggers?"

Mama said, "Charlotte, don't say that word!"

I asked, "Mama, are you saying, Aunt Polly's not your sister, she's your slave?"

She said, "Yes Charlotte! Now hush!" Then she walked away.

I don't remember what else we saw that day. I just couldn't get what Mama had said out of my head.

We went back to my grandparents' home and had supper. Later, I went to Aunt Polly.

"What's a nigger?" I asked her, "What's a slave?"

Aunt Polly sat down beside me and said, "My, my! You must be the dumbest white girl in the world."

I asked, "Why would you say that?"

She said, "Charlotte, I am your mama's slave. I was born a slave, my job has always been to take care of Ms. Abby.

So when she married your daddy, me and Henry was a wedding gift to your mama."

I could feel tears running down my cheeks and stammered, "You're not Mama's sister?"

She smiled as she was wiping my tears away and said, "No, we just love each other like we were sisters, we grew up together."

I began crying even harder as I said, "But you were a gift, how can a person be a gift?"

Aunt Polly looked in my eyes and said, "I'm black, a nigger, a slave. I was owned by your grandparents and they gave me to your mama. I'm not a free person, I have to do what I'm told. I can be bought or sold, just like an animal."

I said, "My mean cousins, Joshua and Abraham, told me what a nigger was. They said you were a nigger."

Aunt Polly said, "Is that why you got in a fight with them last year?"

"Yes ma'am." I replied.

Aunt Polly hugged me real hard and said, "Lord love ya."

I said, "Aunt Polly, you're not a nigger."

She said, "I am."

I said, "Sara's not."

She said, "She is."

I said, "Sara is a slave?"

Aunt Polly said, "Yes."

I said, "I know you have a soul, just like me, you've always taken care of us, you ain't stupid," I continued, "all those things Joshua and Abraham said makes a person a nigger. You're telling me, you're a slave just because you're black?" I asked.

She replied with tears pouring down her face, "Yes child, that's why I'm a slave."

I had never seen Aunt Polly cry, and it broke my heart. My crying turned to sobbing.

Trying to understand, I asked, "The black people that work for my grandparents here in Paris, are they slaves?"

She said, "No, it's against the law to have slaves here."

I said, "So you can stay here and be free, and be just like a white person?"

She said, "Yes."

I said, "You and Sara need to stay here, and Uncle Henry can come be with you."

She said, "Charlotte, you just don't know how the world works. You know old man Johnson, just up the road back home?"

"Yes." I said.

She said, "You've seen his mule, how he treats that poor animal, don't hardly feed it, you see its bones all over, and he uses that whip, beatin' that poor thing, hollerin' for it to work harder. You know he's gonna work that animal until it dies in its harness, and then he's probably gonna be mad at it 'cause it dies. Some people treat slaves just like that. Now, your daddy treats us just like he treats his fine race horses. Now just hush up all this slave talk, it upsets your mama."

I said, "Yes ma'am."

Next, I go to Sara telling her, "You need to stay in Paris."

Sara starts to tell me what she knows of slavery. George, the new blacksmith that works for Daddy and Uncle Henry, has been at the farm for about two years now. Sara is sweet on him. They had shared glances and would talk. They had started courtin'.

George had told her where he came from.

She said, "He was born on a sugar plantation in Louisiana. He lived there until he was about six years old. He don't remember much, except everybody had to work hard from sun-up to sun-down. There was the constant fear of being beat. They were always hungry. He never had a daddy.

He did remember being pulled from his mother's arms as she begged for the Massa not to take her baby. He was scared and crying out for his mama. She was being hit over and over, and him clinging so tight to her that his arms hurt for days where the white man grabbed him tight enough to rip him away from her. The Massa didn't care."

I interrupted Sara and asked, "Sara, what's a Massa?"

Sara said, "Massa is the way some slaves say Master."

I said, "Master?"

She said, "Owner, like your daddy owns me, only he don't make us call him Master. We just call him Uncle William, or Mr. William."

I said, "Did George really tell you all this?"

She said, "Yes, let me finish." She continued, "The overseer didn't care. No white person cared. The other slaves were trying to comfort his mama. There was nobody to comfort him. His hands were tied and he was put in a wagon with the white man that pulled him from his mama. He said he will never forget the look and screams of his mama begging for her baby. After being in the wagon for a long while, he told the white man he had to pee. The man said nothing, and kept driving. George held it as long as he could, then he did it in his trousers. He lay in that wet wagon all day. No food, no water, and no compassion.

That night, when they got to where they were going, the white man was mad because George had peed in his trousers, and on the wagon.

He grabbed a hoe that was close by and beat George with it, yelling, "You filthy nigger, look what you did. I let you ride in my wagon and look what you did to it."

When George woke up the next morning, he hurt so bad he could hardly move.

The man came out and made him scrub the wood on the bed of the wagon. He then loaded George up and they head off again. George slept all of that day. He didn't know how many days they traveled. Then, one night when they stopped, he's taken out of the wagon and another white man comes up and tells a black woman to take the child inside. She takes him into a cabin, tells him her name is Lucy, and she says she will take care of him. She gives him some food and started heating up some water to clean him up, as he's covered in waste and dried blood."

I was shocked, I said, "Sara, that's the most horrible thing I've ever heard in my life."

She said, "Yes it is. So the white man in the wagon was a neighbor that was doing some business down in Louisiana. While there, he was to pick up a slave boy for Mr. Jones. That's who would own George now. Mr. Jones wanted a boy to help his blacksmith. He didn't know the boy would be treated so badly on the way to his plantation, and he was pretty mad at his neighbor too, but the man was just doing him a favor, so he couldn't say much about it. Lucy took care of George. After a few days of eating well and healing up, Mr. Jones came into the cabin.

Mr. Jones said, "George, you look well enough to me, from now on, you stay with the blacksmith, Noah. Noah's cabin is down at the end of the row of cabins, you'll see the blacksmith shop, he's expecting you."

George says, "Yes sir, Massa." and heads to the door.

Mr. Jones asked, "Don't you have anything you need to take with you?"

George said, "No sir, Massa, I don't have anything."

Mr. Jones says firmly, "George."

George stops and turns to face him and asks, "Yes sir, Massa?"

Mr. Jones said, "We're not hard on our niggers around here, as long as you work hard and do as you're told."

George answered, "Yes sir, Massa." as he stood there looking at Mr. Jones.

Mr. Jones said, "Run along now."

George said, "Yes sir, Massa." then left to go find Noah's cabin.

Noah was a stern, older man, with gray hair, and very muscular. That is where George would spend the next thirteen years. Noah teaching him how to be a blacksmith. He started by getting this and that, bringing the horses to Noah, taking the horses back, getting food ready for the both of them, then cleaning up the shop every evening. For a long time George felt like he was Noah's slave, but he learned everything Noah knew. George eventually became a fine blacksmith.

Noah was always telling him, "George, don't worry about the rest of them niggers, you worry about you and me. If we just keep to ourselves and don't bother any of them, maybe we won't be bothered. White folks sure hate for niggers to be talkin', we supposed to be workin'. If we workin' hard, nobody bother us. You remember that boy!"

George said, "Yes sir Noah, I'll remember."

After about thirteen years had passed, Mr. Jones died, his son got the plantation and sold all the slaves.

They were sent to the auction place. They stayed there about a week. The whole time white men came and went, looking them over, like our daddies look over a horse before they buy it.

That's when our daddies bought George, they were looking for a blacksmith. The white men at the slave auction took them to two slaves that were blacksmiths. One of them was George, the other blacksmith was a good deal older, so your daddy bought George.

On the ride home from Georgia, they all talked. George said he'd never been talked to by a white man like your daddy talked to him.

He said Uncle William talked to him like he was a man, not a nigger. He never saw a white man and a black man be so kind and respectful of each other like our daddies. They both explained to him how things worked at your daddy's farm.

Work hard, if you need or want anything, ask for it. Take care of what you have. Be respectful, mind your manners, get along, and you will always have a home, food, clothes... everything you need. When you get too old to work, you will be taken care of. This is your home. This is home to all of us, and we all work together to have what we need. If you can't do these things, you will be sold. Now, if you find a girl, get married, and have babies, it's your job to make sure your family follows the rules. If they don't, and you can't get it in hand, your entire family will be sold. We won't split up a family, it's ugly and wrong. We don't beat people, what's born in the bone can't be beat out the hide. Ask the other workers, they will tell you we are fair and honest. We don't use words like nigger and slave, and we don't put up with sorryness or bad attitudes. Everybody is to be treated with respect."

When Sara finished, I said, "You can't go back to America, you have to stay here and be free. If you stay, Aunt Polly will, then, when me and Mama get back home, we'll send Uncle Henry. Think of it, you could work for my grandparents, and be free."

Sara looked at me and asked, "How is staying here going to be better than going home?"

"You'll be free!" I exclaimed.

Sara said, "If I stay here, I'm just another nigger! At home, I'm Ms. Abby's seamstress."

I said, "But freedom, don't that mean anything to you?"

She said, "No it don't! I have it good at home. I've learned to sew. I can make any dress Ms. Abby wants. Sometimes I make dresses for the other ladies.

Ms. Abby pays me with some of the money she charges for the dresses. I save that money, I've got nearly fifty dollars. That's my money. Nobody gave it to me. I earned it!"

She got up and started to leave the room. Sara and I had never had a cross word, until now.

I said, "Sara, you could be a seamstress here, my grandparents would take care of you, just like I have."

She stopped and turned to me, she had a look in her eyes like she could've hit me. I have never seen anyone as mad as she was.

Sara shouted, "Take care of me? I take care of myself! I don't need you to take care of me. I've learned how to do things that make me valuable. When I get married to George, I will have servants to tend my house and cook. All I have to do is sew and make beautiful dresses. What do you know how to do, ride a horse? You need someone to take care of you. Do you have money? Can you do anything to earn money? No you can't! You just depend on your daddy to take care of you. Then you will find a rich man to marry and he will take care of you! Don't tell me that you take care of me!"

I said, almost begging, "Sara, I'm trying to save you!"

She said, "Save me from what? Marrying the man I love and being happy?"

I said, "Save you from slavery!"

She made a huffing sound and said, "Don't worry about me, you should worry about yourself!"

I asked, "What if George don't follow the rules and y'all are sold?"

She raised her head high and said, "I can never be sold."

I asked, "What makes you think that?"

She said, "I don't think it, I know it."

I asked, "How?"

26

She said, "George wouldn't court me, because he was scared to care about anyone. He asked, what if one of us got sold off? He said he would rather live life alone than go through the pain of being torn away from his family, like when he was a child. So I talked to Aunt Abby, and she gave me a paper saying me and mine can't be sold! See, I know how to take care of me. George and I are to be married this fall." Sara finished smartly.

I said, "I didn't know."

She said, "Nobody knows. It's against the law for me to have such papers. Aunt Abby said she would just give me my freedom papers, they call them manumission papers. The bad part is, if she sets me free, I have to leave within ninety days. The law says a freed slave has to leave the state of North Carolina. I don't want to leave. I talked with George about it and we decided we want to stay on your daddy's farm and have a family. Charlotte, you're my family, I love you. I don't want to be anywhere else. I think I'm the luckiest girl in the world. I have a wonderful family, a wonderful home, and somehow the good Lord got me together with George. What else could I possibly want?"

I quietly said, "Freedom."

She said, "What's freedom? I have more freedom than you."

I said, "I'm sorry Sara, I love you too. I just don't want anything bad to happen to you. Has Mama really done something illegal?" I asked.

She said, "Aunt Abby has been doing illegal things for years. It's against the law for her to teach me to read and write. That's why she always told us not to tell people that we have lesson time every day."

I asked, "Really?"

She said, "Yes ma'am."

I asked, "What would happen if she was caught teaching you?"

She said, "I don't know about the law, but I'm sure there would be hell to pay with the neighbors. George told me, white people, well, most white people don't want slaves learning. It scares them and they think the slaves will start to think for themselves and rise up against the slave holders. White folks are always worrying about that. It's also illegal for us to have money."

I said, "Oh, really?" I had never heard of such things.

The next morning, Mama came into my room, she sat on the edge of my bed, and gently stroked my hair.

She said, "Charlotte, Sissy told me about your conversation last night. I hope this is all done and over with. I don't want to hear another word about it. I also don't want your daddy to hear of it, do you understand?"

I said, "Yes ma'am."

Mama stood up and said, "Now, let's go down for breakfast, and see what Grandmother has planned for the day."

I sat up in bed and said, "Yes ma'am. I'll be right down."

I got dressed and came downstairs for breakfast. It appeared that I had stirred up a hornets nest, so to speak.

Grandmother started telling Mama the evils of slavery and that's why they had decided to live in France, "A more civilized country". She wanted Mama and me to stay in France. Grandmother couldn't believe that in this day and time, a child of hers would still own slaves.

"I'm ashamed to introduce you to my friends, with you being a slaveholder!" she said.

Mama tried to explain about the laws of manumission and how the slaves would have to leave the state.

Grandmother didn't want to hear any of it, she said, "Move here with your slaves and pay them a wage. That's simple enough!"

Mama looked at Aunt Polly and asked, "Sissy, do you want to live here?"

Aunt Polly said, "No ma'am."

Mama turned to Sara and asked, "Do you want to live here?"

Sara replied, "No ma'am."

Grandmother stated, "They are ignorant, they don't know what you're asking!"

Aunt Polly said, "No ma'am, I'm not ignorant, I love Ms. Abby. We are just fine."

Grandmother once again sternly stated, "It's wrong! All of you go home if you like, however, I believe Charlotte should stay here and learn to be a proper lady!"

Mama, looking shocked, asks, "What do you mean?"

Grandmother said, "She acts just like her father, she speaks like a slave. Sara is more of a lady than Charlotte, something must be done before it's too late!"

Mama spoke loudly and sternly, "Mother, Charlotte is not staying here, I will not listen to another word about it!"

I had never heard Mama speak to anybody like that.

Now I really wanted to go home. I wondered, is this how I made Aunt Polly and Sara feel?

This was the extent of our trip to Paris. Lots of arguing over slavery.

The trip home was refreshing, getting out in the fresh air. It took twelve days to cross the Atlantic on the way home. It was nice to have the time to get over the trip, and start to feel more like ourselves. I can honestly say, I will never forget going to Paris.

We arrived home a week before my sixteenth birthday. Daddy and Uncle Henry were waiting for us at the train station. It was so good to see them. They were asking us how the trip went.

We all just put on a smile and said, "Fine."

They knew something had happened. Daddy asked Mama, "What happened over there?"

Mama simply replied, "Oh, nothing to worry about."

I noticed Uncle Henry look at Aunt Polly, she smiled, hugged him, and said, "It sure is good to be home."

I reckon Mama told Daddy, and Aunt Polly told Uncle Henry, because the next morning Uncle Henry asked if he could talk to me for a few minutes.

We walked as he explained how happy he is here with my daddy. "He don't treat people like niggers, or slaves, he treats them like people. If you are a good person he treats you good. If you're no 'count, he won't waste his time with you. That's all a person can ask for. If I took my family and went north, I bet I couldn't find work, or a place to live that's near as good as here. Charlotte, this is home, we're all family. You need to worry about yourself, and not me and mine. Right now, inside the house, your mama is talking to your daddy, 'bout sending you away to school to learn to be a lady. So I think you've got bigger problems than I do."

I asked, "Sending me away... to where?"

He said, "Don't rightly know, seems they got schools for girls to go and learn all these things your mama has been trying to teach you all these years."

I said, "Grandmother wanted me to stay in Paris and learn to be a lady. Do you think Mama wants me to go there?" I asked.

He once again said, "I don't rightly know. I do know your daddy has been telling you for years not to do certain things, and say certain things in front of your mama. You're just hardheaded and want to do only what you want. Now it seems like you're gonna be a lady, like it or not. Your daddy is trying to keep you here, but she says the way you act, is all his fault."

I hugged Uncle Henry and said, "Thanks. I'd better get on up to the house."

I wanted to run, but at the same time, I didn't want to go. I went in the front door and froze. I could hear Mama and Daddy talking loudly, I had never heard them talk to each other like that.

I heard Daddy saying, "Charlotte is a beautiful, sweet girl. She don't need all that gussying up to get a fine husband. One day she will meet a young man, and then she'll start thinking about all the things you've been teaching her about being a lady. Right now she don't care. I'm telling you, don't throw away what you have over something you ain't gonna get. She will resent you if you force this. Charlotte is Charlotte, and I'm proud of her. She's not going anywhere she don't want to go, and that's final!"

Daddy had saved me from being sent to Paris, but at what price? Had I caused the argument between them?

Mama didn't say anything more to Daddy about me going away to learn to be a lady, though she did say it to me. Every day she would say something about my hair, my dress, how I walked, how I talked. Around Mama, I was trying to be the proper lady that she wanted me to be. Though now, it seemed everything I did was wrong.

Finally, I gave in and asked, "Where is this school?"

She was delighted! She said, "They are all over the place now, you don't have to go to Paris. You can stay right here in America!"

I said, "I'll go if Sara goes."

Mama said, "Sara can't go."

I asked, "Why not?"

Mama sighed as she said, "You know why, because she's black."

I said, "If Sara don't go, I won't go."

That was the last time she said anything about it.

I look back now and wondered if Mama was a slave. Not a black slave made to work hard with the fear of being beat. I mean a slave because she was a woman with laws that oppressed her. Social rules that were so ingrained in her that she had no choice except to be a proper lady, with no concern of her own thoughts or feelings, having to be the perfect hostess, with perfect manners, and perfect clothes for every occasion. The huge amount of details a lady is judged on. Having to always smile when greeting someone, always making them feel welcome. That was a fake smile. I knew Mama's smile and that wasn't the smile we saw at home when it's just me, Daddy, Aunt Polly, Uncle Henry, and Sara. When we would go to church, or a pig pickin' and such, it seemed like women and children were to be seen and not heard. Ladies only talked about silly, unimportant things. Children were sent off to play. I was in between, not really being a child anymore, but not an adult either. Being too old to go play with the children, I had to sit with the ladies. I wondered, is this what being a proper lady meant? If so, I wanted no part of it.

3 BECOMING A LADY

February 24, 1859. My sixteenth birthday, Daddy gave me a horse. His name was Logan and he was two years old. He wasn't a full-blooded thoroughbred like his mama was, his daddy was an Indian pony. Daddy bought him from a Cherokee Indian.

I never understood why people didn't like Indians. This man was nice, had a kind look in his eyes, and had long, shiny, black hair. He looked… Regal. His name was Adahy, pronounced, "a-dah-hey". He said his name meant, "In the oak woods". He told me, his people believed a name is the first gift a person gives to their child. That sounded beautiful to me.

He had named his colt, Logan. I figured that was his gift to the colt. He had loved and cared for him from the day he was born. Now he needed money for his family, and he had no choice but to sell him. I could tell it broke his heart. He and Daddy talked for a while, smoked a cigar, and came to an agreement on the price. Daddy watched me interacting with Logan and offered two hundred dollars for him.

Adahy said, "You know that horse ain't worth that much to you. You don't have to do this."

Daddy said, "I want to. Besides, he might not be worth that much to me, but it appears he is to Charlotte."

I promised Adahy, I would love Logan as much as he did, and told him to come by to visit any time he wanted to.

When Adahy left, I heard Uncle Henry tell Daddy, "It was mighty kind of you to pay so much for that horse. Willie, you're a fine man."

It seemed Daddy was always doing things to help people. He did it in a quiet manner that allowed them to keep their dignity.

Logan was a stallion, chestnut in color, with a blaze on his face. There was a bit of a white sock on his left hind foot, and right front foot. When he first saw me he stood up tall, held his head high, shook his head like he was making sure his mane fell right, and puffed out his chest. I had never seen a more beautiful animal.

He seemed to understand me when I would talk to him. He would get these expressions on his face, like a person. He would raise his eyebrows, tilt his head, and move his ears back and forth. I fell in love with him the moment I saw him.

Adahy came to visit a few times. I was always happy to see him. I would show him what Logan had learned to do since his last visit. Things like me riding him, as Adahy had never been on his back. I was the first and only person that had rode him. Logan loved me and was quick to do the things I asked of him. He learned how to bow, and back up on command.

I would tell him, "Go to your room," and he would run to his stall and wait for me.

Adahy acted proud of Logan, but I think it broke his heart more and more every time he saw him. Then, he never came back. I thought of Adahy often, I imagined he thought of Logan often. I'm sure he loved that horse every bit as much as I did.

Once when crossing the creek, something spooked Logan and he threw me, my left foot was caught in the stirrup for a second, and it hurt my leg. Even worse, I had landed on my back on a rock that was in the creek. I couldn't breathe for a minute. Logan ran to the north bank of the creek and stopped. I rolled over and crawled out of the creek. I was scared because I didn't know if Logan was alright. The reins were wrapped around his right front ankle, and he was shaking.

I whispered to him to calm him, saying, "It's alright Lo, everything will be fine, let's just get home." I unwrapped the reins from around his ankle. I stood up, as much as I could, and led him over to a log. He stepped over it with his front legs. I stepped up on the log, and got on him. Breathing and moving was difficult, so I leaned down over the front of the saddle as far as I could, rubbing his neck, talking to him all the way home. "We're gonna be fine Lo, just walk easy. Easy Lo."

Uncle Henry was the first to see us riding up to the house. He hollered, "Oh Lord, somebody go find Mr. William!"

Logan walked right up to Uncle Henry and stopped.

Uncle Henry gently slid me down, carrying me in his arms, asking me, "What happened?"

I could hardly talk it hurt so bad, I said, "Something spooked him, it's not his fault."

By this time Daddy was there, and Uncle Henry was carrying me to the house. Daddy said he had sent for Aunt Polly and the doctor.

After looking me over, Aunt Polly said, "You have a broke rib or two, ain't nothing a doctor can do about that. Let me mix up some white willow bark to help ease your pain."

The doctor got there and gave me some medicine to help the pain. He said, "Polly was right, three broken ribs and a torn muscle in my left leg." He tightly wrapped my leg and ribs.

I told Aunt Polly, "I don't know why he wrapped my ribs like this, I could just wear a corset all the time."

She said, "That's what I was going to have you do. Now, you've got to do what the doctor says!"

It was days before I was up and around. The first thing I did was limp to the barn to see Logan. He had a place that was raw looking on his right front ankle where the reins had been wrapped around. Uncle Henry said he had been putting a salve on it.

I asked, "Will it leave a scar?"

Uncle Henry nodded as he said, "Probably."

I started crying, that beautiful animal would now have a scar.

Uncle Henry asked, "Are you okay, are you hurting? I can carry you back to the house."

I said, "I hurt for Logan, It's sad that he will be scarred forever."

Uncle Henry said, "Darlin', you are more busted up than that horse, maybe you should worry about you for a while."

I said, "I know you're right Uncle Henry, but it still bothers me."

One week to the day, I told Daddy I was going out to ride Logan. He didn't think that was a good idea. I reminded him, that he had always said, "When a horse throws you, you get right back on."

He said, "You did, that day."

I said, "Daddy, I need to do this, just for a few minutes."

He agreed, as long as he could be close by to help me, if I needed him.

I agreed.

Logan's ankle looked better, it had scabbed over. I limped for two more weeks. The ribs, now that was another story. Every breath I took, hurt for at least a month. After that they only hurt occasionally.

When I was better, I was back to riding Logan pretty much every day. His ankle was now healed, but it did leave a scar. It was a relief to get back to normal. I liked riding along the north bank of the Reedy Fork Creek. Even though this was where Logan had thrown me, it was still my favorite place.

On one particular day, I saw a young man riding along the south bank. I would glance over and he was looking at me, and I noticed he kept looking at me.

He hollered over and asked, "Would it be alright if I cross over to your side at the ford?"

"Yes." I replied.

A little further down, we came to the ford. He crossed over, took his hat off with a flourish, held it to his chest, and introduced himself.

"My name is Jeremiah Turner, my family owns the land south of the creek." he said.

"I'm Charlotte Smith, my daddy owns the land north of the creek." I said.

He said, "Oh, I know your daddy, he's a fine man. I knew he had a daughter, I just didn't know she was so grown up and so pretty."

I had never been talked to like that before, and I felt my cheeks getting warm, as I started to blush.

"You don't know me?" I asked. "We went to church together before you left to go to school." I said nervously.

He placed is hat back on his head as he said, "Maybe, but you were just child when I left."

I asked, "How long have you been away?"

"Three years." he replied.

I could feel my cheeks cool a little as I was getting more comfortable, "Where were you?" I asked.

Proudly he said, "The University of Virginia."

I then asked, "Are you home for good, or are you just visiting?"

He smiled as he said, "Oh, I'm home for good." He then asked, "May I ride along with you for a while?"

I said, "Yes." I was happy that he wanted to. I fell in love with him the moment he spoke to me.

"That's a beautiful horse you have there, what's his name?" he asked.

"Logan," I replied. "What's your horse's name?"

"Jefferson, after our third President, and also the founder of the University of Virginia." he answered.

We rode and talked, and before I knew it, he had rode all the way home with me. He helped me off of Logan, shook hands with Daddy and said, "I hope it was alright for me to escort Ms. Charlotte home."

Daddy said, "Of course." They walked off talking to each other, I couldn't hear what they were saying. I didn't know what to think.

When they came back, Jeremiah took his hat off with that same flourish as when he first introduced himself, held it with his left hand against his chest, and asked, "Do you plan to go riding again tomorrow?"

I replied in my most charming, southern, sweet voice, "Why, yes I do."

He smiled and asked, "Might you and Logan be interested in having a picnic with me and Jefferson?"

I looked at Daddy, he just smiled. I didn't know what to say. I was surprised.

"Uh, yes. I would like to have a picnic with you." I managed to answer. "Shall I bring the food?"

He bowed a little, and using both hands he put his hat on his head, left hand at the center, right hand at the back, he ran his right thumb and forefinger down the brim and slid it off the front with a tiny flourish.

Smiling he said, "You bring the food, I'll bring the blanket and find a good spot. Meet you at the ford at 11:30?"

Blushing I said, "Alright, I'll see you then."

He tipped his hat to me and said, "Until tomorrow, Ms. Charlotte!" Without using the stirrup he jumped on his horse and raced off down the driveway.

Daddy laughed and said, "So my baby is going to start courtin', well darlin', there's not a finer young man around. Mighty smart too, he just got home from school yesterday. It sure didn't take him long to find the prettiest girl in the county."

I felt myself blushing again. I kissed Daddy on the cheek and said, "Thank you Daddy."

He said, "Maybe you need to go have a talk with your mama about courtin'. Now go on, I'll tend to Logan."

"I love you Daddy." was all I could muster to say.

That night Jeremiah Turner was all I could think about. He was three years older than me. He was handsome, tall, with big broad shoulders. He reminded me of the statue I had seen in Paris. I thought about his long blond hair, hazel eyes, and his strong arms helping me off of Logan. His large hands around my waist, and the feeling as he looked into my eyes.

The next morning I was so excited! I could hardly wait to see him again. Mama and Aunt Polly were helping me get dressed. They were lacing my corset tighter than normal.

I said, "Mama, that's too tight, I can't breathe!"

"You will get used to it," she said, "you want to look pretty, don't you?"

I said, "Yes ma'am."

She suggested I wear my burgundy riding habit. It had black trim, the sleeves were black below the elbow, and the collar and lapel were also black. It had five green buttons at the wrist, and two bigger green buttons on the back of the bodice.

It was weighted at the hem of the long skirt, so it would hang nicely when I was on Logan. My hat was a black riding hat with purple and burgundy feathers, and wide white lace ribbon that fell to the middle of my back.

Mama said, "You look like a lady. Now you be sure to act like a lady. Don't you let him kiss you!"

Kiss me? I hadn't even thought of kissing until she brought it up!

Mama told me, "He's no boy, he's a man! He's been away at school, Lord only knows what he's been up to. I can't believe your daddy agreed to let you start courtin' a grown man. You and I have a lot of talking to do. For now, you just remember, be a lady."

"Yes ma'am." I replied. "Mama, don't you like Jeremiah?" I asked.

She said, "I think he was a well-behaved boy. I don't know what kind of man he is."

I smiled and said, "I think he's a fine gentleman."

Mama said, "I suppose we will see."

I said, "Mama, did you see him yesterday, don't you think he's handsome?"

Mama smiled just a little and said, "Yes, he is."

Aunt Polly made the picnic lunch, and packed it in the saddle bags. Uncle Henry saddled Logan and tied on the saddle bags. Daddy helped me onto Logan, Mama fussed over how my riding habit was hanging.

Finally, Mama said, "Oh Charlotte, you look very pretty."

I smiled and said, "Thank you Mama." I then rode away to see the man that would become my husband.

Jeremiah got there before I did. Once again he helped me down off of Logan. This time I noticed how tall he was. The top of my head came up to his shoulders.

We stood there with his hands on my waist for a minute, just looking at each other. The sun was shining on his face, and I noticed the tiny gold colored flecks in his eyes, which made them sparkle. I could have stayed right there forever. Then we were startled by the sounds of banging hammers. Daddy and Uncle Henry had decided today was the day to repair the roof on the tobacco barn close to the ford. We both laughed and as he spread out the picnic blanket, I got the saddle bags with the food.

Daddy hollered over, "Don't pay us no mind, we've just got work to do."

Jeremiah tipped his hat to Daddy and said, "I understand, do you need any help, sir?"

Uncle Henry laughed, saying, "No, no, we don't aim to interrupt any courtin', we've just got work to do!"

Jeremiah laughed and said, "Yes sir, I understand. Want to join us for lunch?"

Daddy and Uncle Henry both yelled, "No!"

Jeremiah and I sat down and talked there on the north bank of the Reedy Fork. It was cool in the shade of the trees. The blanket was spread out on the sandy loam soil that grew our tobacco so well. He had picked a spot close to the creek, where we could hear the water rushing over the rocks.

I said, "I like the spot you picked. The soil is soft under the blanket."

He said, "Soil? You're the first girl I've ever heard call it soil. Most girls say dirt."

I smiled as I said, "Daddy says dirt is dead, soil is alive."

"He's right. Your daddy is a smart man." he said.

I had my head down just a little, turned slightly to the right and looked up with only my eyes, trying my best to be cute, I asked, "What did they teach you at the University of Virginia?"

He smiled and said, "Other than dirt is dead, and soil is alive? They taught me about plants, what they need to grow, where they need to be to grow their best, how to grow better crops, and how to keep the soil alive."

I said, "I thought people only went to school that wanted to be a preacher, doctor, or lawyer."

He said, "No, these days you can go to school for botany, like I did. You can learn architecture, you know, how to build buildings and such. If I hadn't been there for botany, I would have taken every architecture class they had, it's so interesting to me. I consider it a leisurely pursuit. All these questions about me, how about you sharing something yourself."

I asked, "What would you like to know?"

He smiled and said, "Yesterday, as I helped you off of your horse, I noticed you had a revolver on your saddle, I noticed it there today." He then asked, "Do you always ride with it, and do you really know how to use it?"

I smiled really big and said, "Yes, I always have it with me when I ride. Daddy wouldn't let me ride off by myself without it. Of course I can use it. Daddy taught me when he bought it for me. It's an 1851 Colt Navy pistol. He thought since I liked riding by myself, I should be able to protect myself from man or beast."

"I have never known a girl to have a pistol, it's bigger than you are, you can't shoot that thing!" he said matter-of-factly.

I said, "Yes I can. I practiced shooting at a tree. When I could hit that, I started shooting squirrels and rabbits. Daddy taught me how to skin, clean, and cook them over an open fire. He taught me to fish too. Uncle Henry says I can skin near 'bout anything. Why can't a girl have a gun?"

He said, "I didn't say a girl can't have a gun. I said, I have never met one that did."

I asked, "Does it bother you? You have a gun on your saddle."

He smiled and said, "No, it doesn't bother me, I think I like that your daddy has taught you to take care of yourself. I have a gun for the same reason. That's a fine looking horse, how long have you had him?"

I smiled and said, "I've had him a few months." I told him the story of getting Logan from Adahy, and of Logan throwing me in the creek.

"Oh, you broke some ribs when Logan threw you off into the creek! Am I hurting you when I help you down off of him? I won't help you down if I'm hurting you!" he said apologetically.

I quickly said, "No, you haven't hurt me, your hands are just below where my ribs hurt. I like it when you help me down."

He was smiling the whole time I was talking, then he said, "I love the way your big brown eyes sparkle when you speak of Logan."

I blushed and said, "I love Logan."

He said, "I hope one day your eyes will sparkle like that when you speak of me."

He didn't know they already did!

He said, "I also like those dimples when you smile."

I said, "Thank you, I like your smile too." I didn't know what else to say. Then I thought, "Your horse is beautiful too, how long have you had Jefferson?"

He said, "I've had him since he was born and I had just gotten him broke before I left for school."

I don't remember much about the food. Ham, bread, and jelly maybe. I just remember wanting this day to never end. I do remember this was the first time I ever cared about how I looked, or what I was wearing. It was strange to me. I was glad Mama had Aunt Polly lace my corset so tight. Now at the age of sixteen, I finally started acting like a lady. Daddy was right, someday I would meet a man and the ladylike ways would mean something to me.

I still didn't want to be the kind of lady Mama and Sara were. Just somewhere in between me and them.

So this became our spot, we came here every day. We talked about us, our families, who we were, who we wanted to be, and what we wanted for our future.

He was the youngest of nine children, only six were alive now. Three had died as infants. His oldest brother John Turner Junior, was twenty years older than Jeremiah. He had run off to California back in 1849, during the gold rush. He writes home and says he's doing well.

Jeremiah said, "Daddy calls Jr. a damn fool, running off across the entire country in search of gold. There's gold right here in northeast Guilford County. Less than ten miles away from this very spot are two gold mines."

William Turner is the second child of the family. Jeremiah says, "He's a hard working lawyer who lives in Charleston, South Carolina, with his wife and seven children."

Margaret Turner, the third child, was named after their mother. She still lives at home. People call her a spinster. I know her from church. She is a charming, pleasant lady.

Mary Turner is the fourth child. Jeremiah says, "She's a pretty lady that lives in Boston with her husband and three children."

Charles Turner, the fifth child, died at one month old, back in 1828.

Joseph Turner, the sixth child, went to the University of Virginia. He's a preacher, and lives close by in Greensborough.

Laura Turner, the seventh child, died at birth in 1833.

Alice Turner, the eighth child, died at five days old in 1837.

Jeremiah Turner, the ninth child, was born on September 2, 1840.

Jeremiah would be the one to stay home and work the plantation, and was happy to do so. He loved farming.

His daddy also had a brick kiln, and did pretty well selling bricks.

In October of 1853, he went by carriage with his daddy to the very first North Carolina State Fair. It was put on to encourage farmers to use better farming methods. There were also horse races, and prizes for jelly making, pickling and such. But Jeremiah was interested in the farming. That day he decided he wanted to go to school to learn to be a better farmer. Every year he went to the fair.

October 9, 1855, the railroad in Gibsonville opened. It was just in time for Jeremiah and his daddy to take the train to Raleigh for the fair.

Going to the fair gave him the opportunity to see things that amazed him, like a cotton gin. They had been around for more than fifty years, but he had never seen one. They also had a grain drill, a corn sheller, and a straw cutter. Even a barrel made by machinery, an apple peeler, and a water wheel. He saw a coat made by a blind girl, whose name was Rebecca. She went to the Deaf and Dumb and Blind Institute in Raleigh. He was most impressed with her handiwork.

Mr. Westbrooks of Guilford County had the largest variety of apples he had ever seen. It seemed as though most people agreed his apples were the best tasting too.

Jeremiah left for the University of Virginia when he was sixteen years old. He was smart and worked hard, as he was eager to get there.

He admired Thomas Jefferson. He said Jefferson said learning is a never-ending process. He liked that. He told me about the University, the rounded roof of the library that they called the Rotunda. He told me of the serpentine brick walls lining the driveway going behind the Rotunda, and the greenhouses where they grew the plants they learned about. It sounded like a wonderful place.

He had ideas of how he wanted to build his home. He said there are ways to make your house cool in the summer. If you face the house to the north and line the driveway with trees, it will funnel the cooler north air towards the house. If you put a copula at the highest point of the house, the hot air can escape. This creates a draft and moves the air making the house feel cooler. Porches should be built all around the house to cool the air before it comes inside. If you have a creek or spring close by, you should divert some of the water and have a springhouse in the cellar. In the summer have your bedroom along the north side of the house, and in the winter your bedroom should be on the south side of the house. To take full advantage of the seasons, every house should have two bedrooms.

I loved listening to him talk, the sound of his voice, his enthusiasm, the way he smiled when he spoke of the future. I wanted to know everything he knew. I wanted to be a part of his future.

He told me of going to Hot Springs, Virginia, when he was on break from school. He said the water was hot right out of the ground, and it had minerals in it that had healing properties. He said he had soaked in the hot water, and also had a mud bath. That's where people rub the mud all over their bodies.

I laughed and said, "You're teasing me!"

He was also laughing and said, "No, really, you let the mud dry and then wash it off. You feel really good afterwards."

I said, "Alright, let's go on the other side of the creek and get some of that red dirt your daddy uses to make bricks, bring it to the creek, make mud and rub it all over us. That's going to make us feel good?"

He said, "No, it's special mud. It has minerals in it. But we can go play in the mud as long as I don't have to explain it to your daddy."

I smiled and said, "Maybe we had better not."

Jeremiah has a ring he wears on his right hand. He says it belonged to his great-great-great-grandfather. This grandfather came from Pennsylvania. That ring is dear to him. He calls it a signet ring. It is gold and has the letter T on it. I like that he wears his grandfather's ring, it tells me that family is important to him. I like the way it looks on his hand, it draws my attention to his large strong hands, and makes me think of his hands around my waist when he helps me down off of Logan.

After about two weeks of our daily picnics, he leaned over and kissed me. This was the greatest moment I had ever known.

He then said, "I know it seems soon, but I want to talk to your daddy about getting married, I mean, if you want to be my wife?"

I couldn't believe it, I was so excited I exclaimed, "Oh yes!" Then I kissed him!

We heard a couple of throats clearing. It was Daddy and Uncle Henry letting us know they were close by and watching.

Jeremiah said, "After I left your house last night, I spoke to my daddy about it. Daddy told me, "Jeremiah lowered his voice, and with a stern tone said, "You be sure, before you ask, you do right by that girl. She's got a good reputation, and you'd better make sure she keeps it!" Changing his voice back to normal he said, "So now, I just need to talk to your daddy."

I asked, "When are you going to talk to him?"

He stood up and said, "There's no time like the present!"

He walked over to Daddy and Uncle Henry, I heard him ask Daddy if he could have a word with him. The two of them walked off together, talking. It seemed like forever, they kept talking and talking. I was looking for a sign or something to let me know what was happening.

Uncle Henry walked over to me, and said, "They sure have been talking a long time, what could that boy have to talk to your daddy 'bout that would take so much time?" Then he laughed and said, "Darlin', I know what they're talking 'bout!"

I looked up at Uncle Henry and I asked, "Do you think he'll say yes?"

He laughed some more and said, "Oh, I'm sure he'll say yea, but I bet he's got plenty of rules and stipulations 'bout it."

I said, "I hope he says yes. I love Jeremiah, Uncle Henry."

He said, "I know you do. We all know you do!"

Then finally, I saw Jeremiah smile, and shake Daddy's hand. I knew Daddy had said yes!

Jeremiah quickly walked back to me. He looked at Uncle Henry and asked, "Excuse me Henry, might I have a moment alone with Ms. Charlotte?"

While reaching out to shake his hand, Uncle Henry said, "Why sure you can!" Uncle Henry then walked away.

Jeremiah smiled and said, "He said yes! We're getting married!" Then he shouted, "Whoo hoo!" He grabbed me at the waist, picked me up, and swung me around a couple of times, then sat me down.

I was laughing and smiling and asked, "When?"

He thought for a second and said, "How about April?"

My smile faded as I said, "April sounds so far away."

"I promised your daddy that I would have a home for you before we got married. I believe I can have it done by April. That gives me nine months to build a house, and for us to gather everything we need for a home," he said, "can you do everything you need to do in nine months?"

I said, "I don't know, what all do I need to do?"

He grinned and said, "I don't know, ask your mama."

Mama was quick to inform me, tradition says, I was supposed to turn him down twice before saying yes. That sounded silly to me. I wanted to marry him, I didn't want him to think I didn't.

Daddy was expecting it, he wasn't surprised. We both had good reputations, as did both families, and nobody disagreed. As a matter-of-fact, our daddies had been talking about when this happens, they would both give us five hundred acres that would meet up at our spot.

The next thing we knew, we were planning a wedding. We had to decide where to build our house. Jeremiah had already shared with me what he wanted our house to be like. He asked me what I wanted. I had never really thought about it. Everything that he had described sounded wonderful. These were happy, busy days.

A month later he gave me an Amethyst engagement ring. It was deep purple. He chose it because it was my birthstone.

4 THE PREMONITION

On August 28, 1859. The Northern Lights reached as far south as Cuba. Mama and Daddy woke me up, and we all went out on the porch to see. It was moon-bright and red outside. Birds started to sing because they thought it was morning. The red light slowly moved across the sky. It was as if the hand of God was reaching out for something, like in the painting by Michelangelo, The Creation of Adam.

Aunt Polly was worried, she said, "Red northern lights this far south, means war or death, maybe both. It's coming, mark my words."

I thought for a second, war means Jeremiah going to fight, was Aunt Polly predicting his death?

I looked at Aunt Polly and shouted, "I don't want to hear any more of your silly superstitions!" I ran upstairs to my room and cried the rest of the night.

The next morning Aunt Polly said, "I'm sorry child, I didn't mean to worry you."

"I know Aunt Polly, I'm sorry too, I'm scared for him." I replied.

Aunt Polly hugged me and said, "I know darlin', we all are. We can't do nothing about it right now 'cept pray to the good Lord, and that's what I've been doing."

September 2, 1859. It was Jeremiah's nineteenth birthday and we had spent the day together. The first half at his parent's house, we had dinner with them.

He then wanted to show me the progress on our house. He was so excited, almost running from one point to the next.

He said, "This is where the parlor will be, this is where the dining room will be. Over here we will have flowers and a brick walkway that goes all the way around the house. As a matter-of-fact, we will have a brick drive from the gate right there where the trees end. It will come straight up toward the house, then circle around a big flower bed, that will have a short brick wall around it. We won't have to walk in dirt or mud and you won't get your dresses dirty. The brick drive will bring you right up to the front steps. Everything is going fine, we're right on schedule to get the walls, roof, doors, and windows done before winter. Then during the winter, I will work on the inside." He laughed as he said, "Daddy had to expand his brick kiln to supply us with enough bricks, but he said he's happy to do it." he finished with that smile of his.

We then went to my parent's house for supper with my family. Aunt Polly had made him a special supper. He said everything Aunt Polly cooks is special. He's such a charmer. I had made him a birthday cake with white sugar, with a lot of help from Aunt Polly. I put nineteen candles on it. It was pretty and it tasted good too! I was quite proud of it.

After supper we all went out on the porch. Daddy and Uncle Henry always liked a cigar and a bit of sippin' whiskey after supper. Daddy offered a glass of whiskey to Jeremiah, which he eagerly accepted. Uncle Henry offered a cigar, he was happy to be offered that as well. He had heard of their cigars, and their whiskey. He had never been offered any, until now.

"Gentlemen, I consider it an honor, thank you both." he said while raising his glass, his face beaming with pride. It meant a lot to him that they were including him in their after supper ritual.

They both nodded and leaned back to enjoy the moment.

Jeremiah sipped the whiskey, then raised his glass again, as in a toast, and said, "This is every bit as good as I have heard." He lit the cigar, and he too leaned back and enjoyed it for a moment, then said, "Gentlemen, I do believe men are correct when they say, you make the finest cigars around."

We ladies had a cup of tea. We all talked and laughed.

Jeremiah said, "This is my best birthday yet."

Just as darkness fell, the Northern Lights crept down again. I couldn't speak, I was scared God was going to reach down and take Jeremiah that very minute. Aunt Polly didn't say anything about what it meant.

Jeremiah looked up and said, "The Aurora sure is beautiful. Maybe God wanted to give me a special birthday gift."

We all sat and watched the red light cover the sky. It lasted until around ten o'clock.

Daddy then said, "Well... let's all let Charlotte and Jeremiah have a little time alone before he heads home."

They all said goodnight, and once again, wished him a happy birthday. He thanked them all for making it a very special day.

After they all went inside, Jeremiah took my hand and lightly kissed me on the cheek. "What's wrong?" he asked.

I said, "The Northern Lights scare me, Aunt Polly says when they're red, it means war, or death."

Jeremiah said, "I always heard it was lucky to see them. So I guess it really means nothing, just a silly superstition."

I looked at him and said, "I know, but it worries me. If war comes, you'll have to fight, what if... "

He interrupted me mid-sentence. "We can't live our lives worrying about what if."

I then said, "I know it's silly, but it scared me the other night, and now it's happened again on your birthday, what if it really is a sign about you?" I continued, "I was thinking, maybe... when you leave... you could go to the barn and wait for me... I don't want to wait until we get married next year."

He squeezed my hand a bit, smiled and said, "Charlotte, as tempting as that is, I can't let you do it. I mean I really, really want to, but not because you're scared of a superstition. Now if you want our first time together to be in a nasty old barn, there's another superstition you need to be aware of."

"What?" I asked, afraid of what he might say.

"The Aurora makes you more fertile." he replied.

I asked, "Really?"

"Yes, that's what people in China and Japan believe. Here's another superstition for you. When I blew out the candles on my birthday cake, I said a prayer. Now my Guardian Angel will take the smoke and prayer from the candles straight to God, and it will be answered. I'm not supposed to tell you my prayer, but I know you can guess it's about you and I being together for a long time." he said.

I felt relieved as I softly asked, "Really?"

He said, "Yes, really. Would you feel better if I sat right here with you until after my birthday has passed?"

"Yes, I would." I replied as I rose to go inside, "I'll go ask Daddy."

He stood up and said, "No, I should ask him." He went inside, and after a few minutes he came back out laughing and said, "Your daddy just told me I could call him William, and he's going to be in his study, until I leave at a quarter after midnight."

He sat back down. I snuggled up to him with my head on his chest, and he put his arm around me. This felt so good, I prayed that he was right. After a while he asked if I was feeling better. I told him I was.

He whispered, "Ms. Charlotte Elizabeth Smith, were you really willing to do that in a barn?"

I replied, "Yes."

He said, "I don't know if that would be a good idea, Logan is in there."

I giggled and said, "Now you're teasing me."

"Yes I am, I suppose if you're willing to go to the barn with me, I can call you Charley, has anybody ever called you that?" he asked.

"No, why would they?" I asked.

"Because it's a nickname for Charlotte." he said.

"You'd better not let Mama hear you call me that, she would have a hissy fit." I said.

He said, "Well Charley, how about if it's our secret. I'll only call you that when nobody's around to hear?" he giggled a little bit and said, "I bet your mama would have a fit if she heard you say hissy fit."

I said, "I know, she don't like a lot of things I say, I reckon she thinks I'm too much like my daddy. I'm proud of my daddy, he started with nothing. Look at how his hard work has paid off. I'm proud to be like him."

He said, "I know, and you should be proud of him. I know I'm proud to say you're going to be my wife. You're like both your mama and daddy. I would say you have the best of both of them. You say stuff like reckon, hissy fit, and yonder, around here, but I've noticed you are quite the lady around other people."

I looked up at him and said, "You reckon?"

He grinned, and said, "I reckon."

I asked, "Do you like for me to act like a lady?"

He said, "I want you to be you! I also want to share something with you."

"What?" I asked.

He said, "I've never been with a girl, you know... like that. At the university the fellas acted like it was something you're supposed to do. Go visit a so called, "loose woman". I didn't like the idea of it being a business transaction. Before I left for school Daddy told me a few things he said I should always remember. Be honest, be fair, keep good company, live my life with the goal that every night when I go to bed, I can sleep well with the knowledge I've done no wrong to God or man. Be a true southern gentleman! I want to be with you more than anything else in this world. We've both waited this long, I think we can wait a little longer. When we're married it will be right. We will take our vows before God and our family and friends. Then we go, to our home, to our bed, and you and I will join spiritually. Not just sex, but love."

I wiped away tears, and said, "That's the most beautiful thing I've ever heard."

He kissed my head, and softly said, "It will be, Ms. Charley, it will be." We heard the clock inside the house strike twelve. I raised my head from his chest. He kissed me and said, "I truly love you."

I said, "I truly love you, you're a perfect southern gentleman, and I'm proud to say you're going to be my husband. I'm glad we're going to wait and make sure everything is right, just like you said."

He kissed me again, and said, "I better head out, I'll see you tomorrow," then whispered, "Ms. Charley."

I smiled and said, "I'll see you tomorrow, Mr. Jeremiah."

He jumped up on his horse, Jefferson, just like always, not using the stirrup. I liked that, and wondered if I could do it.

Maybe I could try it sometime, but make sure nobody's around to see me do it. He, as always, tipped his hat as he said goodnight, and raced off down the driveway.

I went inside and kissed Daddy on the cheek and thanked him for allowing Jeremiah to stay so late. "I Love you Daddy."

He smiled and patted my hand and said, "I love you too, darlin'. Jeremiah is a fine young man."

I had already walked out of the room, then stopped and turned to Daddy and said, "Yes sir, he surely is." I went upstairs and got changed into my nightgown, let down my hair, starting brushing it, all the while thinking of Jeremiah. I went to bed dreaming of the things he told me.

The next day, all my fears were gone. Everything was back to planning the wedding. Sara commented about me and Jeremiah being alone for so long out on the porch. Aunt Polly reminded her of how much time she's been spending with George. Sara didn't want to talk about it anymore.

We later read in the newspaper stories of the telegraph operators running the telegraph off of the electrical current in the air from the Northern Lights. They had shut off the batteries because it was feared the batteries would be damaged due to the currents in the air. The telegraphs still worked. Maybe Jeremiah was right, the lights didn't mean anything.

On October 17, 1859, John Brown and a group of men trying to take over the Federal Armory in Harper's Ferry, Virginia, took hostages. Colonel Robert E. Lee of the 2nd U.S. Cavalry led a group of U.S. Marines to end the raid. They killed six, and captured nine of the raiders. Was Aunt Polly right, was war coming?

Jeremiah took me to the seventh North Carolina State Fair in 1859. We went by train. I had rode the train to Greensborough with Daddy before, but I had never been to the fair. I could see why he loved it so much.

One evening we were at a harvest dance. It was a fun evening. Being engaged, people now treated me as an adult. The ladies decided I needed to know a few things about being married. I was told horrifying things. They said when I get married I am the property of my husband, it's my job to please him in every way, especially sex. I was told it's very unpleasant and just something I must endure. I had no right to say no, if I didn't want to do it, he would just force himself on me, and I could do nothing about it. I would have no rights at all. I couldn't own anything, or have an opinion. The husband is to make all decisions. My purpose is to bear him children and to make a good home, be a charming hostess, and be a lady.

One lady said, "If you're lucky, you will with get with child right away, and he will start visiting the slave quarters, only bothering you when he's ready for another child."

This couldn't be true. It sounded like I would become a slave to Jeremiah. He loves me, he wouldn't treat me like that. I had to talk to him. It was Saturday night, so I could talk to him about it tomorrow. Sunday, our day to spend together.

He was working hard on building the house. Every day I would ride Logan over and take him dinner. We would have a picnic and discuss what was being done and what had to be done next. He worked well into the night and our picnics were the only time we would see each other, sometimes for days. Sundays we had the whole day together. We would go to church, then have Sunday dinner. We would alternate having Sunday dinner with his family and mine, then we had the rest of the day just for us. Tomorrow after dinner with his family, we would have all afternoon to talk.

The next day when we were finally alone, he asked, "What's wrong, you haven't been yourself since the dance last night. Did something happen?"

I replied, "Yes, something did happen. Some of the ladies told me how things would be when we get married. Jeremiah, I don't believe you would treat me the way they say."

He said, "Oh, they are the, shall we say, old-fashioned ladies, that don't like being with their husbands? Charlotte, I love you! I don't know anything about... sex. I have talked to my daddy, I've even talked to your daddy about it, and here's what I've learned. If there is love, and gentleness, it should be pleasurable for both of us. If it's not, you need to tell me, I would never expect you to do anything you don't want to do. I promise I will never hurt you. You need to trust me. Trust in our love."

I said, "I do trust you, I do love you. Why would they tell me such things? They said my purpose is to bear your children, and make a good home. It sounded so bad."

He smiled and said, "Your purpose is to make me happy, as mine is to make you happy."

I said, "You do make me happy. Is it true that some men are like that?"

He said, "Well, somebody's wife told you that, so I guess that's how her husband is."

I asked, "So some men force themselves on their wives, and their women slaves?"

He said, "I guess he does. Look Charlotte, I'm not like that. I think... sex, should be with the person you love, and you are the person I love."

"You are the person I love, I want us to be married, and I want to be with you. Does it also mean I become your property? I can't own anything? I can't have an opinion? How is that different than a slave?" I asked.

He wrapped his arms around me, looked me in the eyes and said, "No, you won't be my property, you will be my wife! You can own anything you want!

You can say anything you like, you have opinions on lots of things, and I love that about you. You're smart, and I love talking to you. I love the way you are so interested in the things I like. I want you to have opinions. You wouldn't be the Charlotte I fell in love with, if you didn't voice your opinions. You will not be a slave! What you describe, that does sound like slavery to me. Which, by the way, I don't agree with." he said matter-of-factly.

I hugged him tight and said, "Really? I don't like slavery either. I have been trying to figure out how to talk to you about it. I don't want to own slaves. I'm told if we free them they have to leave North Carolina, even if they want to stay here and work for a wage. So what are we to do?"

He said, "I can't make Daddy do anything, I haven't thought much about it. I've just been trying to get the house built."

I said, "I haven't said anything to my daddy about it, but as for our place, I think we should offer them their freedom, and they can leave if they want to. If they want to stay, we will guarantee they can have their manumission papers at any time, all they have to do is ask. I know they aren't supposed to have money on them, so we could help them with their money. We could keep a ledger showing how much they have earned, and how much they have spent. If they say they want to leave, we give them their papers and their money. The slaves that our daddies are giving us were all born here. I think we can trust them to keep quiet about it. What do you think?"

He smiled that smile that lights up his face and he said, "See, you have wonderful opinions. That's a great idea. Let's do it!"

I was as excited as when he proposed to me. I hugged him tight, then kissed him and said, "I knew you would make everything right, you're such a wonderful person. I love you!"

He whispered in my ear, "I love you too, Ms. Charley."

I then asked, "Do you think our daddies will be mad about it?"

He said, "Hmm, I don't know. Let's think on it a while before we tell them about it. Maybe we should even wait until ownership of the slaves has transferred to us before we say anything... if we say anything."

I happily agreed, and said, "Yea, no need to stir up trouble. I learned that hard lesson in Paris."

We then went and had a wonderful supper at my parent's house. By this time George was having supper with us at the house every Sunday.

During supper, Daddy said, "Me and Henry have to take a trip for business. We'll be leaving tomorrow morning, we'll be gone a little over a week. Jeremiah, I know you're busy over there building your house, but I would appreciate it if you could find the time to check on the farm for me."

Jeremiah said, "Yes sir. It would be my pleasure."

Daddy asked, "George, you got much work waiting on you?"

George said, "No sir. Don't have any blacksmithing work right now. I was gonna help the field hands, unless something came up."

Daddy said, "I would appreciate if you would go along with Jeremiah, while he checks on the farm, and help him with the house."

George said, "Yes sir, I'd be happy to."

Daddy said, "George, while we're talking, I think it's time you stopped riding that old plow horse. You go to the pasture after supper and pick out a decent horse for yourself. You can't have a race horse or the horses that belong to me, Henry, or Charlotte. That leaves about fifty or so for you to choose from. While y'all are at it, Henry, get him a saddle and bridle."

George said, "That's mighty kind of you Mr. William. I thank you!"

Daddy said, "You're welcome, George."

I asked, "Daddy, where are y'all going?"

He replied, "Never mind that, y'all just keep working on Sara's wedding."

They got home the Wednesday of the following week. They had went down close to Charleston, South Carolina and bought a slave that was to be the cook for Sara and George. As soon as they got home, Daddy sent somebody to get George. While waiting for George to get there, Daddy was introducing her to everybody. Her name was Mae. She seemed like a kind lady, and she reminded me a lot of Aunt Polly. I liked her.

George rode up and stopped short, looked at her for a few seconds, and then began to cry. He jumped off the horse and grabbed her up saying, "Mama, oh Lord, Mama. I thought I'd never see you again."

She was crying too, and asked, "George?"

He said, "Yea, Mama. It's me George."

Daddy said, "Come on y'all, let's leave them alone for a while. George, y'all can visit here on the porch, or Henry will drive your mama to your house, whatever you'd like."

George said, "The porch here is just fine Mr. William. Thank you."

Daddy said, "You're welcome."

As we walked in the house, I don't believe any of us had a dry eye.

After a couple of hours, Sara went out and told them supper was ready.

Mae looked at George and asked, "We gonna eat in the big house with the Massa?"

George said, "Yes Mama. This is Sara, we're getting married Saturday. Sara, this is my..." he could hardly say the word, his voice was breaking up, and he cried, "Mama."

Sara hugged her and said, "I'm so happy you're here."

They came in for supper. While we were eating, Daddy said, "George, I tried to find your family. Your mama is the only one left. Your brothers and sisters died on that sugar plantation in Louisiana. Your mama had eight more children before she was sold to the gentleman in South Carolina."

George said, "I had three brothers when I was sold," he looked at Mae and asked, "so you had eight more babies after me?"

"Yes," she said, "the Massa was the daddy of all of y'all."

George hung his head for a minute then asked, "Did he know we was all his?"

Mae replied, "Yes."

George said, "So he sold his own son, and worked his other children to death?"

Mae once again said, "Yes."

George asked, "How can a man do that to his own children?"

Mae said, "I reckon he don't know the Lawd. The good Lawd the only thang get me through them hard times."

George said, "I've hated him for selling me off, and taking me away from you. Now I hate him even more for what he's done to you."

Daddy said, "George, I understand your feelings, and you have every right to feel that way. Let me share something with you. Hate only hurts you. Hate will destroy you. It don't hurt him a bit. You need to forgive him, so you came move on and live your life and be happy. He will have to answer to God for all he has done. When it's your time to answer to God, you want to have a clean heart. Now, I know it will take some time, since you just found out about all this. Be happy that you have your mama with you, you're marrying Sara, and you have all of us. You're a fine young man, don't let hate turn you into something else."

George sat there for a minute, trying to take it all in, and then said, "Mr. William, I never thought of it like that. Until I came here, I never even cared about anybody, I was scared we'd be sold off away from each other. I don't reckon I need to worry about that now, do I?"

Daddy said, "No George, you don't, you can rest easy. You're with family now."

I realized then at that very moment, how much Daddy didn't care for slavery. I wondered if I could tell him the plan me and Jeremiah had for freeing the people that were to be our slaves. I would speak to Jeremiah about it later.

After supper Uncle Henry told George, "You take your mama home to your house in the buggy, I'll ride your horse and bring the buggy back."

George said, "Thank you, Mr. Henry."

Uncle Henry said, "You're welcome, son."

It's now Saturday, November 12, 1859. I stood beside Sara as she and George were married. Jeremiah stood beside George.

Daddy told Uncle Henry, "I won't have none of this jumping the broom nonsense, Sara is to be married proper in the eyes of God by a preacher. It don't matter if the law recognizes it or not."

Daddy had found out one of his field workers, Zeb, could read and write a little, and he knew the Bible well. Daddy took him out of the fields, and gave him the job as preacher to the workers.

White people in the community weren't invited to Sara's wedding, as Daddy and Uncle Henry knew they wouldn't come, but it didn't matter. The only thing that mattered that day was Sara was getting married. The only work to be done was preparing for the wedding and the party afterwards.

Daddy had made sure everybody had brand new clothes. Fine clothes, like you wear to church.

He told the workers, "Y'all wear these clothes to the wedding and then they'll be your Sunday going to church clothes." He also told them, "Now that y'all are going to church on Sundays, y'all don't have to work for me on Saturdays."

He understood there were things they had to do for themselves. Laundry, house cleaning, and such things, were to be done on Saturdays.

"Sunday is a day of rest for all of us, except for Preacher Zeb!" he proclaimed. Until this day they had always worked six days a week. Now they would work five.

They usually got new work clothes on Christmas. They had never had Sunday clothes. Daddy asked them not to say anything about it to other people off of the farm, as it could cause problems. They all quickly agreed, nobody need know of it.

Mama and Sara had made the wedding gown, it was all white. She looked beautiful.

Aunt Polly and Uncle Henry were as proud as peacocks. Uncle Henry had been planning before last planting season as he planted extra tobacco for cigars for both Sara's wedding, and mine, which was to be in April of next year. Every male over thirteen was given a cigar. Daddy and Uncle Henry made apple cider, slaughtered a hog, and cooked it over hickory coals. Mama, Aunt Polly, and Mae cooked for two days, they made a huge cake. They made everything pretty with big yellow sunflowers, and orange and yellow chrysanthemums.

On December 2, 1859, John Brown is hanged in Virginia for treason.

Christmas was on a Sunday that year. Jeremiah gave me dresses and jewelry. I gave him an autographed copy of A Tale of Two Cities, the new book by Charles Dickens. He was thrilled. I had wrote to my grandparents and asked if they could acquire it for me. It arrived just before Christmas.

Jeremiah picked me up that morning, we went to his parent's house and stayed until after dinner. We then went to Mama and Daddy's.

Sara, George, and Mae spent all day at Mama and Daddy's house. George seemed to like being part of a family.

Mae said, "I ain't never got a Christmas present, thank y'all."

George said, "I never did until I came here. Being with my mama, and spending Christmas with my family is the best gift I could ever get. Thank you Mr. William!"

It was a grand Christmas for everyone.

5 MRS. JEREMIAH TURNER

The evening before our wedding, Jeremiah came for supper.
Everyone gathered on the front porch as Daddy, Uncle Henry,
George, and Jeremiah were all smoking their cigars and sippin' a
bit of whiskey. All the talk is of the wedding. After a while,
everyone leaves and it's just me and Jeremiah on the porch. We
sat there with my head against his chest, his arm around me. This
was my favorite time of day.

I asked him, "Jeremiah, are you nervous about tomorrow?"

He squeezed me a little and asked, "Now what is there to be
nervous about?"

I said, "Tomorrow night."

"Oh," he said as he leaned down and whispered in my ear,
"Ms. Charley, it will be wonderful."

I asked, "Promise?"

He said, "I promise!" He then reached into his pocket as he
said, "I have something for you."

I raised up off of his chest and turned to him. He handed me a
small box. Inside was a shell cameo brooch. The shell was pink
and the carved lady was white, it was in a gold frame.

I said, "Oh Jeremiah, it's beautiful!"

He said, "The lady on it is the Roman Goddess, Diana the Huntress. There is a lot about the myths of her that remind me of you."

I smiled as I said, "Really, what?"

He smiled that smile that lights up his entire face as he said, "Well, she's beautiful, pure, and uncorrupted. She must be outside in the forest and with the animals. She is a huntress but animals are sacred to her, she has the power to talk to, and control them. Jasmine flowers and the oak tree are also sacred to her. Men will fight to the death to be one of her priests', or shall we say, do her bidding. She will attack and kill any animal or anyone that tries to take her dignity. She is regarded with reverence and considered to be a patron of the lower class, and slaves. In her temples, the slaves were granted asylum, she is their protector. All of these things remind me of you. Now, don't you go telling your mama and Aunt Polly all this stuff, they will see it as me trying to get you to be a pagan, which I'm not! I just thought of you when I saw it."

I smiled and said, "I won't tell anyone, it will be our secret. That's beautiful. Is that how you see me?"

He said, "That is exactly how I see you."

I said, "I wish I had something to let you know how I see you."

He smiled and said, "You have given me something that lets me know how you feel about me."

I asked, "What?"

He said, "On our first picnic, I noticed how your face lit up when you spoke of Logan. I hoped one day you would light up like that when you speak of me. Then one day you did. The very next day I asked you to marry me, and you said yes. Tomorrow, you will give me the greatest gift I could ever receive, you'll become my wife."

I said, "On our picnics when you talked about the future, I thought, I want to be a part of your future. Tomorrow you will give me my greatest gift. You'll become my husband, and give me your name." I nestled back against his chest looking at the cameo and said, "I'm going to wear this tomorrow."

He said quietly, "I was hoping you would."

I smiled as I said, "You know, this is the last night you have to leave me and go home. I love the thought of us spending every night together, for the rest of our lives."

On Saturday, April 21, 1860, we were married. I was just a little over seventeen and he was nineteen. Our mama's put on the prettiest wedding for us. They had flowers everywhere and fancy food spread out on two long tables. We were married at Mama and Daddy's house. Uncle Henry had slaughtered a hog and cooked it over hickory coals. It seemed like everybody in the county was there.

Mama, Aunt Polly, and Sara were buffing my fingernails, fixing my hair. Sara rubbed my hair with just a little bit of jasmine scented water, then went to work making a long loose braid, and rolled it into a ball at the nape of my neck. Mama was curling strands of my hair in the front, so I had a few spiral curls that hung loosely on both sides of my face. I ain't never been fussed over so much.

Then Aunt Polly said, "You need something old, something new, something borrowed, something blue, and a penny in your shoe." She continued, "Something old reminds you of your past, your family, where you come from. Something new is for a good future. Something borrowed is to remind you of your family and friends if you ever need any help. Something blue is for faithfulness and loyalty. The penny in your shoe is a wish for good luck."

Then Mama said, "Well, your dress is new. As for something old and borrowed, you can wear these." She picked a bag up off the dressing table and took out four hair combs with green and white jewels on them.

I said, "Mama, I've only seen you wear these a couple of times, how long have you had them?"

She said, "Your daddy gave them to me when you were born. They are dear to me."

I said, "Oh, Mama they're beautiful, I'll be careful with them."

She smiled and said, "I know you will."

Sara said, "I've brought the linen handkerchief I made, it has blue flowers embroidered on it. You can carry it."

I said, "Thank you Sara."

Aunt Polly then said, "I put the penny in your boots. Now put them boots on, and let's start gettin' you dressed. That boy don't wanna wait all day."

I smiled and said, "Yes Ma'am. Thank y'all, I appreciate everything y'all are doing for me."

I put on my white boots. I had never worn white boots before, they buttoned up the side.

Aunt Polly laced my corset tighter than it's ever been. I didn't mind, I wanted to look pretty. I couldn't wear the dress that Mama wore when she married Daddy, it was too small. Mama and I made my dress. The large hoop skirt was all white lace, it had small pink flowers along the bottom holding up the swags. The bodice was pink, trimmed in white lace. It was long in the back and rounded as it came up to my waist in the front, and was fastened with hook and eye closures. It laced up the back with white ribbon. It had a white lace panel that fastened with hook and eye closures to go across my breasts and this had a tiny pink bow on it. Over the top of the tiny pink bow is where I pinned Jeremiah's cameo. It matched everything perfectly.

The bell sleeves were off the shoulder and loose, and they came to the elbow at an angle, then long white lace that reached down to my wrist.

The veil was made of the same lace as the skirt and the trim, in the back it was a little bit longer than my skirt, in the front, it hung just above my waist. Aunt Polly insisted on the veil, she said it hid me from evil spirits trying to keep me from getting married and being happy.

I had white gloves, a matching pink and white lace bag, and a fan. I put the fan and handkerchief in the bag.

I carried light pink camellias, and white jasmine flowers. Aunt Polly had put a little bit of sage in with the flowers for luck.

She said, "The flower colors mean, white, chosen right. Pink, of me, he will always think."

Jeremiah wore black trousers, a white shirt, a red vest, a tail coat, black hat, white gloves, and he had white jasmine pinned to his left lapel. To this day I've never seen a more handsome man.

When Jeremiah saw me, he smiled and took his hat off with that flourish and little bow. He held his hat against his chest, I couldn't stop smiling. Everything was so beautiful.

His brother Joseph, the preacher, performed the ceremony.

We took off our gloves. I handed my gloves, flowers, and bag to Sara. Jeremiah handed his gloves and hat to George.

Joseph asked us to join right hands. I remember Jeremiah slipping the ring on my finger, I was shaking and tears of joy started to flow. While putting the ring on his finger, I nearly dropped it. He lifted my veil and sealed our vows with a kiss.

The rings were made of gold that was mined in Gibsonville. Jeremiah said, "It would always make us feel close to home." They were engraved with our initials and our wedding date.

His parents, John and Margaret, told me I could call them Daddy and Mama.

I asked, "How about Daddy John and Mom Peggy?"

They were delighted.

We spent all afternoon at the party. We said our goodbye's, got into Jeremiah's new white carriage, and George drove us to our new home.

We rode up our tree lined driveway, the trees went all the way up to the brick serpentine walls with the wooden gates.

"In the winter we close the wooden gates to stop the rush of cold air." Jeremiah said with a smile.

The house was made of brick from his daddy's plantation. There was not only a wide porch, or veranda, as Jeremiah would say, that went all the way around the house, there was also an upper porch, or loggia. The front door was five feet wide! It was a set of double doors made of mahogany wood, and each door had twenty-four panes of glass. They were beautiful. There were large windows on each side of the doors.

We pulled up in the carriage, and always the gentleman, he helped me down. We walked up the steps, he opened the doors, lifted me in his arms, and carried me across the threshold.

Aunt Polly had told us, "It's bad luck for a bride to fall going into her new home, so you'd best carry her." I didn't mind, I liked being in his arms.

The entrance hall was wide and had blue and white fabric on the walls. He didn't put me down, he continued up the curved stairs to our bedroom. The bedroom was the most beautiful room, there was blue and white fabric on the walls in there too. On the north wall were french doors that opened to the loggia. They had window panes like the front entry doors.

The bed was huge with a fine crocheted lace canopy that Sara had made. On the bed was a quilt with a double wedding ring design that his grandmother had made for us which was green and white. They must have spent months working on them.

Also in the room was a table, two chairs, a chaise lounge, a large mirror, and a desk Uncle Henry had made. Flowers were everywhere. The room smelled of jasmine. He put me down and kissed me.

The room next to the bedroom was the dressing room. There were two of everything, one for him, one for me. Wardrobes, chest of drawers, vanities with large round mirrors. One lace, three panel dressing screen for me. A wooden dressing screen for him. Behind the screens were wash stands.

I went behind the dressing screen to get into my nightgown. His mama had made it for me, it was white, long, and made of silk, with long puffy sleeves, and buttoned all the way up my neck. It flowed when I walked. There was a dressing gown to match it. I let my hair down, and as I brushed my hair, I realized this is going to be the first time he sees me. My hair down, no hoop skirt, no corset, just me. I was nervous, but excited.

I came from behind the screen and walked into the bedroom, he was in a dressing gown also. He laughed and said he saw more of my skin all day at the wedding than now. He ran his fingers through my hair, he untied the ribbon holding my dressing gown, and slid it off my shoulders, letting it fall to the floor. I untied his dressing gown, and slid it off his broad shoulders, it too, fell to the floor.

He kissed me, looked at the high neck on my nightgown and said, "I'm not undoing all those buttons." We laughed, he ripped it open, and it fell away. He looked at me and said, "You are the most beautiful thing my eyes have ever seen." He picked me up in his strong arms and lay me on our bed, and we joined together spiritually. He was loving and gentle. It wasn't wrong, dirty, or unpleasant. It was beautiful and right, just like he said it would be. I wanted him as much as he wanted me. We fell asleep in each other's arms, waking up to make love a few more times.

The next morning we woke up and made love again. He told me to stay in bed, he would be right back. He returned with a tray full of food, coffee, and champagne.

He asked, "What do you think about having breakfast on the loggia?"

I said, "That sounds wonderful."

I got out of bed and put on my dressing gown. We opened the french doors and went out into the sunshine, the morning was cool and crisp, and if you listened closely you could hear the water rushing over the rocks in the creek where we had our first picnic. Today we had our first breakfast together.

I looked at the tray and asked, "Champagne, for breakfast?"

He smiled and said, "Well, it is a special occasion!"

I giggled, then said, "Yes, it is."

He asked, "What do you want to do after breakfast? Your first day as Mrs. Jeremiah Turner."

I blushed as I said, "Stay right here with you."

Every morning he would bring me coffee in bed. I asked him, "Why does the coffee taste so much better when you get it for me?"

He laughed and said, "I know you don't like strong, really hot coffee, so I mix yours half coffee and half water. It weakens it and cools it. Then to make sure it's just right, I taste it. So maybe it tastes so good to you because it's made just for you, with love."

Our home was a large house with three rooms across and three rooms deep, two stories tall, with an attic, and a cellar. When you enter the main doors, to the left was Jeremiah's office. There was a door connecting his office to the next room which was the men's smoking parlor, and it was connected to the dining room. There was a door going to the left side veranda from Jeremiah's office.

To the right of the main entrance was the main parlor, a door connected it to the next room, the ladies parlor, and a door connected it to the dining room. There was a door going to the right side veranda from the main parlor.

The entry hall went back to the dining room, which ran the width of the house, on the right side of the dining room there was a small room, where food was to be brought in from the kitchen house. The dining room had doors going onto the back veranda, they were like the front doors, two wide, and lots of window panes.

The stairs curved around just past the door going into the parlor.

The kitchen house was off of the back right corner. The kitchen was also made of brick, it had a cast iron cooking stove, and a hand pump for water. The cook had a room in the kitchen house.

To the left rear of the house was the kitchen garden, it was surrounded with a low brick wall. At the back of the house Jeremiah had built a large greenhouse.

Upstairs, there were three rooms on each side of the stairs, and one in the middle on the south side. Our bedrooms were on the west side. Just like Jeremiah had wanted, we used the bedroom to the north in the summer, the middle room was a dressing room, and in the winter we used the south room.

There was a sewing room in the southeast room. The south-side middle room was our library. Every inch of wall space was covered in beautiful shelves to hold the books he collected and held so dear. I had started reading his favorites and had developed a love of books and learning. There was a chess set in the library, he taught me how to play. We spent many hours in that room reading, talking, and dreaming of our future together.

The other rooms upstairs were bedrooms for the children we planned to have some day.

I was afraid to have children, as Grandmother only had one child that lived to be grown, and Mama nearly died having me. Jeremiah was quick to point out that Mama was tiny and frail. I wasn't.

We talked about how to raise a child, and I had told him about Paris, and Mama wanting to send me away to learn to be a lady. We agreed, we wouldn't force anything like that on our children.

We went to the same church our families had always went to, Friedens Lutheran Church, just a few miles down the road, about halfway to Gibsonville.

It was a German Church. The word Frieden means peace. The sermons had been in German until 1840. I never knew our parents could speak German. I had never heard them speaking German. As a child, I never noticed that much about the people at church. They were just our friends and neighbors, we all dressed up, went to church on Sundays and heard the word of God.

Jeremiah explained that both of our families had come from Germany many years ago and settled in Pennsylvania. In 1740, some of the settlers left Pennsylvania and came to North Carolina, some went even further south. The first church building was made of logs, and it was built in 1745. The second is brick, and was built in 1771. It is two stories tall, people can sit upstairs and hear the preacher. They have what they call a sounding board to help people hear. This building is the one we use now. In 1791, the State of North Carolina granted fourteen acres to the church. There are plans to build a new building on that land, across the road.

Sometimes we wouldn't go to church, we would go down to the banks of the Reedy Fork, read the Bible to each other, and talk about what we had read. We would have a picnic and enjoy the beauty of God's creation.

Once we went to Wilmington, North Carolina. While we were there we went to the beach. I had seen the ocean before, but it was a port and on a ship, nothing like this. Oh, the beach... the water meeting the land. It was amazing to me, to see such beauty and power, as the waves would crash against the sand. I had never felt closer to God. It was quiet except for the sound of a few birds, and the waves. Jeremiah and I were the only people there. This seemed to be the most peaceful place on earth. We camped on the beach that night.

When he took me to see the University of Virginia, and to Hot Springs, Virginia, I saw a different side of the beauty of God's creation, the mountains.

The Blue Ridge Mountains look smoky. Like a winter evening, before the snow would come, when smoke from the fireplace hangs low to the ground, and looks blue. The beauty of the mountains, the valleys, the trees, and the blue haze was mesmerizing. Sometimes, you can't tell if it's a mountain off in the distance, or clouds. The beauty goes on for as far as you can see, just like the ocean.

When we saw rays of sunshine shining down from the clouds, I asked, "Do you think that's how spirits get to Heaven?"

Jeremiah looked up and said, "I don't know, maybe that's God looking down, keeping watch over all that he created."

I think both are beautiful thoughts, and both may be true.

Hot Springs, Virginia, was just like Jeremiah had described. The water really did come out of the ground hot. It felt so good, I even tried the mud bath. It did make me feel good. Maybe it was the water, the mud, and the minerals, or maybe it was spending carefree time together, alone.

We were young and in love, we could barely contain ourselves. We made love every morning and every night.

We loved the days when the weather was too harsh to go outside. On those days we rarely came downstairs. We would linger in bed, read, play chess, and talk. People kept asking when we were going to have children. We didn't want children right away, we just wanted to be Jeremiah and Charlotte, not Mama and Daddy.

October, 1860. The last of Jeremiah's first tobacco crop was in the tobacco barns curing. It had been a good year. Thing's couldn't be better. We went to the North Carolina State Fair, and stayed in Raleigh for a few days. Being in the Capital, we heard a lot of talk about secession. It appeared to us, most in North Carolina didn't like the idea of South Carolina leaving the Union. I didn't like hearing about it. Secession meant war, and war meant Jeremiah would become a soldier. I thought back to the Northern Lights on his birthday, and it gave me chills.

November 6, 1860. Lincoln is elected President. North Carolina didn't allow him on the ballot. No slave state voted for him. That should have been a sign as to how insignificant the South could be.

December 20, 1860. The Thursday before Christmas, South Carolina secedes from the Union. Some people celebrated, some cried. At Sunday supper, Daddy, Jeremiah, Uncle Henry, and George, were talking about what it meant for us.

Jeremiah said, "The general consensus in Raleigh is for North Carolina to stay in the Union. Most of the people around here feel the same way."

Daddy said, "Yes, that's true, but most of the people around here, just like us, sell their tobacco in Danville, Virginia. So if Virginia secedes, the people around here might be changing their minds. I'm sure people down along the South Carolina border feel we need to follow South Carolina."

Uncle Henry said, "I think we'd better be planning on having the biggest tobacco crop that we ever had. Maybe grow more grain and food to put back, just in case things get bad."

Daddy asked, "Jeremiah, if it comes to war, are you joining up?"

Jeremiah replied, "I pray it doesn't come to war, but I'm afraid it will no matter what the states of Virginia and North Carolina decide. If North Carolina is involved in a war, yes sir, I will be joining up. I have a duty to protect my wife, my home, and my property."

I felt tears running down my face, I said a silent prayer asking God for peace.

That night when we went to bed, Jeremiah asked, "Have you given much thought to the idea of us having children?"

I said, "No, secession and war seems to be the only thing I can think of these days."

He said, "That's why I'm asking, if war does come, and I leave... I think I would like knowing you are with child. The reality is, we may not have another chance."

I began crying and just nodded. I couldn't speak. From that night on, we didn't take any precautions.

Christmas wasn't very festive that year, the threat of war was all anybody seemed to be able to talk about.

January came, and things kept getting worse. On the ninth, Mississippi seceded. The tenth, Florida. The eleventh, Alabama. The nineteenth, Georgia. The twenty-sixth, Louisiana. February second, Texas.

Then things kind of settled in for a while, with no more states leaving the Union.

February 2, 1861. Jefferson Davis is now the President of the Confederate States of America.

Jefferson Davis was a graduate of West Point. He had a cotton plantation in Mississippi. Had been elected to the U.S. House of Representatives, a position he left to fight in the War with Mexico. While in Mexico, due to his outstanding performance, he was offered the position of Brigadier General, which he declined. He was then elected to the U.S. Senate, a position he held until President Pierce appointed him as U.S. Secretary of War. He then went back to the Senate, where he was outspoken concerning states' rights. He left the U.S. Senate in January, 1861, after Mississippi seceded from the Union.

Lincoln was inaugurated March 4, 1861. Some people in the South had started calling him a "Black Republican."

April 12, 1861. Confederate forces in Charleston, South Carolina, fire on the Union held Fort Sumter. Fort Sumter surrendered on April 14.

April 15, 1861. President Lincoln calls for 75,000 troops to suppress the, "insurrection".

The Secretary of War sent a wire to the North Carolina Governor asking for two regiments for immediate service.

Governor Ellis replied, "Your dispatch is received, and if genuine, which its extraordinary character leads me to doubt, I have to say in reply, that I regard the levy of troops made by the administration for the purpose of subjugating the states of the South, as in violation of the Constitution, and as a gross usurpation of power. I can be no party to this wicked violation of the laws of the country and to this war upon liberties of a free people. You can get no troops from North Carolina."

The Governor sent men to take control of forts. He called for a special session of the General Assembly, drafting proper documents, and preparing for war. Volunteers started signing up.

April 17, 1861. Virginia seceded. Once Virginia seceded, Joseph Johnston was the highest ranking U.S. Army officer to resign.

He was given rank of Brigadier General and command of the Army of the Shenandoah. General's Thomas Jackson and James Longstreet brigades were under Johnston.

Lincoln had offered Robert E. Lee command of the Union Army the day before Virginia seceded. He declined as he felt he couldn't fight against his home state of Virginia. Lee resigned from the U.S. Army. Lee served as military advisor to the now President Davis of the Confederate States of America.

April 21, 1861. Our one year anniversary. I asked Jeremiah, "How about, we go to Paris to visit my grandparents?"

He answered, "With war looming, we can't go right now."

I said, "All this is why I want to go. Let's move to Paris. We can come back after the war."

He smiled and said, "Charlotte, I can't run away and expect someone else to fight to protect our home. I understand you're worried, but it's beyond our control. We have to be strong in our faith in God, and in each other, we will get through this."

I began sobbing and said, "The Northern Lights on your birthday. Aunt Polly said the red meant war, what if it means your death?"

He reached over, put his hand under my chin and lightly pulled my head up, to look me in the eyes, and said, "God's will be done." He hugged me, and held me close for a long time, until I stopped crying.

May 5, 1861. Arkansas seceded.

May 20, 1861. North Carolina seceded. The state chose this date because it was the anniversary of the Mecklenburg Declaration of Independence of 1775.

May 22, 1861. Jeremiah, is now a Cavalry Soldier.

6 JEREMIAH SAYS GOODBYE

Leading up to his leaving, Jeremiah showed me the plans for the stables. They were to be made of brick, be right outside of the serpentine fence, on both sides of the driveway. Each stable would have a small paddock. This was for Logan and Jefferson, and the horses of guests. He explained the plans, and asked if I would like to get the stables built.

I said, "I can do that."

He smiled that smile I love so much and said, "I know you can."

He gave me instructions on how to care for all of his plants in the greenhouses. He took me to Greensborough, on West Market Street, to Donnell's Photographic Gallery. We had our photographs made. I ordered a locket with his picture in it. He wanted a picture of me to carry in his pocket.

The night before he left, we held each other all night, I was afraid to let him go. We didn't sleep. We made love, we talked, and we cried. He took off the signet ring that was so dear to him, placed it in my hand and asked me to take care of it for him. I held it tight and told him I would. He tried talking about the future, when he comes home to me, us having lots of children, a long happy life together. I admired his strength and courage.

I hated my weakness. I decided I needed to be stronger for him. I wouldn't let him see me cry, when he leaves.

Monday, May 27, 1861. Jeremiah stood on the brick walkway, I stood on the bottom step, making me almost his height. He kissed me and said, "I'll write as soon as I can."

I clung to him and said, "I love you Jeremiah Turner."

He hugged me tight, and whispered in my ear, "I love you, Ms. Charley Turner."

He walked to Jefferson, turned to me, took his hat off with that flourish like the first day he had asked me on a picnic, bowed a little, held his hat to his chest and said, "I'll be back before you know it. Don't you forget about me!" He put his hat on just like that first day.

I said, "I could never forget about you! Don't you forget about me!"

Smiling he said, "Forget about you? Never!"

He jumped on Jefferson, like always, without using the stirrup, he tipped his hat and raced down the driveway.

Jeremiah left hoping I was with child. I wondered if he would ever come racing back up the driveway. I couldn't get the Northern Lights out of my head. I went to our bedroom and sobbed. There I stayed, sending away anyone that came knocking at the door, even Aunt Polly. I could hear Sally, the house girl, in the dressing room next door. She would empty the chamber pot and leave a tray with food and water beside my door.

June 8, 1861. Tennessee seceded. The last to join the Confederate States of America.

One day, Sally was frantically knocking on the door, I shouted, "Go away!"

She said, "No Ms. Charlotte, there's a letter from Mr. Jeremiah." I ran to the door and took the letter.

June 12, 1861

My Dearest Ms. Charley,

 I am with the 1st North Carolina Cavalry. For now I am at Camp Beauregard, in Ridgeway, North Carolina. That's northeast of Raleigh, close to Virginia. Everything is disorganized, but it is getting better every day. We spend our days training. Day after day it's the same thing. Some of the fellows here aren't very good horsemen, but I'm told with the proper training they will be. Don't worry about me. Jefferson and I are getting along just fine. I worry about you. I'm sure you are tending the plants. How are the stables coming along? If you have any questions just ask and I will respond with an answer right away. I wouldn't want to be holding up your work. Have you been riding? How's Logan? I know it's too soon, but I still have to ask, do you think you may be with child? I trust you have everything in order. I look forward to hearing from you. I love you!

Truly Yours,
Jeremiah

 There was a little pencil drawing of Jefferson in the upper right corner. I didn't know he could draw.
 I quickly ran to the dressing room, bathed and got dressed. I then headed to the greenhouse. I hope I wasn't so self-consumed that I let Jeremiah's plants die. Sally had been watering them so they were all still alive. I got out my instructions and went to work, tending each plant just like he asked.
 I then headed outside to find Anderson, one of our workers. I found him and gave instructions as how to start the stables. I asked him to get some of the workers to start clearing the area, and I sent a note to Daddy John asking for the brick.

Now I could write to Jeremiah. I went into his office and sat at his desk, and wrote him right away.

June 19, 1861

Dearest Jeremiah,

I was thrilled to get your letter. It does my heart good to know you are well. Your plants are fine. The brick have been ordered for the stable, and the workers have started clearing the area. Right now I am at your desk looking over everything from the past week. It is strange sitting at your desk, however, it does make me feel closer to you. I am fine, and yes, you are correct, I do not know if I am with child. Logan is well, and no, I haven't been riding, but I will today, as I'm going to post this letter. I miss you. I love you!

Always Yours,
Charlotte

I saddled Logan and rode to Gibsonville to post the letter. The Confederacy had taken over the postal service, as of June 1, 1861. They wouldn't accept the old stamps, and I had to buy Confederate stamps for five cents each, it wasn't really a stamp, the postmaster just wrote the word, PAID, on the letter. Logan got a long ride in, as it's eight miles to Gibsonville. I had plenty of time to think. I realized Jeremiah didn't care about the plants or the stables, he just wanted me to have something to do. I would tend the plants, and the stables would be built. I would carry on, for Jeremiah, for us. He wanted to make me feel like I was doing it for him. I wouldn't let him down. I stayed busy. I wanted everything to be just like it would be if he were here.

July 1, 1861

My Dearest Ms. Charley,

   Please never think for a minute that I am fighting for slavery. I know slavery is wrong. I'm fighting for our home, for our rights. I hear men here talking. It is unreal to me how some talk about keeping niggers in their place, or they are fine with freeing the slaves as long as they don't have to treat the niggers as equals. Others say free them, and put them on a ship to Africa. I guess some men need to feel they are superior to another. Most of the time we are just riding and training, it's very boring. I'm sure your days are more exciting than mine. Are you well? Are you with child? How's the farm, the tobacco, the greenhouse plants, the stables? Don't get too comfortable at my desk. The talk around the campfire is this war could be over in a few months. Hopefully, I could be home in time to take the tobacco to market. I love you! I miss you!

Truly Yours,
Jeremiah

   July 7, 1861. North Carolina Governor Ellis dies. It seems that he had suffered from bad health his entire life.

   That same day, Henry Clark is named Governor. He had been the Speaker of the North Carolina Senate. State law at the time made him the new Governor.

July 12, 1861

Dearest Jeremiah,

    I was relieved to get your letter. I heard there had been fighting, I have been praying you were well. I regret to tell you I am not with child. You were so hopeful, it breaks my heart. I am well. The crop is good. One stable is complete and we now are working on the guest stable. I must say Anderson is a fine brick mason. The arched doorways are beautiful. The brick floors are quite nice as well. Your plants are all growing. I would never doubt you, and think you were fighting for slavery. I admire that you have the courage of your convictions. You are willing to go into battle to stand up for your rights, and to fight for our home. I am proud of you. I will be delighted to give you your chair back, as quick as you can get here. I love you! I miss you!

Always Yours,
Charlotte

July 25, 1861

My Dearest Ms. Charley,

　I am delighted to hear that you find me brave. I'm just doing what I feel I have to do. You are right, I am heartbroken to find you are not with child, I was hopeful. I haven't see any fighting as of yet, just training. I've heard of another victory right outside of Washington, a place called Manassas. The citizens of Washington came out, in their Sunday clothes, with picnic baskets, to watch the battle. Reading about it made me think of the Roman's watching death as a sport. How can people, families, go to a battlefield to watch men kill each other? Men fighting for their lives. This should be impossible to watch, I can't comprehend anyone being so dispassionate, all the while placing their own children in harm's way. Their indifference turned to concern, when they left their picnic baskets as our boys won the battle and chased them back to Washington. One of the general's got a nickname. General Jackson of the 1st brigade is now called Stonewall Jackson. It is said that he sat on his horse in the middle of the battle with his hand held high, encouraging his men. He is the reason we won that battle. I hope this letter finds you well. I miss you more than words can say. I long to be with you. Maybe one day soon we will be together, and never have to be parted again. I have to ask about the crop. Is everyone well? I love you!

Truly Yours,
Jeremiah

August 2, 1861

Dearest Jeremiah,

All is well here, everyone is fine. The crop is good, I believe you would be proud. Work here has fallen into a good routine, everybody doing their job, and willing to help where they can. Everything would be perfect if only you were here. I too, long for you. It feels like you've been gone so long. Although sometimes at night I dream of you holding me, I think you are, but I reach for you, and you're not there. These are lonely days. Our bed feels so big and empty. I too, pray we will be soon united, never to be parted. Are you eating well? I hear stories, so I worry about you. Is Jefferson well? I'm counting on him to bring you home safe. The other day, I was in the stable, I was having a weak moment, and I started to cry. I felt Logan put his head on my shoulder. He was so quiet and easy, I didn't know he was that close to me until he touched my shoulder. He just stood there with me while I cried. I wondered, had you prayed for God to comfort me. If you did, thank you. I needed comforting that day. I miss you! I love you!

Always Yours,
Charlotte

August 12, 1861

My Dearest Ms. Charley,

   Soon we will be finished with our training and I'm told we will be leaving for Virginia on Oct 10th, if the fighting is not over by then. I wouldn't mind if it is. I have requested leave before heading to Virginia. I will have from the evening of Friday, August 30th, until the morning of Wednesday, September 4th. Take the train from Gibsonville to Ridgeway, North Carolina. One of my fellow Cavalry men here, Robert Parker, is from just about six miles away. His father will send a carriage to pick you up. I will meet you at their home as soon as I can. Mr. Parker and his wife Jane are very nice. I have had the opportunity to have supper at their home a few times. I know you will like them. If we are ordered to leave, I will send you a wire. Check for a wire before you get on the train in Gibsonville. I pray I will see you on the 30th. I live for the thought of those few days with you. I too, dream of you in my arms. I know you are lonely, and yes, I have prayed asking God to comfort you. I'm glad to hear the crop is good. I am always proud of you, I count on you to keep the farm going. I am eating well. Jefferson is well also. I too, look forward to the day Jefferson brings me home to you. I miss you! I love you!

Truly Yours,
Jeremiah

August 20, 1861

Dearest Jeremiah,

I will be on that train! I will start packing as soon as I post this letter. I will get to be with you on your birthday! I will check for the wire, and I pray you are not sent to Virginia early. I look forward to meeting the Parkers, it's so kind of them to let us stay at their home. As for the farm, this is a very good year for tobacco. The plants are thriving. Once again everybody here on the farm is working hard, they are good people, I'm glad they are here. As always, missing you. I love you!

Forever Yours,
Charlotte

Finally, August 30 has come. I get up early and Daddy drives me to the train station in Gibsonville. There is no wire waiting for me. Happily, I board the train. The trip is uneventful until after the stop in Raleigh. Some of the people that boarded there seemed happy about the war. They were talking about keeping niggers in their place. I remained quiet.

Just as Jeremiah had said, there was a carriage waiting for me. Mr. Parker was an older gentleman, with gray hair, and a gray beard. He had a pleasant smile. He spoke highly of Jeremiah. Mrs. Parker was also older with gray hair, and she was just as welcoming as Mr. Parker. I immediately felt at home.

Mrs. Parker said, "Jeremiah is a fine young man, he has been coming home with Robert on Fridays for the last few weeks.

You are all he talks about. Mr. Parker offered for you to come and stay with us, so you could see him before they leave for Virginia. The boys usually get here around six, you'll have a few hours to freshen up if you'd like."

I said, "Mrs. Parker, you are so kind to give us the opportunity to be together. I will always be grateful. Is Robert your only child?"

She said, "No, dear, he is our youngest. Our two older boys died in the war with Mexico. We have another son, Thomas. He is a year older than Robert, he married a girl from New York. He was a lawyer there, but now... he's a Union Soldier. We have three daughters, all married and living up north. We don't know when we will see them and the grandchildren again. We haven't heard from them in months, with all the changes with the mail, it's hard to get letters. Their husbands are now with the Union Army too. I pray for all of us. It's hard to believe that family is now supposed to be the enemy, because a few people can't resolve their differences among themselves."

I said, "Yes ma'am it is. Jeremiah has a sister in Boston. Her husband isn't with the Union Army, yet. I pray they all get home safe."

She smiled and said, "I like thinking, that up north there is a family that welcomes Thomas into their home, and makes sure he's fed proper, and maybe a chance to see his wife. Same for our daughter's husbands. "Do unto others as you would have them do unto you." We are trying to do unto others as we would have them do unto ours, so I guess we are really doing it for selfish reasons. Whatever the reason, it's the right thing." She took out a handkerchief and wiped away a tear.

I hugged her and then said, "I'm sure there are families looking after them. The country is full of kind and generous people like yourself."

I lightly kissed her on the cheek, stood up and said, "I should go get freshened up, it was quite hot on the train."

She had a girl show me to my room, my bags were already there. I undressed, bathed, got into my dressing gown, and started fixing my hair.

About five o'clock there was a knock on the door and I said, "Come in."

Jeremiah walked in. I jumped up and ran to him. He grabbed me in his arms. I wanted him to never let me go. We held each other tight, crying.

He kissed me and said, "You are the most beautiful thing my eyes have ever seen."

I looked at him standing there in his uniform, I started to unhook his belts holding his sword and gun. I smiled as I said, "I'm not undoing all of those buttons." I grabbed his coat on both sides of the buttons, and yanked as hard as I could, but I wasn't strong enough to rip them apart.

He laughed and smiled that smile that lights up his entire face and whispered in my ear, "I love you Ms. Charley." We held each other, kissing, then he said, "I am dirty and sweaty, I don't want to get you dirty. Give me a few minutes to clean up."

I laughed and said, "Just a few minutes."

He quickly went into the dressing room. I stopped fussing with my hair, let it down and started brushing it.

In a few minutes he came back into the bedroom wearing a dressing gown. He walked over to me and undone my dressing gown as he said, "See, you don't have to deal with all of the buttons, although I do appreciate you trying." I untied his dressing gown. He picked me up and took me to bed.

Later, he told me that Mr. Parker had said that he would have food sent up to us, that there was no need for us to feel the need to visit with them.

We were to cherish the little bit of time we had with each other. We spent the entire time in those two rooms. The Parkers had given us the most precious gift possible. We fell asleep in each other's arms. For just a few nights, when I would reach for him, he was really there.

September 2, 1861. Jeremiah's twenty-first birthday. We spend the day in bed, talking, laughing, cherishing every moment, all the while afraid of what the future holds.

September 3, 1861. Our last night together, he would have to be up early in the morning and leave. As we lay in bed holding each other he, as always, was talking about the future. I told him what Mrs. Parker had told me, about why she had invited us here. He said he knew why, Robert had told him.

I said, "Well... I've been thinking about that. I can't believe their kindness. I've only been concerned with you, the farm, and myself. I haven't thought to do anything for anybody else. "Do unto others as you would have them do unto you." I knew that. I learned it in church, Daddy had told me that many times. It isn't just words from a book, it's the teachings of Jesus. I have to do something, and you might not like what I have decided to do."

He asked, "What have you decided? Do you want to take in soldiers, feed them, and give them the chance to spend a day or two with their wives? I think that's a fine thing for you to do."

"No," I said, "I want to be a link on the Underground Railroad."

He quickly sat up and said, "You must be crazy, you could go to jail for that. We already risk enough with freeing our people and paying them, I can't let you do that."

I replied, "Do you remember when I wanted us to run away to Paris, and you said fighting for our home and our rights is something you have to do? You might not understand, but this is something I have to do. I know you don't believe slavery is right, but you fighting for the South is keeping people in bondage.

I know we tell ourselves you're fighting for a different reason, but can the reasons be separated? You fight for our rights and I'll fight for their freedom. There are a lot of people in Guilford County already doing it. It's not as big of a risk there as it is here." I smiled and said, "There is a way to stop me."

He said, "What way is that?"

I said, "Come home, and make sure I don't."

He smiled at me and said, "Do you promise you will be careful and not take any unnecessary risks?"

"I promise. Do you?" I asked.

He said, "I promise. You cannot write about any of this in letters to me or anybody!"

I said, "I know that. Now, let's not talk about it anymore tonight. We have just one more night together. Only the Lord knows when or if we will ever be together again."

We spent a wonderful night together, we woke early the next morning and made love once more, then, Jeremiah got up and went into the dressing room. He came out looking so handsome in his uniform. He then kissed me and said, "I noticed you are a bit skinny, you need to eat! I need to know you will take care of yourself. You know I'm still hoping for a child. You need to be healthy and strong to have a baby."

I said, "I will. I need to know you will take care of yourself too. I love you Jeremiah Turner!"

He smiled that smile and said, "I love you." Then whispered, "Ms. Charley Turner." He opened the door and quietly left.

7 DO UNTO OTHERS

The Parkers invited me to stay a few days, but I felt I had to get home. I had work to do. As soon as I was home, I asked Anderson to come into Jeremiah's office so we could talk. I asked if he was familiar with the Underground Railroad. He was. We talked about how I could help. He said sometimes there are runaway slaves that spend the night on the farm already. The workers don't let them stay in their houses out of fear, so they show them to the barn and get them food. It's not very many, and just once in a while.

I asked, "How do we let the runaways know if it's safe to stop here?"

He said, "Songs. When they hear certain songs they know which way to go, if it's safe to stop, or if they need to keep moving, and such things."

I said, "Start singing those songs if you know them, if you don't, then learn them! Bring everyone straight to me. They will stay here in my house until they are fed, tended to, and it's safe to travel. No slave catcher can force their way into a white man's home looking for a runaway, so this is the safest place for them.

Although, I would like for you to stay here in the house on those nights. I would feel better knowing there is a man in the house. Do you know how to use a gun?" I asked.

He said, "I ain't never shot one ma'am."

I said, "Well I'm going to teach you. You know we both are in a lot of trouble if anybody finds out. I will be arrested and they will probably hang you. You still want to do it?"

He smiled and said, "Yes ma'am. Everybody here will want to help. We all trust each other. Ain't nobody here said anything about you and Mr. Jeremiah paying us and offering our freedom papers anytime we want them. You good people, Ms. Charlotte."

I smiled, patted him on the shoulder and said, "You are too Anderson, all of the people that work here are good people, and I'm glad you're here. Now as Jeremiah once told me, "there's no time like the present." Let's go teach you how to shoot."

"You know how to shoot a gun Ms. Charlotte?" he asked.

I said, "I do."

He said, "I declare! A woman that know how to shoot a gun!" He chuckled. "I thought I'd seen it all, but I guess I was wrong!"

Anderson was a large muscular man, around thirty years old. He was born on Daddy John's plantation. He was sweet on Sally, the house girl. I asked if they had plans to marry.

He said, "Yes, we talked about it when you was gone, we was planning to ask you if it's alright."

I said, "Anderson, you don't have to ask me, ask Sally."

He said, "I already did ask her, she say, she wants to marry me. Is it alright with you Ms. Charlotte?" he asked.

I said, "Anderson, you are a free man, Sally is a free woman. Y'all decide what you want to do. Just let me know so we can fetch the preacher from over at Daddy's farm to marry y'all proper. Then you can move in here with Sally. That works out real good. When were you thinking about getting married?"

He smiled and answered, "Right away ma'am."

I said, "You go tell Sally, lets practice shooting, then I will go see Daddy about the preacher."

I taught him and all the other adults on the farm how to shoot.

Anderson and Sally were married. It was nice to have a reason to celebrate. I missed Jeremiah. Part of me was sad that life here goes on without him, but I know it has to. He wouldn't like for life to come to a standstill, awaiting his return.

Gradually but steadily, it seemed as though there was always singing around the farm, and it wasn't long before the runaways started showing up. We tended to their wounds and gave them warm food. Some were just tired from all the running and needed a safe place to rest, before moving ahead on their arduous journey.

Jeremiah and I continued writing letters to each other. I couldn't tell him everything that we had been doing on the farm.

October 10, 1861

My Dearest Ms. Charley,

    We have completed our training, it is now time to join the war. We are going to Virginia. I will write to you as I know more. Please don't fret over me. I know you have plenty to keep you busy. I know you are working hard. I am eating well and taking care of myself and Jefferson. I hope you are taking care of yourself. I miss you more every day. I think the more miles between us is going to make me miss you even more, already at times, it's more than I think I can bear. Sometimes I feel that I would give up everything, even life itself for one more night with you in my arms. I know it's wrong of me to write to you in moments of weakness, but sometimes I am overcome with sadness and I must let you know how much I love you, and how much I miss you. Once again I must ask. Are you with child? It preys on my mind, we might not have any more chances for you to have my child. I sometimes daydream of you with my son in your arms, I think of us having started our family, me coming home, our family growing. I have to keep looking to the future. Please remember the further north I am, and the more we move around, it's harder to get mail, pretty near impossible sometimes. The time between getting letters will be longer, but please keep writing, never think I have stopped writing, the letters will eventually get to us. I need to know you're safe. Keep praying, keep thinking positive, and keep working hard. I love you!

Truly Yours,
Jeremiah

October 16, 1861

Dearest Jeremiah,

I love reading of you wanting to hold me in your arms. I don't consider it a weakness to let a person know they are loved, or that you miss them. I, also, would give anything to be in your arms. Once again, it breaks my heart to say, I am not with child. It is a beautiful thought, me holding our son, us starting our family, and you being home. Maybe God isn't ready for us to have children. Maybe we have much work to do in our lives before we are ready for children, God knows what's best for us, doesn't He? You are right about the miles between us, knowing that you are already in Virginia makes me miss you even more. I didn't know it was possible to miss you more than I already do. I try to stay busy as to not think too much, sometimes I do break down and cry. Then I think you wouldn't like the thought of me crying, so I gather myself and get busy. Anderson and Sally were married last Saturday. He now lives in the main house, I'm sure it makes you feel better knowing there is a man in the house. Everything here is going just like we planned. Some of the tobacco has been sold, and more has been put in the barns. We've gotten a good price. It has been a good year for tobacco farmers. You take care up there in Virginia. I understand about the mail. I will never stop writing to you. Know you are always on my mind. I love you!

Forever Yours,
Charlotte

I went to see Daddy after posting that letter. I sat in his office and told him everything about freeing the people on our farm, and helping the runaways.

He wasn't as surprised as I thought he would be. He did ask if Jeremiah was in agreement with it all. I told him Jeremiah didn't like me taking the risks, but he understood.

Then Daddy said, "Why are you telling me this, I shouldn't know, no one should know!"

I shifted in my chair a little bit, took a deep breath and said, "Well Daddy, I would like for you to do the same."

He looked directly into my eyes and said, "Do the same? What do you mean? You want me to hide runaway slaves?"

I said, "Daddy, I want you to give all of your people their freedom. Freedom isn't something to be bought and sold. It's a God given right. It's not for any person to take away from another. Nobody has to know you have done it. It's... it's just the Christian thing to do. Do you remember teaching me, "Do unto others as you would have them do unto you?" Would you want to be owned by another man? I know you are a kind man, the people here love you, I'm sure they would all want to stay and work for you. The only difference is, they would know they could leave if they wanted to, and you would pay them. Look at how much money you have made because of Uncle Henry and all the others. Uncle Henry is one of the smartest men I know, shouldn't he be allowed to make decisions for himself? You know he would stay here, but he would feel like a man. A man that takes care of his family. He deserves that, they all do."

By the time I had finished talking, tears were rolling down my cheeks.

Daddy sat in his chair, and turned away for a minute. When he looked at me, he too, had tears running down his cheeks. Then, after composing himself, he finally said, "You're right. How did you and Jeremiah work this out?"

So I filled him in on what we were doing, when I got to the Underground Railroad part, I told him that right now I was just letting them stay, I wasn't helping them get to the next place. I needed his help for that.

I said, "I need you and Uncle Henry to take people to Reidsville. They would stay at my house, and I would let you know when they are ready to move on to the next stop."

He said, "Will you think any less of me, if I have to think on this for a day or two?"

I walked over to him, kissed him on the cheek and said, "Daddy you're a fine Christian man, I could never think badly of you."

The next day Daddy and Uncle Henry came riding up to my house. Uncle Henry got off of his horse and picked me up as he hugged me and said, "Thank you darlin', all that hard headedness you got in you finally paid off for me and mine. Your daddy is a good man, and he has a good girl too. That Jeremiah is one lucky boy. That is, if he can put up with you and that hard head."

I smiled, kissed him on the cheek and said, "I love you Uncle Henry."

He said, "I love you too darlin'."

Daddy wiped his cheek. I think it was tears. Once he gathered himself, he said, "Me and Henry are going to be making a lot of trips to Reidsville in the future, you reckon you got anything that needs to be going along with us?"

"Oh Daddy! Really?" I said. "Y'all come inside, let's have some coffee and figure out all the details."

Anderson and Sally were thrilled that we could now provide safe transport for runaways to Reidsville.

Anderson shook Daddy's hand and said, "You a fine man, Mr. William. A fine man."

December 25, 1861

Dearest Jeremiah,

    Today is Christmas. I wonder if you are alive. If you are alive, are you safe, are you warm, where are you now, and are you eating enough? The winter is lonely without you. It's cold here, and even colder without you to hold me close. I'm staying busy working hard all day, so there's no idle time to spend thinking of myself. But when night comes and I go to our cold, empty bed, I miss you more than I can describe. I have tried to spend some time in the evenings in the library reading, but I can't. I see your books, your chess set, and your chair. I smell the wood and leather. It all makes me ache for you. I remember how we always loved that room. All the laughter, the conversations, the dreams of the future, it all seems like a distant memory. Every part of this house reminds me of you, and everything in it reminds me of you. I finally understand your desire for a child. A real, living, breathing part of Jeremiah Turner. Will we ever have another chance? Sometimes it feels as though it was all a dream. Are you real, were we ever really together? I try to remember what you told me so long ago. Trust in God. Trust in our love. Merry Christmas Jeremiah! I love you!

Forever Yours,
Charlotte

December 25, 1861

My Dearest Ms. Charley,

As of today, I have been in four skirmishes. No major fighting, so I am told, although when I am being shot at, it seems major to me. Camp life is wearing thin. The same thing, day after day. It's cold. No blanket can warm me the way you did last winter. Just four days ago we were twenty-five miles from Washington, then we started moving away. I follow orders, but I feel I could be of more use elsewhere. I think I would be a better scout than cavalry. I have requested it. I will let you know. It will make it harder for your letters to find me. I must seek change, the camp life is unbearable to me. I pray you are safe. I hope you have been receiving my letters, and always remember, I will never stop writing. I never knew Christmas could be such a sad and lonely time. Do you remember when last year we thought Christmas wasn't very festive after South Carolina set us on this course? I am so happy we decided to leave the decorations up and try to carry on. I have been trying to spend the day just reliving last Christmas, with you, in our home. Warm, beautiful, and full of love. I remember you were wearing a red and white velvet dress. Your hair smelled of jasmine, just like the day we were married. We had mistletoe hanging in every doorway. Running cedar draped over every porch rail, banister, and mantle. That huge tree, which we thought we'd never get through the door. How nice it was to decorate with you. I must admit, I was quite proud when our parents came to supper and complemented you on our home. My lady Ms. Charley, I love you!

Truly Yours,
Jeremiah

I couldn't tell you how many slaves we hid and transported. We told them we didn't want to know their names, where they came from, or their plans after they leave us. We wouldn't let them know anything about us either, so if they got caught they wouldn't have any information about us, or the other runaways. I saw unbelievable things. I don't understand how one human could do such things to another. Most of the runaways were tired and hungry, and they usually needed shoes and clothes, and they always needed rest. Sometimes they would stay a while and work to earn money, before heading north. Daddy and Uncle Henry made at least one trip a week to Reidsville for me. They thought it would be best not to tell Mama, Aunt Polly, and Sara. I continued to get the outbuildings built as Jeremiah would tell me in letters what he would be working on if he were home.

We cleared land for more tobacco, used the wood for barns, fence rails, and some for next year's firewood. We also grew winter vegetables.

We spent a lot of time carding cotton, breaking flax, spinning the yarns and working at the loom.

We were also busy killing hogs, scalding them to remove the hair, butchering, salt curing the meat, then smoking it. The smell coming from a smoke-house is heavenly. It's also hog breeding time. We would put the boars with the sows now, and come early spring they will be having their babies, as it take three months, three weeks, and three days for a sow to have babies.

During the winter, it takes longer to tend the animals, we would have to break the ice so the animals could get water. We would also be busy feeding hay and grain, and cleaning the stables every day. It's cold for them too, so they also want to stay inside.

January is the time to start burning off and tilling the small patches of land for the tobacco seedbeds.

In February you mix the tobacco seeds with a bit of soil and sow the beds. We would stake them and then cover them with linen, making a little shelter to protect the seed. It takes six weeks for the seedlings to mature. During that time, we prepare the fields. Plowing, disking, and mounding up the furrows. With luck and good weather, by the beginning of April we are ready to transplant from the seedbeds to the fields. We would use three people per row. One to walk along the furrows with a pole and make the holes, the second person plants it, and the third person waters it. I had never known how much work went into growing tobacco.

As a child at my parents home, I only helped with these kind of chores until I grew tired of them, then I would go to do something more pleasant. As a grown woman with my husband gone to war, I felt I had no choice but to work alongside everyone else. I never knew hard work. Sometimes, I think the workers felt pity for me. I appreciated their kindness toward me, and I loved them for it. I believed they loved me too.

The biggest effect the war had on our part of North Carolina was it took our men away. The city of Greensborough was growing and thriving due to manufacturing goods for the war. Not as many people farmed as they now had jobs in Greensborough, so those of us that chose to continue to farm, had to grow more. We simply couldn't grow enough tobacco. Normally we would grow enough food for us and the animals. Now any extra food that was grown could be sold at a good price.

Spring of 1862. Around here, buttercups are the first flowers to bloom. They always make me think of Easter. The red buds are the first trees to bloom. Our first signs of new life. They are followed by the dogwoods.

Aunt Polly would always say the dogwood blooms were a symbol to remember that Jesus died to save us from our sins. The white flower is for purity and innocence, the shape of the flower represents the cross he died on, the brown spot on each petal represents the blood he shed for us, and the center is like a crown of thorns to remind us of his pain. I had never read anything about that in the Bible, but I always think about it when I see a dogwood blooming. Maybe she's right. The tree looks dead in the winter and then it seems to be reborn in the spring, just like Jesus on the third day. Maybe God wants to remind us each spring that Jesus died for us, and through him we can all be saved.

I wonder if our country can be saved. How many people must die before hard-headed men will talk peace? I also wonder how people can fight a war, with both sides claiming God to be on their side. Is God with Jeremiah, or does God see Jeremiah as being on the side of evil? I tell myself, God knows what's in Jeremiah's heart. Jeremiah doesn't keep his fellow man in bondage and he's not fighting for that. God knows, he must know...

Jeremiah is now a scout. In his letters he explained to me, some would call him a spy, but he is always in his uniform, so that makes him a scout. He rides ahead and reports back to his commanding officer of what he sees. Troops, how many, which way they're heading, what they have with them, cannons, supplies, and so on. With good scouts, commanders should not be surprised by their enemy. His letters now seem a bit more positive. That, in turn, makes me more positive.

March of 1862, the Confederate Congress passed a resolution recommending tobacco farmers plant food crops instead of tobacco. Our money had already been spent on tobacco seed, not to mention all the work we had already done preparing for planting the tobacco.

I, like many around me, felt we had no choice but to grow the tobacco. We did plant extra food crops, like corn, potatoes, a wide variety of vegetables, and herbs. The herbs were for making medicine, like Aunt Polly had taught me. We also used herbs for making sausage, and to give bland food some flavor. We grew almost everything we needed, there was very little that we had to buy at the store.

I would get letters from Jeremiah, he seemed to like being a scout. He would tell me how he was being careful to avoid the enemy. Sleeping lightly with his back to a river, as to offer a little protection. Traveling off of the main roads, listening, always being aware of what is going on around him. Being that he was a country boy, it was easy for him to determine if sounds were made by man or animal. Jeremiah was a smart man, he could take care of himself. I had a renewed faith he would make it home from the war. Maybe spring does that to a person. Signs of new life everywhere gives one hope.

When spring arrived, it seemed like every day an animal on the farm was having babies. The pigs, cows, chickens, goats, and the horses. It takes a horse around eleven months to have a baby. Before Jeremiah had left, he had bred Logan to his best mare. She gave birth to a colt that looked just like Logan. I was so happy at first, and excited to write to Jeremiah. I watched the mare strutting around the paddock with Little Lo, as I called him, showing him off to the world, but then it made me cry. That's what Jeremiah had been hoping for. That I would be here with his son. I didn't want to write the letter, but I knew he would be asking about the mare and I would have to tell him anyway. Like he has always said, "There's no time like the present". I wiped away my tears and went inside and wrote the letter.

Spring also means more work. Everyone helped, even the children. They didn't have to work, they wanted to.

I asked a few of the women to go to the main house and help Sally with the cooking, and we would all eat together.

Anderson said, "A lot of people won't care too much for you working in the fields and letting all of us eat in your fine home."

I replied, "Anderson, I don't care what people think. We are just trying to get by as best we can, and we save a lot of time by all the food being cooked in one place all at once, and all of us eating together. Besides, I enjoy the company. So the hell with those that don't like it!"

Anderson had a shocked look on his face as he said, "Ms. Charlotte!"

"I'm sorry Anderson," I replied, "I'm no lady, I reckon I never really was."

He grinned and said, "You a fine lady, Ms. Charlotte, a mighty fine lady!"

"Thank you." I replied.

What good was it to be a lady now? All the things that Mama insisted I learn, how to act, how to dress, and how to fix my hair. Putting on big parties and going to parties, always looking and acting like a lady.

Mama explained, "Children have birthday parties and attend other parties to learn how to be a lady, or gentleman. The purpose of the party is to practice your manners and social skills."

All that meant nothing. Now I had to rely on the things Daddy taught me. I think the last time I cared how I looked, was when I was dressing the morning Jeremiah left the Parkers house. I came home and went to work. No hoops, no fixing my hair, I just braid it and tie it up at the back to keep it out of the way. I wear old dresses, they're only going to get ruined. I wear an apron and a kerchief on my head to try to keep some dirt off me and my hair. When I go to the post office to mail a letter to Jeremiah is the only time I take a few minutes to dress.

I put on a riding habit and a hat. I stopped going to the general store. Anderson, Daddy, and Uncle Henry get the things I must buy. They also bring letters from Jeremiah. I stopped going to church. We have our own services here. I don't like the way some of the people look at me. There's always rumors of the war. Everybody talking politics. I just can't bear it. I get my information of the war from Jeremiah's letters, The Greensborough Patriot, and news Daddy brings when he is in Reidsville or Danville. I know these things are facts. I can't listen to the rumors. It seems that some people enjoy telling bad news, truth has no meaning to them.

Summer came, and the weather turned dry. We were all praying for rain. When I was a child every time it rained Daddy would say, "The Lord has blessed us with some rain."

Now I understood why he said that. We had to carry water to the fields from the ponds that Jeremiah had dug. It was back-breaking work for all of us. Those ponds saved the crops that year. In addition to carrying water we had to hoe the weeds, push dirt up around the plants, and remove the tobacco worms. They are big, fat, green worms, some people call them hornworms. There is only one way to remove them, you have to pick them off by hand. The children seemed to enjoy this task. As the plants begin to mature, you have to top and sucker the plants. Topping is removing the flower buds on the top of the plant. Suckering is removing the little buds further down the plant, they emerge due to the topping. Doing this makes the plants put growth into the leaves, not the flowers.

June 1, 1862. Johnston is wounded at the battle of Fair Oaks. President Davis replaces him with General Robert E. Lee. Lee renames the army, The Army of Northern Virginia.

Robert E. Lee married Mary Custis, the daughter of George Washington Parke Custis, which was the son of President George Washington's adopted son. The Lee's and the Washington's were distant relatives.

Robert's daddy, Henry "Light Horse Harry" Lee, served with Washington and also with General Nathaniel Greene at The Battle of Guilford Courthouse during the Revolutionary War. He retired from service at the rank of Lieutenant Colonel, and became a delegate to Congress. He gave the eulogy at President Washington's funeral. He also served as Governor of Virginia.

Robert E. Lee graduated from West Point in 1829, second in his class. He was a highly respected soldier, earned three brevets for gallantry, and acquired the rank of Colonel. Lee returned to West Point as Superintendent from 1852 to 1855. He then left West Point and returned to the Army, where he took a position in the Cavalry. He has a reputation as one of the finest officers in the United States.

June 16, 1862. Abraham Lincoln signs the Compensated Emancipation Act. I had a hard time understanding, until this day there were about three thousand slaves in Washington? They were freed well over a year after the war had started? I thought the people in the North didn't have slaves. They were freed by the United States Government, which paid the slave holders to free them. The newly freed slaves were offered one hundred dollars each to leave the country. I don't know how many of them took the money and left.

Jeremiah's letters still continue to be positive. We have spent Christmas, my birthday, our anniversary, and soon his birthday, apart. He doesn't say a lot about fighting. He talks mostly of riding a lot, meeting people here and there, some that offer a hot meal. He sleeps in barns as to be close to Jefferson in case he has to leave abruptly. He makes it sound like an adventure.

I could do the things he describes. We could be together. What was it that Sara had said to me in Paris? The only thing I knew how to do was ride a horse, how would that help me? I could go to Jeremiah and be a scout, the thing I do best is ride. It's silly to think of such things. Women aren't allowed to fight in the war.

August, time to start pulling tobacco. You take a few leaves off at a time, starting with the bottom, take them to the barn, tie them to tobacco sticks and hang them in the barn to cure. We pull tobacco from the plants every week or two. When the tobacco is cured we open the barn, and leave it open for a couple of days to allow the dried tobacco to absorb the humid air, so it won't crumble when it comes out of the barn and it's untied and taken off of the sticks. Then it's allowed to absorb moisture for a few more days, taken to the pack house where it's laid out, graded, bundled, and finally loaded into the wagons and taken to market.

From early August to November this was life on our farm. Then it's hog killing time and it all starts over again.

September, 1862. Lincoln signs the Emancipation Proclamation, a document stating, that as of January 1, 1863, if the fighting continues, all slaves in the rebellion states are free. That seemed to just inflame the situation. The Confederate States of America says the United States of America is a separate country and has no authority to declare such a thing.

Another Christmas passes without Jeremiah.

December 25, 1862

My Dearest Ms. Charley,

    This Christmas I am with Stuart's Cavalry. We conducted a raid in Dumfries. We captured wagons full of supplies. We chased a cavalry regiment through their own camp! We took everything of use to us as well. Stuart left six of us behind to operate on the enemy's outpost under the command of First Lieutenant Mosby. It has been an exciting Christmas. I have enjoyed talking with Mosby. He also went to the University of Virginia. He was a lawyer before the war. He didn't care to leave his family and fight in the war, but felt he had a duty to defend his home. He is small in height and weight, but seems large in ideals and morals. He carries himself in a way that makes one think of him as a larger man. He holds his head high, speaks quietly but firmly, and he smiles a lot. I admire him. People seem to want to be in his company. His blue eyes seem to demand respect. From what I have seen, I would say he is a brave man. We share a love for reading. He is an intelligent man, and I have enjoyed our conversations. I feel that Stuart sent us on this raid as to take our minds off of Christmas. It has helped, but then the quiet time comes and there is no other thoughts except of you and home. I hope you have a joyful Christmas. It is such a lonely time. I pray you have spent the day with our families. I close my eyes and I picture you, I miss your smile, your laugh. I miss the feel of your head resting on my chest, I can almost smell the jasmine. What a wonderful way to end a day. I live for the moment when we will be together, and I can whisper in your ear, "I love you, Ms. Charley."

Truly Yours,
Jeremiah

December 25, 1862

Dearest Jeremiah,

Another Christmas without you, it is more than a person should have to bear. I pray you are warm tonight. I visited with Mom Peggy and Daddy John this morning, followed by a visit to Mama and Daddy's. Sara and George were excited to tell everyone she is with child. They were so happy. Happy like we once were. Mama, Aunt Polly, and Mae, all saying they're going to be grandmas. I am happy for them, for all of them. I tried my best to put on a happy face. I smiled and hugged everyone, and after what seemed an acceptable time, I made an excuse of not feeling well and left. It is so hard to feel happy about anything, or for anyone. The few times I have felt happy, it is quickly followed by guilt. Why should I have a moment of happiness, when you are suffering so? I wish there were a way for us to be together. How much longer can this last? There seems to be no end in sight. It seems hopeless. I look forward to tomorrow, just another day, a day filled with work. I love you Jeremiah!

Forever Yours,
Charlotte

8 ATTACKED

January 1, 1863. The Union declares all slaves in the rebellion states free. The Confederacy doesn't recognize it.

I have decided to continue to plant tobacco. Just like last year. We had cleared more land that we could use for growing food. I felt we needed the money from the tobacco, because prices are still up and it would be foolish to turn down guaranteed money.

In February, Jeremiah's letters explained that he is now with Mosby, in a partisan unit called the Rangers. It's not regular Cavalry, but a small group whose purpose is to harass the enemy, destroy supply lines, and force the Union Army to pull men away from the front where the major fighting is, to protect their rear. He's not in camp. The rangers are spread throughout the countryside, housed by regular people, until Mosby sends for them. Mosby has no use of a sword, he thinks they are outdated, and useless to him and his men. They all carry .44 Colt army revolvers, taken from the enemy. They wear them on belt holsters and some carry an extra pair in their boots. Mosby thinks if a man is close enough to you to use his sword against you, shoot him!

March 2, 1863. Anderson is in Danville with Daddy and Uncle Henry. I am awakened in the night by a huge man climbing on top of me. He's saying horrible things. I suddenly realized what was going on. I tried to fight him off while I pulled a large knife from under the pillow, I stabbed him in the back over and over until he fell dead on top of me. I rolled the dead man off of me, and he fell onto the floor.

I don't know how or why, but I was very calm. I got up and looked at the man. I didn't know who he was. He was a white man, dressed in rags. Was he one of the low-life ruffians roaming the countryside? Why did he come here? I looked around the room and noticed the door to my dressing room was open. I looked inside, my jewelry box is on the floor. I go to the dead man and felt in his pockets and pulled out my jewelry. I stand there covered in the dead man's blood. I have to get him out of the house. I used the rug his body was lying on, and I started to drag him out of my room and down the stairs. As I drug him down the stairs his head is banging on each step. Thump, thump, thump. Sally comes in to see what the noise is, she covers her mouth so as not to scream. I wondered for a second where had she been, but realized I had been very quiet until now. She couldn't have known anything was going on.

She asked, "Are you alright Ms. Charlotte? Is that your blood? Who is he?"

I replied sternly, "Sally, go back to your room, you don't want to know anything about a white man being killed, you could be hanged for it!"

"No," she replied, "you need my help."

I stood there for a few seconds, and then said, "Alright, help me get him out of here."

We dragged the dead man out of the house, down the path to the hog lot, and rolled him over to the hogs. His body won't be there in the morning.

We went back to the house. Sally warmed some water and brought it up for me to wash the blood off. She then put clean sheets on the bed. She said the mattress didn't have blood on it.

We went downstairs to check the windows and doors to see where he came into the house.

He had broken a small pane in a window along the back of the dining room, and then, as best we could see, he had reached in and unlocked the door. We found something to put over it for now. There would be no going back to sleep after that.

When daylight came, I went to the hog lot to get the dead man's clothes and burned them and the rug, while Sally washed my gown and sheets. Anderson got back to the house late in the afternoon.

I told Anderson and Sally, "I need to go see Jeremiah's cousin, Jessie Kime. I'm going to see if he will come to stay here with us for a while. We need to have a white man around here. I'll be leaving early in the morning. It's a day's ride, and I'm sure Jessie's mama will let me stay the night. I'll head home the following morning. Don't worry about me, I've got my gun. Anderson, you make sure there is a gun in every house on the farm. Make sure the men hide them and only get them out if they are protecting lives. Do you understand what I mean?"

Anderson answered, "Yes ma'am." then asked, "Don't you think you should get your daddy to go with you?"

"No, I need to talk to Jessie alone." I answered, "I'll be fine. You take care of things here. If anybody comes looking for a large white man you ain't seen nothing! Do you understand?" I asked.

"Yes ma'am. We ain't seen nobody around here!" he answered.

I slept some, though lightly, that night. It was comforting to know that Anderson was in the house. I was eager to see Jessie, so I left early.

I had only been around Jesse a few times, but when Jeremiah was preparing to leave, he told me I could always count on Jessie. So I rode to right outside of Liberty, close to Richland Church.

Jessie was a good bit older than Jeremiah, and he wasn't nearly as tall.

His hair was starting to gray, and he had mutton-chop side burns. He had lost an arm in the war with Mexico, but even with the one arm gone, he was a cheerful man. It was dusk when I got to his house. He lived with his parents. Mr. and Mrs. Kime were happy to see me. We ate supper, and they asked about Jeremiah, and after catching up with each other, I told them why I came.

I said, "There have been some ruffians prowling around the house, and I would feel better if a white man was there. Jessie, I came to ask if I could get you to come stay at the farm."

Jessie quickly answered, "Yea, we can leave in the morning."

Mr. Kime said, "That sounds like a good idea."

Mrs. Kime nodded in agreement.

The next morning as we were about to leave, I said, "Jessie, before we leave, I need to tell you that I've been hiding runaway slaves."

Jessie said, "A lot of people around here are doing that." Then he asked, "Do you think maybe it's slave catchers prowling around?"

"No, it wasn't a slave catcher," I answered, "I'll tell you all about it on the way."

On the ride back, I told him the real story.

With Jessie there, everybody seemed relieved. Things continued as normal as we worked, and hid runaways. Jessie understood the people there were free and paid to work. He worked too. It surprised me how much work a one armed man could do. He did suggest we make the men's parlor a bedroom for him. He said he didn't think it would be proper for him to sleep upstairs, and being downstairs he could hear if anybody was trying to come into the house. I thought that was a fine idea.

After about a week, I told Jessie, Sally, and Anderson, that I planned to leave. I desperately needed to see Jeremiah. He couldn't come to me, so I would go to him.

They all thought it was a bad idea, but I didn't care. I wasn't asking permission, I was telling them. They could carry on with everything just fine without me. If they needed anything, go see my daddy. I asked that they not tell Daddy or Daddy John for a few days. I didn't want anyone trying to stop me. I had to do this. This is what I had planned when I asked Jessie to come stay. I had to make sure Jessie knew how things were done on the farm, and feel that I could trust him to run the place, like I had. I trusted him.

I had Jeremiah's signet ring in my hand, then I took my engagement ring off of my finger and handed both to Sally, and said, "I trust you will keep these safe, I don't have to tell you how dear they are." I figured it was safe to keep my wedding ring on.

Sally, crying softly, said, "Ms. Charlotte, won't nothing happen to them."

Anderson said, "Ms. Charlotte, I can take you, or your daddy can take you. You shouldn't go by yourself."

I said, "Thank you for your concern Anderson, but I plan to do this myself. I have Logan, my pistol, and my knife, and I know how to use all of them."

Jessie sat quiet for a few minutes, then finally said, "I understand you needing to see Jeremiah with everything that has happened. I think you have made your plans and ain't nothing gonna to stop you, so all I have to say is," then he asked, "what is your plan? Are you just gonna to get on that horse and ride sidesaddle to northern Virginia?"

I said, "I haven't thought about riding sidesaddle or not. I plan to leave in the morning and ride from town to town, until I get there."

Jessie then said, "That won't work. A woman traveling alone these days is an easy target for the ruffians and such. You will end up robbed, raped, and most likely dead.

Now a young man traveling north to join up wanting to fight alongside his older brother, might have a better chance of making it. The first thing you need to do is cut off your hair, then put on some men's clothes. Not fancy clothes, just some work clothes, and you can't ride sidesaddle, that's for sure." he finished.

"I can do that," I said, "What else should I do?"

He continued, "Well, don't talk to people unless you have to, you can probably travel on the main roads until you get to Charlottesville. You still have to be careful, but I haven't heard about Union soldiers being that far south. After Charlottesville, you should stay off the roads and maybe travel at night. Where are you planning on going, and how do you figure you're gonna' find him?"

I said, "His last letter came from Middleburg. I'll go there and find him. It will take me about three weeks to get there, so I'll have plenty of time to figure it out."

Jessie said, "Alright, let me get you some of my clothes. Maybe you should wait to cut your hair until you get to Danville. You can stay with friends and with your hair cut off they will have more questions, they might even send a wire to your daddy and try to stop you."

"That's a good idea," I replied, "I'll braid my hair and let it hang down under my shirt and wear a hat, and with the collar turned up on my coat, people won't notice my hair. I'll tell friends I'm traveling to Charlottesville to visit Jeremiah. Everyone knows I've always been a tomboy, so they shouldn't pay much attention to my men's clothes."

9 THE LONELY JOURNEY

I left home on Sunday, March 8, 1863. I had rolled up a change of clothes in my bedroll. I had a compass, canteen, saddlebags filled with food for me and Logan, and a few cigars for Jeremiah. I had made a little pocket on Logan's saddle for hiding the money I carried with me. I thought one hundred dollars would be plenty for the trip. I carried a knife on my belt underneath my coat. My gun was in my boot. I jumped on Logan without using the stirrup and raced down the driveway.

By that afternoon I was outside of Reidsville, and it had started to rain, hard. I thought I would stop in and visit with Ms. Patience for a while and wait for the storm to pass. Ms. Patience was actually Mrs. Walton Reid. Her husband was also off fighting in the war. They had been friends of my family for as long as I could remember. She was a tall woman with brown hair and a lovely smile. I knocked on her door, she was shocked to see me looking as I did. I explained that I was going to Charlottesville to visit Jeremiah and thought dressing like this would be safer.

She agreed. I asked if I could visit with her until the storm passed.

She said, "You will stay here tonight. It's cold out and that storm isn't letting up anytime soon. I'll send a boy to tend to your horse. You go on upstairs and get out of those wet clothes. I'll have some warm water and clean clothes brought up to you."

"I can't ask you to do all that for me," I replied, "I thought I could just visit for a while, until the storm passes."

"Charlotte, I'll not take no for an answer." She said, "Now get upstairs and stop dripping all over my rug. It's the first room on the right."

I smiled at her and said, "Yes ma'am. Thank you so very much."

I quickly got cleaned up and put on the dress she had sent up for me. Supper was on the table when I came down, I hadn't eaten anything since breakfast before leaving home. I didn't realize I was so hungry until I smelled the food. I was grateful for her kindness and friendship. We had supper and talked for a couple of hours. She hugged me as I set off to my room for the night. The bed was a comfortable feather bed with feather pillows like home.

I didn't sleep much that night. The next morning I was up, dressed in my men's clothes and gone at daybreak. She was still asleep when I left. I will always appreciate her, and I hoped she understood I had a long way to go, and I couldn't stay and visit. I did leave a note, thanking her for her kindness and hospitality. Mama would want it that way.

The morning was cold and damp. There were still heavy, gray clouds overhead, but the sky was blue off to the west. I was glad when the clouds cleared and I felt the warm sun. Logan kept a steady pace and we made it to Danville by afternoon.

Once there, I spent the night with the family of Mr. Jones, a gentleman that bought our tobacco every year.

Being around friends and talking about good times, kept me from dwelling on the journey ahead. Mr. Jones told me I could probably stay the next night with his sister Martha, who lived in Chatham, Virginia.

Martha was a nice lady, with dark hair and maybe a few years older than me. She reminded me of Mama with her lady-like ways. She told me trying to hide my hair wasn't fooling anyone. I asked her to cut it for me. As she started cutting, I cried. I thought about Mama using a wooden comb as she combed my wet hair, as she would say combs are for wet hair, brushes are for dry hair. Mama had told me to brush my hair every morning and every night.

She would say, "Young men like long hair. They find it pretty and take it to be a sign of good health, healthy enough to bear children. A ladies hair is her crowning glory!"

My hair was now just touching my collar. As I looked at myself in the mirror, I thought about how Jeremiah loved my long hair. Would he still think I'm pretty now that it was gone? That night I braided some of my hair into two watch chains, one for Jeremiah, and one for me.

I stayed at Martha's house for two days. She gave me bandages and suggested I bind my breasts. She gave me other advice, don't play with your hair, don't swing your hips when you walk, and walk with a purpose.

On the fifth day of my journey, I left Martha's house. I was trying to retrace the route I had traveled with Jeremiah when we went to Charlottesville to visit the University of Virginia.

I got close to one of the places we had stayed, I thought to myself, "As grand as that house is they won't let me stay." I asked some slaves working in the field if they could tell me of a safe place to stay the night. I spent that night in a slave house. I slept in a hole in the dirt floor.

These wonderful people didn't have much food, but they shared what they had. I was grateful, but saddened by the fact that people were forced to live like that, and forced to work so hard, while the people that benefited from the hard work lived in such a grand place and ate whatever they desired. This place reminded me of the story Sara told me about George. I felt ashamed. I shouldn't have accepted their food, I left most of the food I had in my saddlebags with them.

The next day after a long ride I made it to Lynchburg, Virginia. I stabled Logan and checked into the Western Hotel. I signed in as Charley Turner. I stayed there two days. Both me and Logan needed the rest.

In the hotel restaurant I ordered their famous french toast. Many years ago Thomas Jefferson had told them how to make it, and he had ordered it for everyone in the restaurant. People loved it, and it was added to the menu. I had it before, when I stayed here with Jeremiah, sometimes we would have it at home.

Monday I made it to what I think is the Buffalo River, which means I should be halfway between Lynchburg and Lovingston. I spend my first night outside. The weather was good, and enough moon-light so I could see a bit. I felt comforted by the sound of the whippoorwill calling, "whip-poor-will, whip-poor-will," over and over, it was a sound I was used to hearing at home. I missed home, but there was no turning back. I had to see Jeremiah.

I caught two small fish. I tried to remember what Jeremiah said in his letters about building a small fire and what kind of wood to use. Hardwoods like oak or ash don't smoke and spark as much as softer woods. I was getting cold and a large fire would have felt nice, but a large fire draws attention. I had the river to my back, and it didn't look like it was going to rain. Logan was hobbled and grazing. I heard a fierce, low, throaty growl. It got louder and higher pitched. I'm not sure what it was, but it scared me.

It sounded mad. It wasn't a bear, maybe a wolf, or a bobcat. I heard it a couple of more times, and decide it's a bobcat. Bobcats are usually quiet. It must have seen me and was trying to scare me away. I couldn't really tell where the sound was coming from, it sounded like it was all around me. What should I do, leave, stay? I try to calm down and think. Jeremiah had talked about camping and wild animals. Slowly I rolled up the legs of my trousers, I needed to get the fish scraps away from me. I crossed the river and threw the scraps on the bank and came back. I brought Logan over next to me. Jeremiah had told me that bobcats hunt from dusk to around midnight, then again right before dawn. I wasn't sure. Was that what he had said about bobcats or was it wolves? I hear it again and tell myself, that's what he said about bobcats. If I stay awake until well after midnight I'll be fine. I have my gun in my hand and I rest my head against Logan's left front leg. I'm too scared to sleep. From now on I'll travel at night and sleep in the day. After daylight I went to sleep. I slept until late afternoon. I caught and cooked more fish, saddled Logan and set off.

Traveling at night was difficult and slow going. I wasn't on the road, just right off of the road in the woods. I couldn't see well but Logan was sticking to the animal paths and I tried to keep the road in site. I heard a few birds before dark, after dark I heard a wolf and that bobcat. I just kept moving. I figured if something got after us Logan could outrun it or I would shoot it. I didn't want to shoot unless I had to, there was no need to draw attention to myself. By morning I could see a few houses. It had to be Lovingston. There was a small inn there. I stabled Logan on the street level and checked into a room on the second floor. I ate some food and went to sleep. I slept until four in the afternoon, ate, got Logan ready and rode all night again. We had gotten into the mountains and it was getting colder.

There was snow on the ground, and it was harder on Logan. The ground was rocky and we moved quietly and slowly.

It was now Sunday, and we rode into Charlottesville. Riding at night and sleeping during the day, it took us four days to get there. Once again I stable Logan and check into a hotel. I am two-thirds of the way to Middleburg. One more week and I should be there. So far people have left me alone. I guess they are used to young men coming through, looking to join in the fight. I've been honing my skills when I'm around people. I try to act like I belong, I walk straight. I try not to disguise my voice, I just try to speak strong. I leave the next evening.

It's now been five days since I left Charlottesville, and traveling is still slow, I figure it might take me an extra week to get to Middleburg. I stop to make camp. It has become routine now and I'm not scared anymore, I feel there is an end in sight. Logan is unsaddled and grazing, he paws at the ground to move snow away so as to get to the grass. I was slowly sneaking up on a rabbit with a rock in my hand. I'm startled by the rabbit being shot. It was Yankee Scouts, two of them. I stood still, not sure what to do. I've thought about this for the past couple of weeks, I hoped it would work.

After what seemed like minutes, I asked, "Who are y'all boys with?"

They didn't answer.

One finally asked, "What's a reb doing out here by hisself, and out of uniform?"

I say, "I ain't out of uniform, yea I'm a southerner, but I'm headin' north to join the Union. I come from a poor family and I ain't gonna die fightin' to help rich folk keep slaves. My brother went to West Point, and he stayed with the Union, said he took a oath. I'm heading north to join up with him."

One asks, "Who's your brother?"

"Colonel Henry Lee," I replied. He had been a friend of Jeremiah's. He really was a southerner that had went to West Point and stayed with the Union. I prayed they didn't know him, hoped they had heard of him, should be a good chance with him being a colonel.

One asked the other, "Zeb, do you know a Colonel Henry Lee?"

Zeb looked like he was thinking, then said, "Yea, I've heard of Colonel Henry Lee. He's a good loyal Union man."

I then asked, "Y'all want me to skin and cook that rabbit?"

Zeb said, "Hell yea boy, I'm hungry."

I cooked the rabbit as they unsaddled their horses, it looked like they were planning to stay here for the day just like I was. I told them my name was Sam Lee. I came from a little town called Liberty, down in North Carolina. I had just turned sixteen years old, and I thought I was old enough to fight if I wanted to.

One man was named Joe. I knew the other was Zeb. They both had fine uniforms, it looked like it was the first time they had put them on. They had McClellan saddles, Union bridles with running martingales. Both had two Colt revolvers. I silently prayed they were more tired than me.

Then Zeb said, "I know where Colonel Henry Lee is camped, we'll take you there tonight."

I said, "I'd be much obliged, that'll sure save me a heap of trouble. I figured I was gonna have to look through hells half acres to find him." I was thinking, how am I going to get out of this?

We ate, I cleaned up the mess, and they fell asleep. I reckon they believed me and felt comfortable. After they had been asleep for about an hour, I figured it was time to saddle Logan and quietly leave. As I placed the saddle on Logan...

"What are you doing?" Joe asked. Zeb was still asleep.

I said, "I'm gonna go get some feed for my horse. I'll be right back!"

He walked up to me and stood with his face only inches from mine and said, "I think you're a reb, trying to get away from us. You're my prisoner and the only place you're goin' is to a Union prison." He was reaching for his revolver and turned his head and as he started to holler to Zeb, I snatched the knife from under my coat and sliced his throat before he could holler. He was bleeding like a stuck hog. He was staggering around, making a low, gurgling sound. I ran to Zeb as he was waking up, not sure what was going on, he pulled out his gun. As I jumped on top of him and sliced his throat, he fired his gun, hitting me in the left arm. He then grabbed his throat and started making that same gurgling sound. I had never hurt so bad. I wanted to scream out in pain, but I knew the shot would draw attention if anyone was around to hear it. If they heard a woman scream they would surely come looking to see what was going on. I wrapped my arm, took their clothes and one pair of boots and rolled them in my bedroll. I put on the other pair of boots. I took their Colt revolvers, ammo, money, and horses. All I left there in that meadow was two dead men in their long underwear. I figured it was best that whoever found them, wouldn't know they were soldiers right away. I saddled Logan with a McClellan saddle and Union bridle. I then put Logan's rig on one of the Yankee horses. With all three of the horses saddled, I left riding Logan and leading the other two horses. It was very painful but I was scared and I had to get out of there. I pushed Logan hard. After a while I switched to riding a Yankee horse, to give Logan a rest from carrying me. I then changed again, and then back to Logan. I passed Culpepper, that meant I was only halfway from Charlottesville to Middleburg. I had to stop, I felt so tired and sleepy. I looked at my arm, the blood had soaked the bandage and was dripping, I retied it.

I found a small meadow, I needed to stop for a short rest.

I lay down over the saddle, rubbed Logan's neck and talked quietly to him. "I'm sorry Lo, you're a good boy, I hope I didn't run you too much. We'll be okay, we just need to rest. We'll be okay." I guess I feel asleep, or fainted... I woke up to the sound of a girl's voice. I opened my eyes and saw a thin, blonde haired girl standing there talking to me. The breeze was blowing her hair, with the sun behind her. I thought she was an Angel that had come to take me to Heaven. I must have bled to death. She took Logan's reins and started walking. She led us to a house.

Her mama helped me off of Logan, and as the lady was helping me into the house, the girl took the horses into the barn. We went into a bedroom and I saw myself in the large mirror. I was covered in blood. My blood. Their blood. I felt tingly, I felt hot, like I was going to be sick to my stomach, everything started getting dark, the lady was talking to me but she sounded far, far away...

I woke up and I was in a bed, the lady was talking to me telling me everything was going to be alright. I remember this happening a few times. I could hear people talking, but I couldn't move, I couldn't open my eyes. I would try, but couldn't. I thought I was talking to the people, but they didn't seem to hear me. Was I dead? Then one time I spoke, and she answered me.

"How long have I been here?" I asked.

The lady answered, "Two weeks. The doctor came by and fixed up your arm, said you was lucky Janie found you when she did, just a little longer and you would have died. You've lost a lot of blood."

"I'm not dead?" I asked. "I thought the little girl was an Angel."

She smiled and said, "We like to think of Janie as our little angel. No dear, you're not dead, you came close, but you're still alive. I have to ask, why were you dressed like a boy, what were you doing with them Yankee horses and uniforms, and a bullet in your arm?"

I told her the whole story.

She said, "Lord all mighty, bless your heart little girl. John can get you to Middleburg and in the hands of the right people. But for now, you need to stay put, until you get a little strength."

I said, "Thank you ma'am. Who's John... and what's your name?"

She said, "I'm Lucy Thompson, John is my husband. Janie is our granddaughter. Her mama ran off, and her daddy, our son, is fighting in the war."

She was a short woman, I guessed her to be around sixty years old. Her hair was starting to gray. She had a few wrinkles, mostly when she smiled, which she did a lot. Janie was ten years old. She came in and visited with me for hours every day. She was the prettiest little girl I had ever seen. Her pretty blue eyes sparkled when she talked about her daddy. John was also starting to gray, he wore a full beard like the Quakers I had seen around home. He also had a few wrinkles, and he was a pleasant man. He spoke highly of Mosby and his men.

Finally we left for Middleburg. John wanted to take the wagon so I could rest. I insisted on riding Logan, it would be faster. I left the Yankee horses at his place, they were tired and worn out, at least for now anyway. I also left Logan's old saddle and twenty dollars, it was the least I could do for their inconvenience. It took us two long days to get to Middleburg.

John left me at the very large home of the widow Johnson, an elderly lady that I guessed to be in her eighties. Her hair was all gray, and she wore it up. She had high cheek bones, and was short and thick. Something about her reminded me of Adahy. She was a kind lady. She said that she could get word to Jeremiah, as she knew Mosby and his rangers well. She was furious with Mr. Thompson for allowing me to travel.

She said, "That girl is too weak, the trip could have killed her."

He made a little laughing, huff sound and said, "You see her face? All that bruising and swelling came from her trying to get up and leave. She fell and hit her face on the corner of the table then fell to the floor. We got her back in bed. Little Janie sat beside her bed dipping a cloth in cool water, wringing it out and putting it on her face, over and over again trying to get the swelling to go down. The next day she said she was leaving. That girl was determined to get here, she was coming to Middleburg with or without me. I think that horse of hers is just as determined as she is. She had nearly ran them horses to death that day Janie found her. The two horses we left back at the house are still weak. When her horse saw her he perked up, and was ready to go. There was times on the ride up here, she would lay down with her head on his neck and he never broke stride. She could have been asleep some of that time, as far as I know. Maybe now that she's here, you can get her Jeremiah here, and she can rest and recover... good luck."

Mrs. Johnson helped me to a bedroom, helped me get undressed, into a nightgown, then she helped me into the bed.

She said, "You say put. I'll be right back with some food. I will send for your husband. You said his name is Jeremiah. Would that be Jeremiah Turner, from Guilford County, North Carolina?"

I sat straight up and asked, "Yes ma'am. Do you know him?"

She smiled and said, "I sure do, he's a fine young man. He's handsome too. So you're Charlotte! Such a beautiful name," she said, "for such a beautiful girl. You're a lucky girl to be married to such a gentleman, but I reckon he's a lucky man to be married to a girl that's willing to do what you have done to see him."

I said, "Yes ma'am, I'm Charlotte. I am lucky to be married to him. How long do you think it will take to find him, and for him to get here?"

She replied, "Can't rightly say, but I reckon as soon as he hears you are here, he'll come running as fast as his horse can get him here. You rest now. I'll be back shortly."

I said, "Thank you, Mrs. Johnson, I appreciate everything you're doing for me. Is Logan okay?"

She said, "You might as well call me Helen. Who is Logan?" she asked.

"Logan is my horse." I replied.

She answered, "Logan is fine. He's in the barn eating and resting right now."

10 JEREMIAH WALKS IN

Two days later, Helen helped me down the stairs, I was tired of lying in bed. I wanted to get up for a while. I sat in the main parlor in front of the fireplace wearing a nightgown with a dressing gown over it and a quilt on my lap. I was reading the newspaper. There was a knock on the door. I heard Helen talking to someone. I looked to the doorway and Jeremiah walked in. I jumped up and into his arms. It was just over six weeks since I had left home, and one day before our anniversary. It had been one year and seven months since we had been together. He quickly made me sit down as he had been told about me being shot. He had lots of questions. I lay my head against his chest and sobbed. I hadn't let my feelings out since the night I was attacked and killed that man. Now there was no holding back the tears. He held me tight while I cried. I felt his tears fall on my face. After I couldn't cry anymore. I told him everything, killing the man that was attacking me, feeding him to the hogs, getting his cousin Jessie to stay at the farm, my journey here, killing the two Union Scouts, getting shot, nearly dying, falling and busting up my face, riding the two days here lying on Logan.

He was shocked. Then asked, "Why didn't you write me and tell me about the man?"

I replied, "I had to see you to tell you. He... he tried to take me, but I killed him before he could."

He hugged me close and whispered in my ear, "My dear Ms. Charley, how I love you."

We sat there quiet for a few minutes, just holding each other. Then he asked, "How are you feeling?"

I smiled weakly and said, "I'm tired and cold, and I can't seem to get warm."

He said, "Wait right here for a minute."

He walked out of the room and I could hear him talking to Helen. In a few minutes he was back. He picked me up and carried me upstairs to the bedroom I had been staying in.

He said, "You need some rest. Sleep will do you good. Let me get you to bed, I'll hold you close until you wake up. You'll be warm and safe, you can rest easy now."

As soon as he got in the bed and wrapped his strong arms around me I fell asleep. When I woke up it was morning, he was still holding me, just like he said he would.

He smiled that smile that lights up his entire face and said, "Happy third Anniversary."

I smiled like I hadn't smiled in years, and said, "Happy third Anniversary. I can't believe I am here, in your arms, on our anniversary."

He said, "You need food, you're all skin and bones. I'll go down and get us some coffee and breakfast. It's been a long time since I've brought you coffee in bed."

I smiled and said, "That sounds wonderful."

He said, "You're still weak, don't get up and move around until I get back."

I said, "I need to get up and go into the dressing room as soon as you leave, I need to, relieve myself."

He said, "I will walk with you and leave you there, I'll come back in here, and you call for me when you're ready to come back. You shouldn't be walking without me close by, you might faint. You've lost a lot of blood, it takes a lot of time to recover from that."

I said, "I'm embarrassed to talk of such things, but thank you."

He helped me up and then when I was ready, he helped me back to bed. Then he went downstairs. It wasn't long before he returned with a tray of food. It smelled so good, I can't remember the last time food smelled so good to me. He handed me a cup of coffee, I started to cry again.

I said, "It's been so long, I was beginning to think I would never see you again."

He said, "I know, sometimes I would feel like that too. The war just goes on, with no end in sight."

I said, "Let's not talk of the war. Let's enjoy being together."

We ate breakfast, and talked. We found there wasn't much to talk about that didn't somehow involve the war.

Finally I said, "Let's not talk at all, you come back to bed and we can be together. I have missed you so."

There was that smile again, as he said, "As tempting as that sounds, you are in no condition for that. You can't stand up without feeling faint. You almost died, you need to give your body time to heal. Look at yourself, I bet you don't weigh ninety pounds. There will be time for that when you're better. We've waited this long, we can wait a little while longer."

I looked down at myself and said, "I know I must be a sight, all skinny, shot, bruised up, and my hair cut so short. It was silly of me to suggest it, how could you want to be with me now?"

He laughed as he pulled me close and said, "You are still the most beautiful thing my eyes have ever seen!

I want to be with you more than anything, but it would be wrong, I would feel like I was taking advantage of you, and I could never do that. We are here together, I will be here tending to you. When you are well, we will join together, just like the day we were married."

"I love you Jeremiah." I said as tears filled my eyes.

He then whispered, "I love you, Ms. Charley."

So we talked, I told him about Daddy freeing his workers just like we had. How Daddy and Uncle Henry would transport runaways to Reidsville. I told him of the wounds we tended, giving food, clothes, shoes, and a safe place to the runaway slaves. How most came from horrible conditions, and felt that running away was the only way they would survive, even with all the dangers of being hunted like an animal. I told him of when I slept on the dirt floor in a hole, and how those kind people, who had hardly anything, shared their food with me.

I said, "I hear of some people that go to other churches talk and say the Bible teaches us that keeping slaves is God's plan, and is right and natural. How can one look into the eyes of another and decide, you will be my servant? How can these same people beat a person even worse than they would beat an animal? This part preys on my mind, how can a white man that sees blacks as a different species, rape a black woman? These are the kind of people the northerners hate. I hate them too. If it weren't for their kind we wouldn't be at war. I noticed during my journey here, every black person I met was nice to me, very pleasant. The white people? Some were nice, some were rude, some indifferent, and some downright mean. I thought on that a lot as I rode. I realized the black people were nice to me because I was white, and they had to be. Sure, some may have been genuinely nice, but some may not have liked me, and they couldn't say anything, they had to act nice just because I'm white.

They aren't even allowed their own feelings. White men have taken everything from these people."

He talked about how he despised camp life. He said, "A lot of people die in camp from disease and illness. More men are dying from that than from fighting in the war. There is hunger, drinking, gambling, fighting, and prostitution. I never involved myself in any of those things. I was glad to be made a scout. I knew I had the skills to do the job well. Excuse me for bragging, but I am a fine scout. I guess Captain Mosby thinks so too. He chose his men and I am glad to be one of them. Oh Charlotte, I can't wait for you to meet him, and I will be glad for him to meet my beautiful wife. I have great respect for him, so much so, maybe my next horse will be named Mosby!" He finished, bright eyed with a huge smile on his face.

I said, "Look in my saddle bags, I brought you a handful of Daddy and Uncle Henry's cigars."

"Maybe Captain Mosby would enjoy one." Jeremiah said.

"Captain?" I asked. "He's moving up quickly, the last letter I got from you he was a Lieutenant."

He said, "He was promoted to Captain last month. He does enjoy a good cigar. It seems he picked up the habit from Jeb Stuart. Let me tell you about a raid we went on last month, I wrote you a letter but obviously you weren't home to get it." He continued, "We rode beyond enemy lines at Fairfax County Courthouse. The town was occupied by thousands of Union soldiers. There were thirty of us, counting Mosby. He gave orders to spread out and take prisoners. I was to go with Mosby. We went to a large house, Mosby knocked on the door, a window opened, and someone asked, "Who's there?" Mosby said he had a dispatch for Brigadier General Stoughton. In a minute the door was opened, the man said, "You're not Union, who are you?"

Mosby grabbed him by his night shirt and whispered, "Mosby", in his ear. The man quickly took us upstairs to the Generals bedroom. A light was lit and there was the General, fast asleep, lying on his stomach. Mosby yanked back the covers, lifted the Generals nightshirt, swatted his bare backside then told him to get up and get dressed, he was now a prisoner. The General wanted to know who this person was.

Mosby asked, "Have you ever heard of Mosby?"

The General said he had.

Mosby said, "I am Mosby, Stuart's Cavalry has possession of the Courthouse, be quick and dress." We left the house with the General. We reached our rendezvous point, the others were waiting for us. They too had prisoners and horses. We simply rode out of town. Stuarts Cavalry wasn't there, it was just us." he finished with a smile.

I was amazed! I said, "You're teasing me, no one could have done that!"

He grinned as he said, "No one but Mosby! Rumor has it, Lincoln heard about it and said, "We can replace the General, but I sure hate losing them horses." Jeremiah laughed. Then he said, "Mosby has explained his tactics are based on Light Horse Lee. You know, General Lee's daddy."

I said, "Oh, I've read about him."

We must have been talking for a long time because the house servant, Eve, knocked on the door and told us dinner would be ready in an hour, she asked if we needed anything. I said I needed water for bathing. She said she would bring it right up.

Eve was a dark skinned black girl about my age. Average height, a good weight. She was very pretty, and she carried herself in a way that reminded me of Sara, elegant. Shortly afterwards, she knocked again and said the water was in the dressing room.

I asked Jeremiah to help me to the dressing room, which he did.

Once in the dressing room, he said, "I can't leave you in here alone to wash, you might faint, let me help you." He removed my nightgown, picked up the cloth and soap and bathed me. He then helped me get the clean gown and dressing gown on. He carried me to the bed.

He then asked, "Will you stay right here until I bathe? It will only take a few minutes."

I smiled and said, "I'll be right here waiting, I promise."

He came out clean and fresh, he then picked me up and carried me downstairs to the dining room.

Helen and her cook thought eating bloody foods would be good for me since I had lost so much blood, so we had liver. It was battered and fried like chicken, but is was still liver. I hated liver, as a child I would never eat it, but I felt to refuse would be useless, let alone rude, so I smiled and tried to get plenty of the cooked onions in with each bite to make it more tolerable.

Helen said, "For dessert we are having goose pudding. It's an old recipe my mama used to make." She smiled and sat up a bit taller as she continued, "Rumor has it Martha Washington used the same recipe."

I forced a small smile, then asked, "What's in goose pudding?"

She said, "Now let me try to remember, of course it has blood from a goose... and it has oatmeal, sugar, I can't remember everything else. I do remember as a child I loved it. Mama didn't make it often, so it was a real treat."

I felt sick to my stomach. I looked over at Jeremiah, and he was smiling at me, like he was about to laugh. After almost empting the sugar bowl into my goose pudding, I was able to finish it. I was relieved when the meal was over.

We went into the front parlor to visit. Helen told us about growing up in in late seventeen hundreds.

Her parents knew the Washington's, the Jefferson's, and the Lee's. Jeremiah couldn't believe he was actually talking to someone that knew Thomas Jefferson. She told us of growing up in a new country, getting married, having children. She had eleven children, all lived to be adults. Now, six of them were dead, the other five were scattered around the country, rarely came home, or bothered to write. That is why she housed the rangers. She enjoyed the company, she felt like she was helping. It was exciting and made her feel young again.

I grabbed Jeremiah's arm and said, "I need to let Mama and Daddy know that I'm here and safe. I can't believe I haven't sent them a letter yet."

He said, "I sent a letter as soon as I received word that you were here."

I was so relieved, and said, "Thank you."

"Charlotte dear," Helen said, "You might need to get some rest. Eve will come up and let y'all know when it's about time for supper. Jeremiah, are you taking care of our girl?" she asked.

He said, "Yes ma'am." He looked at me and smiled as he said, "With you feeding her and me tending to her, she'll be up and around in no time."

Helen said, "That's what I'm hoping for. For supper we are having roast beef!"

Jeremiah picked me up, carried me upstairs, and lay me on the bed. He asked if I was sleepy. I wasn't, so we talked until supper time.

I could smell the bread baking, it reminded me of being in Aunt Polly's kitchen. It seemed like she always had bread baking. I would come in and she would slice the still warm loaf. She knew my favorite part was the end piece. She always smiled when she handed it to me. I would spread fresh churned butter on it.

Sometimes I put strawberry preserves on it, but most of the time I liked just warm bread and butter.

Eve knocked on the door and told us that supper would be ready shortly. Jeremiah once again carried me downstairs to the dining room.

Supper looked and smelled so good. There was a huge roast, mashed potatoes, black eyed peas, beets, fresh baked bread, and beside the bread was a butter crock.

Helen asked Jeremiah to carve the roast, which he happily did. The roast was very rare. As Jeremiah lay the end piece on my plate he smiled and winked at me. It was the most cooked part of the roast.

Helen said, "Jeremiah, you should give her a piece that's rare, that end is cooked a bit much."

Jeremiah said, "I will, Charlotte's favorite part of the roast is the end piece, her next piece will be rare."

Helen nodded as she said, "That sounds fine."

I didn't ask for a second piece, and dessert was more goose pudding. I said, "I'm too full from that fine supper to have dessert."

Helen and Jeremiah both agreed that they were too.

11 MEETING MOSBY

After a week of eating all the bloody foods, I had to admit, I was feeling much better. I didn't feel faint every time I stood up. That night was like our wedding night. I felt like I had been living for this moment. The sharing of our love, joining together spiritually, the touch, the tenderness, something private, personal, only to be shared with each other. I now felt alive again. We lay in bed, my head on his chest.

I said, "I know you were disappointed to get the letters telling you I wasn't with child."

He stroked my now short hair and said, "I was, but now I feel like we have another chance, we've already started trying again."

I said, "Helen told me I probably wouldn't get with child anytime soon. She said it could take months before we have a chance."

He said, "Don't worry about that, you just concentrate on getting better. We can still enjoy each other, no concerns of children right now."

I said, "I was reading those marriage manuals that we ordered before we were married. Some of them say, to have... sex for pleasure is a sin. Sex is supposed to be for procreation only. Do you think since we had sex... for pleasure, God is punishing us by not giving us children?"

He put his hand on my chin and gently raised my head so he could look me in the eyes and said, "No, I do not think God is punishing us. Sex between a husband and wife for pleasure is not a sin. It is a gift from God. Nowhere in the Bible does it say otherwise. God is not punishing us. We will have children. You most likely won't be with child when you head home, but we will have other chances, we will have children."

I was still looking into his eyes as I said, "I'm not going home until you do. If I get with child, I reckon our baby will be born right here in Virginia. I am the only person in my family to be born in North Carolina. Maybe our babies are supposed to be Virginians."

He said excitedly, "What do you mean you're not going home until I do? That's crazy! You can't expect Helen to let you stay here until the war is over. What about the farm?"

I calmly replied, "The farm is fine. I don't expect Helen to let me stay here. I want to be one of Mosby's Rangers."

He laughed and said, "You are crazy, you can't be a ranger!"

"Why not?" I asked.

He said, "You're a woman! You can't fight."

I still remained calm as I said, "I can't fight? What about the three men I killed?"

"That's different, you didn't have a choice." he replied.

"You have a choice to kill or not?" I asked. "If you choose not to kill, doesn't that mean you die?"

He said, "Well, yes, but you're my wife. How can I do what I have to do, and take care of you?"

I said, "I can take care of myself. I'm staying. I want to talk to Mosby."

He laughed and said, "Alright, if Mosby will take you on as a ranger, I'll not say another word."

I settled my head back on his chest and said, "Good, I have a great horse, I can ride. I already have the revolvers, saddle, boots, and trousers that I took from those two Yankee Scouts. All I need now is to meet Mosby."

He said, "I think you will enjoy meeting Mosby, but I'm afraid he is going to disappoint you."

"We'll see." I replied.

Jeremiah had received thirty days leave. During that time, he took care of me and I grew stronger.

On May 10, 1863. Stonewall Jackson dies. He had been wounded at the Battle of Chancellorsville in Virginia on the second day of May, by one of his own men. His left arm had been amputated in an attempt to save his life, but there were complications. He died on a Sunday.

Jeremiah hung his head and quietly said, "I'm sure if he was aware of it being a Sunday, he was happy to go that day, as he was a deeply religious man. His left arm, that was the arm he held up at Manassas. This is a terrible blow to the Confederacy."

A week before Jeremiah was to leave, I asked him, "How do we get a message to Mosby?"

He said, "I have sent word asking him to come here for supper at his convenience, he will be here when he can."

I said, "I need a dress. I can't meet Captain Mosby wearing a dressing gown."

Jeremiah smiled as he asked, "Tell me, why would a Mosby Ranger need a dress?"

I smiled and said, "You'll see." I went to find Helen.

I asked her, "Where can I get some proper ladies clothes?"

She said, "Right across the hall, dear, is a room full of beautiful clothes that belong to my granddaughter, Dolly. She married a Yankee and she lives in Philadelphia now. She just left everything here. You should be able to wear the clothes, if they don't fit, I can alter them for you."

I went into the room and it was full of beautiful clothes. I had plenty to choose from. I was delighted to find light brown hair pieces, I can look like a girl. I picked a red, green, and ivory plaid dress. I had never cared for plaids, but I really liked this one. It had ivory bows to hold up the swags of the overskirt, as to show about eight inches of the ivory lace underskirt that hung down to the floor. The waist, of course, was to be tight. There was an ivory lace insert that went across the breast and buttoned in place, like my wedding dress. The pagoda sleeves were close fitting up top and really large at the bottom. I picked out white lace gloves to wear with it.

The next afternoon Eve knocked on the door to tell us Captain Mosby was there. Jeremiah told her he would be right down. I asked Eve to help me dress. She helped me dress quickly.

I walked into the room as gracefully as I knew how. I acted and spoke in my most charming, southern way, offering him my hand and said, "Why Captain Mosby, it is such a treat to meet you, Jeremiah speaks so highly of you."

Jeremiah looked at me with a confused look on his face, and relieved, as he must have thought I had changed my mind about asking Mosby to take me on as a ranger.

Mosby stood up, bowed slightly, took my hand and kissed it, and said, "Jeremiah told me he had a beautiful wife, but I never pictured someone as lovely as you. I trust you are feeling better. Jeremiah also told me of your injuries, such a sad thing for a beautiful lady as yourself to be shot.

I do hope I come across the Yankee scoundrels one day soon, as I would love to seek revenge for you."

I smiled my most charming smile, my head slightly low and tilted to the right, looked up with just my eyes and said, "Why thank you Captain Mosby, it's so kind of you to offer, but not necessary, as I left both of them dead wearing only their long underwear in that meadow beside the creek."

His blue eyes grew big as he looked surprised and said, "I had heard about two Yankee Scouts being found dead down near Culpepper, their throats were cut, wearing just their long underwear, all their belongings gone. Are you telling me that you did that?" he asked.

I smiled as I said, "Why yes Sir, I did. I killed them, took their things, and headed out of that meadow as fast as my horse Logan could carry me. Those Yankee horses were plumb tuckered out. I had to leave them behind, useless animals," I said with a smile, "I suppose Yankee's don't put much stock in a good horse. You being a southern gentleman, I'm sure you appreciate a fine stallion." I lay my hand on his arm as I said, "It's a while before supper, let's go to the stables. I would love for you to see Logan, he's as fine of a horse that ever came out of North Carolina. As a matter-of-fact, we could go for a quick ride!"

He held out his arm as to escort me, as he asked Jeremiah, "Do you mind if I escort your lovely wife as we all go to the stables?"

Jeremiah stood up as he said, "Of course, I don't mind at all."

Helen sat there smiling as I believe she knew what I was up to. We walked to the stables, Logan saw me and shook his head as to straighten his mane, and whinnied to me, as he always did.

Captain Mosby rubbed Logan on the neck and said, "Ms. Charlotte, he is one fine looking animal. So you enjoy riding, do you?" he asked.

I said, "Why yes Sir, as a matter-of-fact I do."

Jeremiah said, "I'll start saddling the horses. Charlotte, you can go change into a riding habit if you'd like."

I smiled at him and said, "Yes, I would like to change, thank you, I will be only a few minutes." I turned to go inside.

Jeremiah said, "Charlotte dear, there isn't a sidesaddle here."

I replied, "That's fine, I can make do with the McClellan."

I went inside, quickly changed into men's clothes, and pulled on the Yankee boots I had taken. I put on a hat and quickly went back to the stable. The horses were saddled and ready to go.

I walked over to the gentlemen, looked off to the east and saw a grove of trees in the distance, and said, "I'll race you to the trees!"

Mosby, looking surprised, asked, "Ms. Charlotte?"

I smiled and said, "You can call me Charley. Want to race?"

He grinned and said, "Yes Charley, I believe I do."

"Let's go then!" I said enthusiastically.

I went running up to Logan and hopped on not using the stirrup, and yelled, "Yah!" Logan took off like, "a bat out of hell", as Daddy would say. There was a four-rail fence bordering the yard, Logan sailed over it with ease, I didn't look back to see what the men were doing, I was focused only on getting to the grove of trees before they did. Logan loved to run, I knew he liked running as hard as he could and stopping only when he reached his destination. He didn't slow down as we approached the trees, we got right next to the trees and he slid to a stop, his rear nearly touching the ground, then he turned around and snorted. I sat there and waited for the men to get to the trees.

Mosby said, "Charley, I do believe you are right, he is a mighty fine animal. I must also admit you're quite a rider. I have never seen a lady ride like that. You ride better than a lot of men I know."

I smiled and said, "I have always loved riding, I know how Logan does things as he knows what to expect from me. I believe us to be a fine team."

We all headed back to the stables, once there, Jeremiah said he would unsaddle the horses, Mosby stayed to help. I went inside to change my clothes. I came downstairs within minutes, once again looking like the lady Mosby had met earlier. The gentlemen had just came inside. They were laughing and talking about me and Logan.

Mosby once again took my hand, kissed it as he bowed and said, "Ms. Charlotte, I can't help but to think you had purpose in that demonstration outside. What do you have on your mind?"

I said, "Captain Mosby, I believe I can be of great use to you as a ranger."

Jeremiah stood there with that confident smile of his, just waiting for Mosby to turn me down, then it would all be over and I would have to go home.

Mosby stood there for a minute like he was thinking, he kind of nodded his head slightly as he said, "Charlotte, I believe you are right."

Jeremiah quickly said, "No, now wait a minute, this can't happen."

I firmly replied, "I do recall you saying, if Captain Mosby agreed to accept me, you would say no more."

"I didn't think he would have a woman as a ranger!" Jeremiah exclaimed in almost a panic. "Captain Mosby, she's my wife. I can't allow this. How can I carry out my duties and protect her?" he asked.

Mosby calmly said, "Jeremiah, I think she can be an asset to the Confederacy. It appears to me that she can take care of herself." He looked at me and said, "I like that you can appear to be a boy, very convincingly, and also such a charming lady.

I could use that. I suppose I wouldn't have to send you to get yourself some Yankee revolvers?"

I smiled and said, "No Sir, I have four of theirs and one of my own, and of course my knife."

Mosby smiled and said, "Your knife, I suppose you're pretty handy with it if you killed both of those men with it."

I replied, "Yes Sir. Actually, I killed three men with it. One at home, that's why I left to come here. The two men along the way, well, I had no choice. Once I got here, I figured if I had to kill to stay alive at home, I might as well stay here and fight alongside Jeremiah. There's a funny story about that knife. My daddy gave me that knife. The third time it was used was to kill that man at home. The second time it was used, a neighbor had asked Daddy if he could borrow his knife, Daddy handed it to him, and the neighbor picked an apple off of the tree, cut off a piece, put it in his mouth and said, "Mr. William, this is a fine knife." Daddy said, "It ought to be, it's only been used twice, yesterday I castrated hogs with it, and now you're cutting that apple with it." The neighbor handed Daddy the knife back. My daddy loves telling that story, he always laughs, as he never cared for that particular neighbor. Then Daddy gave the knife to me. When Jeremiah left, I started putting it under my pillow, along with my revolver. Turns out that was a good place for it. Daddy also taught me how to shoot."

Mosby said, "Ms. Charlotte, you are a fascinating lady. Jeremiah, you have failed to tell me of your wife's charming ways." He then asked, "Does she always get what she wants?"

Jeremiah said, "Yes Sir, I believe she does. I certainly thought that would change this evening, but once again, she has found a way. I trust you won't be placing her in harm's way."

Mosby said, "Jeremiah, I will treat her as any of the other rangers and use her only when her skills are required.

Ms. Charlotte, I think it best if most think of you as a man. No need for word to get out that we have a female ranger. Is that agreeable to you?"

"Yes Sir." I replied.

Helen then said, "Supper is on the table. She then whispered to me, "Charlotte, my dear, you amaze me. I didn't know what you were up to, but I figured whatever it was, you knew what you were doing."

I smiled and said, "Thank you Helen."

We all then sat down to eat, once again rare roast beef, this time Helen asked Captain Mosby to carve the meat. I was glad, as I figured Jeremiah would have waited until he had gotten to the middle of the roast, the dripping blood part, to serve me.

As we were eating Mosby said, "Helen, would you find it agreeable for Charlotte and Jeremiah to stay here with you?"

Helen said, "I'd like that very much. We get along well, and there is a room full of clothes upstairs for her to use. I'm excited, this is going to be fun!"

Mosby laughed and said, "Helen, you always delight me. Now you won't be giving away our secret to anyone will you? Not even General Lee. I know you and his mother were dear friends, and he always enjoys a visit with you when he is nearby."

She said, "Oh no, I won't be saying a word about it to anyone."

The rest of the evening was pleasant. Mosby had planned to stay the night.

Mosby said, "Jeremiah, your leave is up next week, go to the other place you have been staying and gather your things. Come back here, I'll send for you when I need you."

Jeremiah answered, "Yes Sir."

Mosby then asked, "Charlotte, will you be ready for duty next week?"

"Yes Sir." I answered happily.

"I'll send you a gray jacket, I believe you have acquired the rest of your uniform?" he asked.

"Yes Sir." I replied.

Jeremiah asked, "Captain, would you like to step out on the porch and have a cigar? Charlotte brought a handful of her daddy and Uncle Henry's cigars for me, and I would like to share one with you. You'll not find a finer cigar."

Mosby said, "Yes Jeremiah, I would enjoy that, a good cigar and fine conversation is a nice way to end an evening."

They went outside. I was hoping Jeremiah wouldn't change Mosby's mind. Helen and I sat inside talking about dresses and such things. After a while the gentlemen returned. We all said our goodnights, and went to our bedrooms.

Jeremiah was furious! He said, "There is no way you're doing this!"

I replied, "There is only one way I'm not doing this! We can both go home! I'm not going to be separated from you again, I can't live like this!"

He said, "Charlotte, you could be killed. Your daddy probably already wants to shoot me."

I calmly said, "Where you go, I go. You did say if Mosby accepted me you wouldn't say another word."

He retorted, "I said that because I thought he wouldn't! You know that! Charlotte, I don't want to argue with you about this, you need to go home!"

I said, "We go home together, now or later, but whatever happens we face it together. Jeremiah, please understand, I can't go on without you. Life at home is empty, meaningless, all I do is work and try not to cry, thinking and wondering if you're alive. I have to be with you, if it costs me my life then, "God's will be done". Until then, at least we are together.

When you got the letter I wrote to you telling you I was leaving home and coming here, I know it bothered you, but just remember how worried you were when six weeks later I wasn't here. Were you thinking, something has happened, is she safe, is she dead?"

He said, "Yes, that's exactly what I was thinking, and I was right, you had been shot and was near death."

I said, "That feeling of worry and anguish, is what I felt every day from the time you rode down the driveway leaving to join up, until you walked through Helen's door."

He sat down on the bed, hung his head a bit, and said, "I can't imagine feeling that, day after day. I guess I never thought about it from your point of view. I always thought as long as I knew you were safe at home, we would get through all of this. I understand, but I still disagree."

I walked over and sat beside him. I slid my hand under his and said, "I will be careful. You said Mosby is good at choosing the right people for the job at hand, he might not ever send me anywhere. Please, let's not fight. Let's go to bed and enjoy being together. We should cherish every moment. Jeremiah, I'm sorry if this hurts you, I'm not trying to hurt you. I love you."

He smiled and said, "I love you too, Charlotte."

I was a little heartbroken that he didn't call me Ms. Charley, but I understood. We went to bed and just held each other all night.

12 A MOSBY RANGER

The next morning at breakfast, Mosby said, "Charlotte, I would like to see how you shoot. Would you mind a small demonstration after breakfast?"

I replied, "I wouldn't mind at all, as a matter-of-fact, I think I would quite enjoy it."

After breakfast he asked, "Could you change into the men's clothing you had on yesterday evening?"

I said, "Yes Sir, I'll be down in just a minute." Within five minutes I was back downstairs and ready to go prove my shooting skills.

Jeremiah said, "I'll saddle Logan for you."

Mosby quickly said, "Jeremiah, I know you are a gentleman, I admire that quality in you. However, my rangers should be capable of saddling their own horses."

I said, "I agree." I quickly got Logan saddled. I walked to Mosby and asked, "What would you like me to do?"

He said, "I am going to nail this piece of paper onto that tree off to the right of the fence. I want you to leave out of this yard and jump over that fence just as you did yesterday. Only this time, right before you jump the fence, shoot the paper, as you are jumping the fence, shoot the paper, and as you are landing, shoot the paper. Hit it all three times, and I will be most impressed."

The paper was about the size of his palm. He walked about forty feet away from the fence and nailed it to the tree. I waited for him to come back.

He stood there for a second and said, "Whenever you are ready."

I walked to Logan and tied his reins into a knot at the end. I came back to Mosby and said, "I'm ready."

I ran up to Logan and jumped on him without using the stirrup, and yelled, "Yah!" Once again he took off like a bat out of hell. I dropped his reins, the knot I had tied kept the reins from falling. I reached into my boot with my right hand, pulled out my revolver, cocking it with my left hand, I fired as Logan was starting his jump. I was squeezing him with my legs to hold on. In mid-jump, I fired the second shot, as his front feet touched the ground, I fired the third. I then put the gun back in my boot, picked up the reins, turned around, jumped the fence and came to a stop right where I had started.

Jeremiah and Mosby were smiling. Mosby walked over to retrieve the paper, I had hit it all three times. They were both impressed. I said, "My daddy taught me how to shoot. Jeremiah taught me how to hit what I was shooting at."

We all laughed, and walked with Mosby into the house as he said goodbye to Helen. I liked Mosby, he was everything Jeremiah had said, he was the kind of man people enjoyed being around.

After Mosby left, Jeremiah asked me, "Would you like to go with me to retrieve my things, and meet the family I have been staying with?"

I said, "I would love to."

He said, "Before we go you need to know a few things, when you're dressed like that people will think you are a boy. You need to be ready to hide at a moment's notice. Here is where we hide." He walked into the study to a bookcase, pulled it open like a door. I followed him into a tiny room. He latched it closed from inside. "It's very important that you stay still and quiet. Helen will tell you when it's safe to come out. Never go out until she tells you it's safe, no matter what you hear." He unlatched the door, and we stepped out into the room. "When you're dressed as a girl, there's no need to hide. Helen is going to start telling people her niece has come to live with her. She will still call you Charlotte."

I followed him to the stable, he saddled Jefferson, we jumped on the horses and started down the driveway.

He asked, "Where did you learn to get on a horse like that?"

I smiled and said, "I learned it from you."

He smiled and shook his head, then he continued with his instructions, "You need to always be aware of what's around you and who is around you. There are soldiers out looking for us, you need to be able to out-shoot and out-ride them."

I said, "I can do that."

He said, "I'm sure you can. I need to know you will do what you're told. I do out-rank you, Private Turner!"

I said, "Yes Sir, 1st Lieutenant Turner!" as I saluted him.

He said, "That's not how you salute, this is how you salute." He showed me a few times until I got it right. "However, we are not in uniform, so no salute. Understand?" he said very seriously.

"Yes Sir!" I answered.

He said, "A few other things for you to think about, don't stand with your hands on your hips, that's how women stand. A man stands with his legs apart, and usually his arms are crossed at his chest. Men like to lean on things, a fence, a post, a tree. They usually lean back against things or to the side, but they don't lean over a wagon and put their chin in their hands. It doesn't matter with that coat on, but a man wears his belt lower than a woman. A man usually carries stuff on his shoulder, most of the time with only one hand. If anybody picks on you, you need to give as good as you get."

I nodded and said, "Thank you."

"You're welcome." he replied.

We finally got to the house where he had been staying, it was just past noon. They were all happy to see Jeremiah, and they welcomed me as a new ranger. Mr. and Mrs. Burns were an older couple with five young grandchildren, four girls and one boy.

Mr. Burns shook Jeremiah's hand as he asked, "How is your wife? We've been worried about the both of you ever since you got word she was hurt."

Jeremiah said, "She's just fine now, she had a rough time, but she's fine. Thank you for asking."

Mr. Burns said, "Glad to hear it! Jeremiah, we're gonna miss you. You take care of yourself, we'll be praying for you to make it through the war."

Jeremiah said, "I'll be praying for your family as well. I'm sure Mosby will be sending another ranger for you to house here. He's well aware of your loyalty and he also knows you need the help here on the farm."

Mr. Burns looked at me and said, "Charley, we'll be praying for you too, son."

I said, "Thank you."

155

Jeremiah said, "They are nice people, I will miss them. I have to admit I enjoyed the farm work. They will be fine though, I'm sure Mosby will have someone else there in a day or so."

I hadn't thought about the people needing Jeremiah. I had thought the people housing the rangers were the ones helping, I hadn't thought about them needing help. I felt bad for them.

I said, "Jeremiah, I apologize, I hadn't thought about what my actions were doing to other people. I have been consumed with being with you, I never thought it could hurt someone else."

Jeremiah said, "I understand. No need to apologize. I didn't write about them in my letters as not to give any information that could be used against them by the Union if my letters were intercepted." He smiled as he said, "I'd rather be with you."

I smiled back and said, "I reckon Helen could use some help around her place too."

He said, "Yes, she sure can."

We got back to Helen's house just in time for supper.

On the morning of June 16, Helen tells us we will have guests for dinner.

I asked, "Guests, who?"

She smiled as she said, "Major Mosby and General Stuart."

I said, "Major?"

Helen said, "Oh he's been promoted since he was here last."

"Oh, General Stuart." I said, "Jeremiah, how am I to dress?" I asked.

Jeremiah laughed and said, "I'm not sure."

Helen said, "John", she was referring to Mosby, "said the General would appreciate you wearing a dress."

I said, "Yes ma'am." A couple of hours after breakfast I went upstairs to get dressed, as I was wearing a dressing gown. I was nervous to be meeting a general. I was worried he was coming here to tell me I couldn't be a ranger.

I had a hard time choosing a dress. Finally I decided. The bodice was pearl colored, trimmed in black ribbon, the black ribbon had daisies sewn onto it. There was a pink ruffle next to the black trim. The skirt was two pieces, a pink ruffled underskirt, topped with a pearl overskirt that matched the bodice. It too, had the black and pink trim. In the front, a large amount of the pink underskirt was showing. In the back the overskirt hung down forming a short train. I chose a few hair pieces, and attached them to my hair, I then added a couple of pink and black hair combs and I was ready to have dinner with a general. I felt sick to my stomach. I calmed myself. I heard someone at the door. I put my gloves on, took a deep breath, and headed downstairs. I entered the main parlor. Jeremiah was there wearing his uniform, he looked so handsome. There were two other uniformed men talking with him. I reached out my hand to Major Mosby as I said in my sweetest, southern voice, "Why Major Mosby, it's so nice to see you again. Who is this handsome gentleman with you?"

Mosby said, "Ms. Charlotte, may I present General Stuart."

General Stuart, with his hat in hand, took my hand and kissed it, then said, "Ms. Charlotte, it is my pleasure." He looked to Jeremiah and said, "Lieutenant Turner you are a lucky man to have such a lovely wife."

Jeremiah said, "Thank you very much, Sir."

Mosby had something wrapped in cloth, he smiled, handed it to me as he said, "Ms. Charlotte, I wanted the pleasure of giving this to you."

I took it, opened it, and my face lit up, it was my Confederate jacket. I was relieved and excited. Still, I remained calm and said, "Thank you very much, Sir."

General Stuart was a much younger man than I had expected. I figured if he was commander of the entire Army of Northern Virginia Cavalry, he had to be an older man.

He was about the same age as Mosby. Jeremiah later told me Stuart had just turned thirty years old. Mosby would be thirty in December. He was dashing, he wore a gray cape with red lining, a yellow sash, his hat had an ostrich plume, and he smelled of cologne. He may have been handsome under all that facial hair. I never cared for beards and sideburns. It made me glad Jeremiah was clean shaven.

Helen announced that dinner was ready. General Stuart held his arm as to escort me, as he asked Jeremiah, "Do you mind if I escort your lovely wife to the dining room?"

Jeremiah said, "Of course not Sir."

We all went into the dining room. Stuart held my chair for me, then seated himself. He was a flirtatious man, liked to talk, and he laughed a lot.

He said, "I am from Patrick County, Virginia. My great-grandfather, Major Alexander Stuart, commanded a regiment at the Battle of Guilford Courthouse, along with Light Horse Lee. Lieutenant, aren't you from Guilford County, North Carolina?"

Jeremiah answered, "Yes Sir, I am. Our home is less than a day's ride from the site of the battle. My great-grandfather also fought at Guilford Courthouse."

Stuart then asked, "Ms. Charlotte, where is your family from?"

I answered, "My parents are from around Danville, Virginia. I am the first in my family to be born in North Carolina."

Stuart asked, "How did the two of you meet?"

I said, "Our families own adjoining land, and have always went to the same church. I guess we have known each other all of our lives." I smiled as I looked at Jeremiah and continued, "Only he didn't pay any attention to me until he returned from the University of Virginia."

Jeremiah laughed and said, "That is true Sir, she was only a child when I left, I came home and found this charming creature riding along the north side of the river bank, I immediately asked her if I could cross over to her side, and have been taken with her charms since I crossed that ford. It's impossible to say no to her. Lord knows I've tried, but she has always charmed me into her way of thinking. The evening before we were married I gave her a cameo with Diana the Huntress carved into it. I thought Charlotte had some of the same attributes as Diana. She has never failed to prove me wrong on that."

"Well Jeremiah, from what I hear, you're not the only one." Stuart said. "Ms. Charlotte, would you be agreeable to a riding and shooting demonstration after dinner?" he asked.

"Yes Sir, I'd love to." I replied.

Stuart laughed a little and said, "Lieutenant, we seem to have something in common. My lovely wife Flora, first caught my eye with her riding skills. She too likes to shoot. Ms. Charlotte, you must meet her."

I said, "I look forward to it."

Stuart said, "Major, I know your beautiful wife Pauline enjoys riding, I've never inquired if she enjoys shooting."

Mosby said, "She's never cared for shooting, she does enjoy riding. I do believe our wives have a lot in common. Ms. Charlotte, you just missed Pauline, she had been close by here for a while, but she's gone home now. I did enjoy seeing her. I must share this story. One night while she was here, the Yankees burst into the house and came into the bedroom, but all they found was Ms. Pauline in her nightgown. They searched all over, but they didn't search high and low, if they had, they would have found me in the black walnut tree outside of the bedroom window."

We all laughed.

I asked, "How long have y'all been married?"

Mosby said, "Pauline and I were married December 30, 1857. So we've been married for about five and a half years. We have a daughter and a son."

Stuart said, "Ms. Flora and I were married November 4, 1855. We've been married about eight and a half years. We have," his face changed like sadness had enshrouded him, "had… a daughter named Flora, she died last November. She was five years old. God has never put a prettier child on this earth. I also have a son. As a matter-of-fact, the Lord has seen fit to bless us, as my wife Flora is now with child. How long have you two been married?"

Jeremiah said, "You have our sympathies Sir, I have heard your daughter was a lovely child in looks and demeanor. Charlotte and I were married April 21, 1860. We were fortunate to recently spend our third wedding anniversary together. We have no children, as of yet."

After dinner Jeremiah offered both Stuart and Mosby cigars.

Mosby said, "Jeb, you're going to love these cigars, I must say it's the finest cigar I have ever had. Ms. Charlotte's daddy makes them."

Stuart said, "I must try one, I do love a fine cigar." He looked at me and said, "We will be outside, you go get changed as I am looking forward to seeing you do what Mosby described."

I said, "Yes Sir." I went upstairs as they went outside. Eve helped me change. I came down within three minutes. They were at the stables enjoying the cigars as I walked up.

Stuart said, "So this is Charley? Well Charley, show me what you can do. The paper is already nailed to the tree."

I said, "Yes Sir." I went in the stable and saddled Logan quickly, and led him outside. I walked over to Mosby and said, "Major, tell me when you are ready."

Mosby looked at Stuart, and nodded. Stuart nodded back. Mosby said, "Now!"

I ran and jumped on Logan and fired the three shots as Logan was jumping the fence just like I had done before. I turned Logan toward the tree with the paper, and I snatched the paper from the tree as Logan ran by, we jumped the fence and came running up to the men and Logan slid to a stop, once again his rear almost touching the ground. I jumped off and handed the paper to Stuart. He looked at it, and said, "I don't believe I have ever seen that done before."

I asked, "Would you like for me to do it again, Sir?"

He said, "No, not now, but I may ask you to do it from time to time as I did quite enjoy it. Where did you learn to ride like that?" he asked.

I said, "Well, Sir, I have been riding a horse since before I could walk. Jeremiah taught me how to properly jump. He likes fox hunting, and I wanted to hunt fox. He said I needed to be a better jumper, so he taught me. Also, Logan is a good horse and will do anything I ask of him."

Stuart said sternly, "If you can't take care of yourself and follow orders, you're out, no matter how sweet and charming you may be."

"Yes Sir." I replied.

Stuart then turned to Jeremiah and asked, "Lieutenant Turner, will her being along affect your performance?"

Jeremiah said, "No Sir. She can take care of herself, as long as she follows orders, I have no issue with it."

Stuart said, "Good. I look forward to reading the good reports from Major Mosby. Every time I read Charley Turner performed well, I will take extra satisfaction knowing our fairer sex is helping to whip the Yankees." He then said, "We must be on our way. Oh, this is a fine cigar, if you could acquire some for me, I would greatly appreciate it."

I said, "I will write to Daddy tonight and ask if he has any to spare."

Jeremiah saluted, Stuart and Mosby returned the salute, said goodbye and left.

Jeremiah said, "I had better get inside and out of this uniform, and you out of those clothes. I liked the dress you wore to dinner, could you put it on?"

We both changed, he came out of the dressing room as I was walking into the bedroom. He walked over, kissed me lovingly and said, "I'm so proud of you. I would hate to be the Yankees on the other end of your guns."

I smiled and said, "Thank you, you have no idea how much that means to me."

He said, "Yes I do."

The next day General Stuart is in Middleburg. We hear gunfire. Jeremiah changed into his uniform and told me to say inside with Helen. He ran out the door. He came back around about eight pm. He was tired, but fine.

He said, "General Stuart was nearly captured while having dinner. Thank God someone warned him. Stuart managed to get to safety and sent in his men. Some of us took cover behind the stone fences surrounding people's yards, as we fought the 1st Rhode Island Cavalry, while more of Stuart's men surrounded the town. They scattered, it looked like they headed south. I figure Stuart's men will take care of the rest. I'd better get out of this uniform."

He went upstairs, got cleaned up and returned to the parlor. Helen told him we were waiting for him to return so we could have supper together.

At supper I noticed he was back to himself. It was as if he had removed the battle along with the uniform. Then he washed himself physically and emotionally.

I asked, "How do you run outside to shoot and kill men, come back inside, get cleaned up, and then return to your normal self?"

He looked at me very seriously and said, "You do what you're trained to do, then thank God you were able to come back alive, and put it out of your mind. Can you do that?"

I said, "Yes I can. Just as I thanked God when you came back alive. I understand, when under fire I have to keep my emotions under control. Yes, I can suppress things for a long while."

The fighting continued for a couple of more days.

June 20, 1863. Fifty northwest counties of Virginia are welcomed into the Union as the new State of West Virginia.

We went about our daily lives. One day in early July, Jeremiah read in the newspaper an account of a battle in Gettysburg, Pennsylvania. Both sides suffered unbelievable casualties. The Union won the three day battle. The North Carolina 26th lost entire companies. By day three, what was left of the 26th was all but destroyed. They called it Picket's charge, but Pettigrew and Trimble were leading their men on the same charge. Picket and Trimble were Virginians, Pettigrew, a North Carolinian. North Carolina suffered unimaginable losses.

After reading it, Jeremiah said solemnly, "This is going to destroy moral. No Confederate wants to hear that General Lee or General Longstreet made a mistake and sent our boys to slaughter. It said General Stuart was late arriving. When he was here, he was following General Lee's orders, there is no way he could have been expected to be in Pennsylvania before Lee. The newspapers need to get the facts right and not print rumors. Our men don't need to doubt orders. Major Mosby is going to be furious about these accusations against Stuart!" he exclaimed.

The next day a man arrived. He spoke with Jeremiah for a minute and left.

Jeremiah closed the door, and walked into the parlor to join me.

Jeremiah said, "Tomorrow night, are you sure you can do this?"

I said, "Yes Jeremiah, I'm sure. What are we to do?" I asked.

He said, "We will rendezvous with Mosby outside of town, he will then give us our orders. You are to do everything he says, you don't give an opinion, just follow orders. This is a matter of life and death. Charlotte, promise me you will follow his orders."

I said, "I promise."

The next night we saddled up our horses and left, we met up with Major Mosby and twenty other men. He quickly introduced me to the others as Charley Turner, Lieutenant Turner's younger brother. He then told us there were supply wagons about three miles east. We were to go in, take prisoners, and the wagons. We attacked at one in the morning. Everybody was asleep except for the pickets. We went around them. Quietly we rode up, when we were about fifty yards from the wagons, Major Mosby gave a signal and all the men took off toward the wagons yelling like the devil was after them. I started hollering and Logan kept pace with the others, our guns were drawn and we were shooting up in the air. The sleeping soldiers didn't have time to get their guns and there was nowhere to run. They put their hands up over their heads to surrender. We rounded them all up in a group. We got them on their horses and tied their hands. Major Mosby assigned three men to take the prisoners. The rest of us were to hitch up the wagons, tie our horses to the back and drive the wagons. We delivered the wagons to where Major Mosby had told us to. Jeremiah and I returned to Helen's house right before daylight.

Jeremiah said, "You did well, you followed orders. This time they weren't shooting at us, most of the time they are. You remember that."

I said, "I will."

We went to bed and he wrapped his arms around me and whispered, "I love you, Ms. Charley."

That was the first time he had said that since Mosby had accepted me as a ranger. It was the sweetest words I'd ever heard.

I snuggled up closer and said, "I love you, Jeremiah Turner." He kissed me and we made love before going to sleep. I was glad to be here in his arms. We slept until noon.

Helen was smiling when we came down for dinner. She wanted to hear all the details. I told her what had happened.

She said, "It will get exciting, don't worry."

Mid-July, 1863. I got a letter from Mama. Sara had a baby boy. They named him William Henry Smith. Sara and the baby were well. I immediately wrote back to congratulate Sara and George. In my letters home I hadn't said I was a ranger. I simply said I was staying with someone and it was safe, Jeremiah was close by and I was able to see him often. I followed the advice from Jeremiah and didn't give details.

The next week we were to rendezvous with Major Mosby again. Once again, supply wagons were in the area, and there were more of us this time. Mosby said these wagons were carrying guns, and there were more wagons than the last time, therefore more men. We quietly headed out.

On the way Mosby said to me, "Last time we were lucky and weren't shot at. We will be shot at tonight. You'd best be ready, did Jeremiah tell you to use your Yankee revolvers before your old one?"

I replied, "Yes Sir. Jeremiah, I mean Lieutenant Turner, has had me practicing shooting two revolvers at the same time."

He nodded and said, "Lieutenant Turner is a smart man, you have a lot to learn from him. How did you do?"

I said, "I did well. I still hit the target all three times, just like with my older revolver."

He said, "Good to hear."

We attacked the same way as before, we rounded up our prisoners, hitched up their wagons and was heading out, when all of a sudden, we were being attacked. There were about ten of them. I guess they had been the pickets and formed up to try an attack to save the others from being taken as prisoners. Our rangers in charge of the prisoners and wagons tried to keep going, as men were scattering about shooting at us. Jeremiah and I were on opposite sides of the wagons. We killed or wounded most of the men. Jeremiah suddenly yelled as he fell from Jefferson, he was still being shot at. I spurred Logan, and yelled, "Yah!" Logan jumped and cleared the wagon, landing on the other side where Jeremiah was shooting, while trying to get back on Jefferson. I was firing the entire time. I killed the remaining two, then it was over. I turned to Jeremiah, he was on Jefferson and bleeding from his left shoulder.

He said, "Let's go!"

We took off as fast as the horses could go. When we finally stopped, I tied his shoulder as best as I could. We headed for Helen's. Once again, it was right before daylight when we got there. I told Jeremiah to go inside, I would unsaddle the horses and be right in. When I got inside Helen was asking Jeremiah if he could make it upstairs while she went to get water and bandages.

I said, "I'll help him." I put his right arm over my shoulder and helped him upstairs. He had lost a lot of blood. He was bloody in the front and the back. I guess the bullet went all the way through. I started undressing him as soon as I got him to the bed. Helen arrived with the wash basin and bandages. I was cleaning him up as Mosby walked into the bedroom.

Mosby asked, "How are you Lieutenant Turner?"

Jeremiah said, "I'm fine, it went through. I just need to get cleaned up."

Mosby said, "Looks like you lost quite a bit of blood. No need to worry, I'm sure these ladies can take care of you. You both performed well. The two of you killed ten men and saved our boys lives tonight. Jeremiah you're on leave until you heal up. Charlotte, you are not. I will send for you if I need you."

We both answered, "Yes Sir."

Mosby left. After Jeremiah was cleaned up and bandaged, I got cleaned up and into my nightgown. I snuggled up to him from the right side so as not to hurt him.

I said, "Thank God you're alive, for a second there, I thought you were gone." I wiped away my tears and said softly, "I love you."

Jeremiah smiled that smile that lights up his face and said, "I love you. I thank God you were there. I might not be here if you weren't. I can't believe Logan cleared that wagon and you killed the two men before he landed. I heard you yell, "Yah", and I knew what you were going to do. I suppose we do make a good team. Thank you, Ms. Charley."

I said, "I only did what you taught me to do."

Early the next morning there was a knock on the door. Eve said someone had left a package for us. I got out of bed, went to the door, took the package and thanked Eve. I carried it to Jeremiah and asked, "What could this be?"

Jeremiah smiled and said, "I have a pretty good idea, open it."

It was full of Union money, Yankee greenbacks. I said, "I don't understand, who sent us this money?"

Jeremiah said, "Mosby. There must have been payroll in one of those wagons last night. When we capture payroll, he divides it evenly between the men."

I counted the money, it was four thousand dollars.

Jeremiah said, "There were thirty-five of us last night, so I guess we took seventy thousand dollars from them. Plus all those guns, wagons, and mules. I was the only one of us injured, none of us were killed. It was a good night. I would like for you to take three thousand of that and give it to Helen."

I counted out the money and took it downstairs to Helen, she refused it. I told her Jeremiah wanted her to have it. We agreed to put it in the room behind the bookcase. She would use it if she needed it.

Three days later I was to rendezvous with Mosby. Jeremiah simply said, "Follow orders and come home."

I said, "I will."

There were only four of us that night, we rode and watched to see what the Union Army was doing. Reconnaissance, gathering intelligence. I got the feeling Mosby was teaching me. I returned to Helen's just before daylight. Jeremiah was awake, waiting for me. He had been awake all night. For the rest of the week I rode reconnaissance.

On the eighth night, Mosby said, "Turner, take Brooks with you, head south, and circle the entire camp, meet me back here in three hours. I want to know everything you see."

I said, "Yes Sir." I looked at my watch, it was midnight. We did as ordered and was back at the rendezvous point right on time.

Mosby asked, "What did you see?"

I told him we saw six pickets and told him where they were. Ten wagons, all covered. Thirty horses.

He said, "Good work, head home."

I said, "Yes Sir."

Jeremiah was waiting up for me, as he had all week.

The next day Major Mosby comes for dinner. Mosby asks, "Jeremiah, how are you feeling?"

Jeremiah replied, "Very well Sir."

"I wanted to check on you, I am glad you're feeling well." Mosby said.

Jeremiah said, "I'm ready for duty. I am confident I can perform my duties."

Mosby said, "I admire your sense of duty, however, maybe we should give it another week or so."

Jeremiah said, "Yes Sir, whatever you think is best."

Mosby said, "Yes, I think a little more healing time is best. I also wanted to tell Ms. Charlotte, Brooks, the man that rode with you last night, is a Lieutenant. He reported you carried out your orders and delivered accurate information. You seemed confident in your actions. I believe his words were, "Charley is a fine addition to the rangers". I am promoting both of you. Jeremiah you are now a Captain. Charlotte, you are now a 2nd Lieutenant. I hope you both are as pleased as I have been pleased with your actions as of late."

We both thanked him. I then handed him the package of cigars that Daddy had sent.

He smiled and said, "I will see that General Stuart will receive half of these. Thank you. Oh, I have personal news that I wanted to share with the two of you. My wife Pauline is with child. She may come up to visit next week, if she does, I would like for the two of you to meet her. Maybe Helen would have us over for supper."

Jeremiah shook Mosby's hand and said, "Congratulations Sir."

I then took his hand and said, "Congratulations, I'm excited to finally get to meet her."

After Mosby left, Jeremiah said, "Congratulations, 2nd Lieutenant Turner."

I smiled as I said, "Congratulations, Captain Turner."

A week later Mosby and Pauline came for supper. Pauline Mosby was a pretty lady. She had a sense of humor that matched that of her husband. She too, had a love of reading, and she seemed quite intelligent. Mosby appeared proud to be married to such a lady, and Pauline appeared proud to be married to such a gentleman soldier. It was instant friendship. I could picture us being lifelong friends and gathering every once in a while after the war. I pray we all survive and it becomes reality. They were excited about the child they were expecting, I must admit I was a little jealous. I think Jeremiah felt the same.

August 24, 1863. While on a raid Major Mosby is shot in the side and thigh. The Major would be alright, but he would need about a month to recover.

During this time we continued to raid the supply wagons, took horses and equipment, disrupted communications, intercepted dispatches, derailed trains, and destroyed bridges. Anything to cause trouble for the Union Army.

September 2, 1863. We spent Jeremiah's twenty-third birthday on a raid, without Major Mosby.

October 9, 1863. Virginia Pelham Stuart is born. Jeb and Flora are delighted to have a daughter.

That fall, Mosby is promoted to Lieutenant Colonel. Winter, cold, snow, rain, and darkness didn't stop us. This was the best time for us. Most people didn't want to be outside, and we met with less resistance. I guess it was times like these that earned Mosby the nickname, "The Gray Ghost", well, and the fact that we seemed to be everywhere, and then nowhere.

November 19, 1863. Lincoln goes to Gettysburg, Pennsylvania for the dedication of a National Cemetery. He gave only a two minute speech, it is called a failure. This cemetery was for the Union Soldiers that died in that three day battle back in July.

A while after the battle, a northern politician walking through the site of the battle noticed weather was revealing the corpses of the dead, he claimed to be appalled and started to work on getting a cemetery for proper burials. The State of Pennsylvania bought the land and had the Union dead removed from the battlefield where they were originally buried, and reburied at this cemetery.

Confederate dead were left in the hastily dug graves on the battlefield.

December 8, 1863. John Singleton Mosby Jr. is born. Mosby was proud to tell us he has another son.

On the same day, a Proclamation of Amnesty and Reconstruction offer pardons to participants of the rebellion. Swear an oath to the Union and go home. If 10% of the 1860 registered voters of a state take the oath, and accept that slavery is abolished, the state can then start to reconstruct their government. Lincoln is basically inviting the states back into the Union. Some in the U.S. Congress don't agree with Lincoln's generous terms and try to come up with another plan. Lincoln veto's their plan.

In 1863, Jeremiah and I spend Christmas together for the first time since 1860. We helped decorate Helen's house. I missed home, my family. This was the first Christmas I had been away from Mama, Daddy, Aunt Polly, Uncle Henry, and Sara. I haven't even seen Sara and George's baby. I wanted to be home so badly I cried. I had to stay here. I must be with Jeremiah. The thought of the Northern Lights makes me feel like I had to spend every possible moment with him. I try not to think of home and family, it hurts too much. We went to bed that night and held each other tight. I knew he missed his family as much as I missed mine. It had been two years and seven months since he had left home. Once again, I was glad when Christmas had passed.

I looked forward to when Christmas would be a happy time once again, spent with all of our loved ones, and not having to be separated from anybody.

I thought back to the Christmas before the war. Running cedar on the porch rails and the mantles of the fireplaces, the smell of the greenery in the house. Me wearing the red and white velvet dress, my long hair all put up and pretty. Jeremiah, wearing black trousers, a white shirt, a black coat, blue vest, and a red ascot. I believe he had worn a pearl stick pin. I went to sleep in his arms dreaming of that Christmas.

In early 1864, Louisiana, Arkansas, and Tennessee accept the terms of the Proclamation of Amnesty and Reconstruction that was offered in December. The U.S. Congress didn't recognize the States. Fighting continued in these States as the politicians argued.

February 24, 1864. We spend my twenty-first birthday together. It's a quiet day and night at Helen's house. I wondered if my family missed me as much as I missed them.

We continued our raids.

March, 1864. Flora Stuart is visiting, we finally get to meet. She is a pretty lady, intelligent. It was wonderful to spend time with her. She reminded me of Mama. She smiled, was polite and charming, but something made me feel like she was sad. I guessed it was because this was her first visit with Jeb in over a year. Flora brought the children with her. Jeb Jr., or Jimmy, as they called him, was not quite three years old. Virginia was five months old.

That night when we went to bed Jeremiah said, "Flora has a hard time."

I asked, "Because of their daughter dying?"

He said, "Of course that, but I was talking about her family. Did you know her daddy is the Union General, Philip Cooke?"

I asked, "The Cavalry General?"

Jeremiah said, "Yes, he's the man that entered West Point when he was fourteen years old, graduated at eighteen years old, wrote a cavalry manual used by the Union and the Confederacy. Flora has a brother and brother-in-law that resigned from the U.S. Army and joined the Confederacy. Her daddy and one brother-in-law stayed with the Union. General Stuart doesn't allow her daddy to be mentioned around him. As a matter-of-fact, little Jimmy's name was changed to Jeb Jr. when her daddy refused to join the Confederacy. Jimmy was originally named after Flora's daddy. General Stuart seemed to have taken it personally."

I asked, "Why did General Stuart take it so personal, wasn't General Cooke from out west?"

Jeremiah said, "General Cooke was born in Virginia, right here in Loudoun County. He had been living out west for years."

"Oh. Is Flora's brother Brigadier General Cooke of the North Carolina 27th Infantry?" I asked.

Jeremiah said, "Yes, and her brother-in-law is Surgeon General of the Confederacy, Dr. Charles Brewer. His daddy and some of his brothers are with the Union, and two brothers joined the Confederacy along with him. It's so sad to see families spilt like that."

I asked, "Have you heard from your sister in Boston?"

He replied, "No, Mama says she hasn't heard from Mary in years now. I guess we all need to rest easy in the fact that she is in Boston, there's no fighting up there. Her husband isn't in the army. They should make it through just fine."

We snuggled up to each other and said goodnight.

13 GENERAL GRANT

March, 1864. Lincoln pulls General Grant from Tennessee and promotes him to Lieutenant General. Grant is the first man to hold this rank in the United States since George Washington. Lincoln wanted it known that Grant was over the entire Union Army and answered only to the President. Grant's Army is called the Army of the Potomac.

General Stuart told me that General Grant had graduated from West Point. Before the war he was dear friends with James Longstreet, who is a general with the Confederacy. In December, Longstreet had taken his twenty-five thousand troops to the so-called western theater of the war, out in Tennessee. I guess it was fortunate for them that Grant was brought to the east. Grant had proven himself in battle, even with some people falsely claiming him to be a drunkard.

General Stuart liked telling entertaining stories, like Daddy. I liked listening and learning. He told me many of the men on both sides were graduates of West Point.

Some were there at the same time, and close friends. Even if they weren't acquainted, all being West Point graduates, they considered themselves brothers, forced by circumstances to fight against each other.

As he talked I couldn't help but think of his father-in-law.

In early April, Longstreet is recalled back to the eastern theater. There is a chance he will have to come face to face with his old friend.

Mosby learns that General Grant is going to Washington every week to meet with Lincoln.

Mosby says to me, "You find out when he goes and you be on every train he is on. You be that charming lady I first met, make friends, gather information. You're not there to kill anyone, just to gather information. You're a smart girl, and I expect you will do well. I will be here upon your return every week for the details."

I said, "Yes Sir."

April 4, 1864. Grant makes Phillip Sheridan commander of the Army of the Potomac's Cavalry Corps. He was moved from the Western theater to the Eastern.

April 9, 1864. Grant tells General Meade, "Wherever Lee goes, you go."

I return from a trip to Washington, Mosby is waiting for me.

I tell him, "I met General Grant, he was a gentleman to me. We chatted about relatively nothing until I excused myself as I had noticed a lonely looking man that had boarded the train with the General. I dropped a handkerchief, and of course he picked it up. I thanked him and asked if I might sit with him for a minute, as I felt a bit faint. He said of course, took my arm, and helped me to a seat. I told him I was looking for my husband who is with Sheridan, but I didn't know where to find him, I then began to cry, saying I haven't seen him since the war started, and I must find him.

He felt so sorry for me, he said he could get me with a supply train next week that will take me straight to Sheridan. I may have to spend a night in Fairfax, but that would be the only delay."

Mosby asked, "When is this supply train to be in Fairfax?"

"Wednesday night." I replied.

Mosby smiled and said, "Good work, any idea how big the supply train is?"

I said, "About thirty cars."

Mosby then asked, "How did you like Washington?"

I smiled as I said, "I liked it just fine Sir, as I met a nice lady who is making me a dress. I go for a first fitting next week."

He laughed a little and said, "I guess every lady deserves a new dress every now and then, don't you agree Jeremiah?"

I said, "Oh no Sir. It's not that I needed a dress. I needed to meet the lady that is making the dress. It seems she makes all of Mrs. Lincoln's dresses. Her name is Elizabeth Keckley. She was a slave, she bought her freedom, moved to Washington and started her own dress shop. Her dresses caught the eye of Mrs. Lincoln, they have become friends. Elizabeth helps runways, so I told her I had come looking for her help, as maybe she could help me get runaways out of Virginia. She looks forward to seeing me next week when I get fitted for my new dress."

Mosby and Jeremiah seemed amazed. Mosby said, "On your first trip to Washington you met and made a friend of someone close to the White House. How?"

I again smiled as I said, "Before I left home, I helped runway slaves. I happened to see a man and his wife that had stayed at our house for two or three weeks, they had been beaten badly, I took care of them and arranged transportation to the next stop. They took me to Elizabeth and told her about me helping them and many others. We had plenty to talk about."

Jeremiah beamed with pride.

Mosby smiled as he nodded his head and said, "I knew you would be a valuable asset. Good job! When do you return to Washington?"

I said, "Next Friday, along with General Grant. It will be safe, as the man that told me about the supply train, should be with the supply train, so I guess by Friday, if he is a smart man he will be a prisoner, if not, he'll be dead."

Wednesday night we take the supply train. He wasn't a smart man.

On my next trip to Washington, I don't speak to General Grant on the train, I don't want him to recognize me. I just speak to the people around him looking for someone that likes to talk. I have found, I don't have to do very much talking, mostly listening. I figure the less I talk, the less people will remember me.

I met with Elizabeth and we talked for hours. I ask about the dresses she makes for the First Lady. She likes talking about her work. She is very talented. I also ask, what's Mary Lincoln like? Is she like we read in the newspapers? She tells me Mary is a nice lady, most accounts of her aren't accurate. I ask if she has met the President and what's he like? She gives a favorable description of him as well. I tell her I had better be on my way. I'd like to see her again soon and meet some of the people that can help me get runaways to safety. She asked me to come back next week. Mrs. Lincoln has invited her for tea and she would like for me to join her. I get the time and date and set off to board the train with General Grant. I read the newspaper on the return trip, well, I appeared to read, as I am listening to everyone around me.

I get to Helen's house, and once again, Mosby is waiting for me. I tell him everything about going for tea next week. I also had information of telegraph lines that have been repaired and are once again operational.

The next night the telegraph lines are down again.

The rangers are still raiding and gathering information. We make frequent attacks outside of the town of Fairfax and along the Potomac.

April 17, 1864. Grant ends prisoner exchange, he feels it is prolonging the war.

April 27, 1864. Northern Armies break winter camp. Fighting gets heavy, quick. Grant is determined to end this. It appears his strategy is to simply win with numbers. The Union has more men than the South. If one of them die for every one of us, they win. The people of the North start to feel the pains of war, with so many of their boys dying. People start demanding that Lincoln remove Grant. Lincoln refuses.

May 5, 1864. The two day battle of the Wilderness starts.

May 6, 1864. Some say Lee defeats Grant, others say Grant defeats Lee. Some say it was inconclusive. I guess it depends on what side you're looking at it from. Longstreet is wounded, shot by one of his own men. The bullet went through his neck and shoulder. He can't move his right arm. Grant doesn't retreat, he advances to Spotsylvania Court House.

May 8, 1864. Lee and Grant are fighting at Spotsylvania Court House.

May 9, 1864. Grant sends Sheridan's Cavalry to take Richmond.

May 12, 1864. Mosby comes by to tell us that General Stuart was wounded yesterday, he died today. Stuart's Cavalry had been fighting against Sheridan's Cavalry. Sheridan was trying to reach Richmond, the battle was called Yellow Tavern. The fighting had been going on for about three hours. Stuart was on his horse firing at the Union troops, encouraging his men. He was shot by a Union private, and taken from the battlefield. Mosby was visibly shaken, as he and Stuart were great friends.

Mosby said, "He was taken into Richmond to the home of his brother-in-law, Doctor Brewer. President Davis visited with him. They say his last words were, "God's will be done.""

I heard those words and chills went down my spine, just like seeing the Northern Lights on Jeremiah's birthday. I started to cry. That was what Jeremiah had said to me, before he left to join the cavalry. I had said to him that he could be killed, and he replied, "God's will be done". I looked at Jeremiah, he knew why I was crying.

Mosby continued saying, "Stuart died before Flora reached Richmond. General Lee said, he feels like weeping when he hears Stuarts name."

Mosby placed his hand on mine and said, "Jeb was a fine soldier, a good man, and a true friend to all of us, he deserves a few tears. He might would have liked the thought of a pretty lady, here and there, crying over him."

I couldn't tell him I was crying because I think Aunt Polly would have said that was a sign, meaning Jeremiah wasn't going to make it through the war. My crying turned to uncontrollable sobbing, I had to leave the room. I went to our bedroom.

A few minutes later Jeremiah came into the bedroom and he said, "I told Mosby I should check on you. He's gone now."

I was lying across the bed still crying. He walked over to me, and I sat up. He put his arms around me, hugged me tight, and said, "Charlotte, it doesn't mean anything, a lot of people say that."

I said, "I try not to be superstitious, but I got chills when he said it. I couldn't control my crying. I know it's silly, but deep down I have a feeling of... of doom. Is that feeling superstition, or a warning?"

He said, "I think its superstition."

I said, "I pray that you're right."

179

He said, "A few days before the battle, Stuart wrote to General Lee and recommended Mosby be promoted, he was always thinking of others. Yes, he was a fine man. I am going to miss him."

I said, "I'm going to miss him too."

May 13, 1864. While in Washington I learn the Union Army starts burying their dead in the front lawn of Arlington House, General Lee's home. I go to tea at the White House and meet Mrs. Lincoln. Mr. Lincoln comes in for a moment, kisses his wife on the cheek, and greets Elizabeth. Mrs. Lincoln introduced me to him.

He takes my hand and slightly bows, and asks, "Ms. Charlotte, judging by the way you speak, I would guess you are from North Carolina, am I correct?"

I answer, "Yes Sir, I am from Guilford County, North Carolina. Most of us there don't care for the institution of slavery so my loyalties lie on the side of freedom. For years now, I have been helping slaves get to freedom. That is how I came to make the acquaintance of Elizabeth. I applaud you on the Emancipation Proclamation. I look forward to the time when the war is over and we are all free."

Mr. Lincoln said, "I too, also look forward to that time. It was a pleasure meeting you. I hope to see you again, as I think it's good for Mary to have friends that are not involved with the war."

I said, "Thank you Sir, it was an honor to meet you. I too, hope to see you again."

He left the room, we ladies chatted about gossip and rumors. After a while we left.

Grant wasn't on the return train, I heard he was on his way to Fredericksburg, his troops were to meet him there.

When I returned, I told Mosby and Jeremiah about meeting Lincoln.

Jeremiah asked, "What did you think of him?"

180

I answered, "I thought, would it end the war if I killed him? I decided, no it would not, and that was not my orders. So I smiled, and acted like a lady."

Mosby quickly said, "You're right. Follow orders. I don't want you killing anyone on these trips to Washington unless you have to, as to avoid being captured or killed. Do you understand?"

I said, "Yes Sir."

Mosby then said, "I imagine it's about time you showed up with a runaway or two. Any ideas on where you can find some?"

I replied, "Yes Sir, I wrote to Daddy and he has put me in touch with the proper people. We will house people here, and then I will take them into Washington. These will be people that have been at our home in North Carolina. I can get them safely into Washington, and they can vouch for me to Elizabeth. If they choose to go further, Elizabeth can make the arrangements. Sir, do you have a problem with me helping runaways?"

Mosby said, "No, I've never cared for slavery."

It turned out that Helen didn't care for slavery either. The people at her house weren't slaves, they were paid workers. She hadn't told us because, well, as she said, "I have a few secrets of my own." She thought the idea of hiding runaway slaves just made life more exciting!

May 19, 1864. Lee and Grant battle again for days, southwest of Fredericksburg. They call it an inconclusive battle.

Sometime in early June, there is a photographer traveling around, and Jeremiah and I get our picture made, we are both in uniform.

The next day I go to Washington with three runaway slaves. I speak to General Grant, as when he looked at me, I thought he may be thinking they were my slaves. I told him I was taking these runaway slaves to Washington. I introduced myself as Charlotte. I told him the same thing I had told Mr. Lincoln.

On the return trip, General Grant came to where I was sitting and inquired if he might join me. I, of course, agreed.

He said, "I mentioned meeting you to the President," I smiled as he said, "the President spoke highly of you and your efforts, so I guess I'll be seeing you regularly."

I, still smiling, and talking in my sweetest, southern voice said, "I certainly do hope so. I feel much safer being on a train that you are on."

He said, "I see you're wearing a wedding ring, are you married to one of our boys?"

I leaned forward as so only he could hear me, lay my hand on his forearm, and said, "Oh no Sir, I'm not married. I wear the ring because I have found, men are more likely to leave you alone if they think you're married."

He nodded a bit and said, "You sound like a smart girl. The President commented he liked the sound of your voice." He spoke quietly and looked out the window as he said, "I suppose both he and I are taken with the way you southern ladies talk. It has always been pleasing for me to hear." He turned to me and said, "I apologize, I'm getting sentimental. For a second, I was thinking of my own dear wife."

"Oh," I asked, "has it been a long time since you've seen her?"

He said, "I just left her. She's in Washington. I just always hate leaving her. She is such a dear, sweet woman. Maybe you could meet her. She hasn't been in Washington very long, and she's lonely. She could use a friend."

I said, "Why, General Grant, that sounds absolutely wonderful! Like my daddy always says, one can't have too many friends."

I didn't gather much information on that trip, but I had helped three people get to safety, and also gained the trust of General Grant. Mosby was pleased.

June 15, 1864. Arlington House is designated as a military cemetery. Some people wanted to be sure that if General Lee survives the war, he wouldn't have a home to return to.

On my next train trip I learned, Grant had given Sheridan orders to move into the part of Northern Virginia that some people now called, Mosby's Confederacy. His orders were to live off of the land and lay waste the so-called breadbasket that fed the Confederate Army. Civilians and their homes were now considered targets of the Union Army. I also meet Julia Grant.

August 13, 1864. Jeremiah and I are to rendezvous with Mosby. We attacked a large wagon train. They didn't even notice us until we were upon them. Then it was over. We had hundreds of prisoners, horses, mules, supply wagons, and one hundred and twenty-five thousand dollars. Two of our men were killed and three wounded.

September 14, 1864. Colonel Mosby is wounded, it is said a bullet hit his belt buckle and went into his abdomen. He was taken to his father's house to recover. We continued our work. He returned to us three weeks later.

September 22, 1864. Six men are captured in Front Royal, Virginia. An eyewitness told the newspaper, six men were murdered. Anderson, Love, and Rhodes were shot, one other of whose name they didn't know. Carter and Overby were hanged. The Union said they were all rangers. Henry Rhodes was not, he was just a boy, his mother begged for his life, asked them to take him prisoner. As they sharpened their sabers, they threatened to cut his head off if she came closer, and then they would cut off her head too. They murdered him in front of his mother, along with the others. Union Generals Torbert and Merritt had turned the men over to General Custer for execution.

The Richmond Examiner reports, "When the rope was placed around Overby's neck, by his inhumane captors, he told them that he was one of Mosby's men, and that he was proud to die as a Confederate soldier, and that his death was sweetened with the assurance that Colonel Mosby would swing in the wind ten Yankees for every man they murdered." Later another one of our men was hanged, there was a note pinned to him that read, "This will be the fate of Mosby, and all his men."

October, 1864. We have derailed trains, torn up the railroad, burned bridges, and all communication from Manassas to Salem is cut off. General Lee is pleased, he sends a message to Mosby, expressing his satisfaction, also asking that Mosby do all in his power to stop that railroad from being rebuilt. We also destroyed the railroad at Front Royal. Sheridan went there with ten thousand troops. He was to get them on a train and then they were to meet up with Grant. When they arrived in Front Royal he found a rail bed without iron. They stayed there for three days waiting for the railroad to be rebuilt. It couldn't be rebuilt, so they would have to march to Alexandria. Railroads had become Sheridan's weakest point, so it was Mosby's favorite target. Sheridan then started putting more men to guard the railroad, therefore making it harder and more dangerous for us. We managed to find weak points.

One clear evening, we were to derail a passenger train. Derailing a slow moving train would mean that, more than likely, no one would get killed, just bruised up a bit. We removed a rail. We were to lie down on the bank of the railroad and keep quiet. Then, there was the train. It got to the cut track and crashed. The boiler burst and hot cinder went everywhere. It looked like all of hell had opened up. Passengers were screaming, Mosby directed us to help the people to safety, and set the cars on fire, but quickly, as we needed to get out of there.

Some people complained about the treatment. Mosby told them to speak to their General Sheridan, as it was his business to protect them. We also found payroll on that train. One hundred and seventy-three thousand dollars. Once again, it was divided among the rangers. The payroll clerks were accused of working with us and were arrested. Later that same day we captured another train about ten miles west of Harpers Ferry, West Virginia. The railroad owners accused Sheridan of not giving them enough protection. To maintain communications between Washington, Baltimore, and the Shenandoah Valley, more troops had to be brought in to guard the railroad. We had achieved our objective.

We both were promoted, Jeremiah to Major, and I became a 1st Lieutenant.

Word was sent to Mosby that we shouldn't attack certain trains as there would be women and children on them. Mosby thought it wrong for the Union to try to shield themselves with women and children. He replied, he didn't understand that it would hurt a woman or a child anymore to be killed than it would hurt a man.

Also, General Longstreet has returned to duty after a long recovery. He still can't use his right arm.

November 6, 1864. Mosby ordered seven prisoners executed, to be chosen by drawing lots. People called it Mosby's, "death lottery". One that drew the lot was just a boy, Mosby didn't want to execute a child, the boy was excused and someone else drew the lot. Only three men were actually executed by hanging. Two were shot in the head and left for dead, they lived. Two, somehow escaped. To me this wasn't a failure, I thought it just proved the rangers weren't murderers.

November 8, 1864. Lincoln wins re-election. Mrs. Lincoln tells me I must get an escort and come to the Inaugural Ball.

I say I will.

When I tell Jeremiah and Mosby, we discuss my going to the ball. I would need an escort. Is it safe for Jeremiah to be going into Washington? Is there information there to be gathered, or just a bunch of people celebrating and drinking? We would all think about it and talk again next week.

November 11, 1864. Mosby sends a letter to General Sheridan stating, that since the murder of our men, we have taken over seven hundred Union prisoners. But hereafter, any prisoners we take will be treated as our men are treated.

No more of our men were murdered. All the rangers had a special hatred for General George Armstrong Custer, after he executed our fellow rangers, and one innocent boy.

By December, Sheridan was in winter quarters at Winchester. A large portion of Confederate General Early's men had been moved to Petersburg. We kept Sheridan's troops busy watching and waiting for us, their sleepless enemy, to capture, or kill them.

Mid-December, 1864. Mosby sees an old friend, they talk for a while, he is a surgeon. Mosby tells him he is in need of a good surgeon, as he is of the opinion that his current surgeon prefers fighting. They agree and Mosby has Doctor Monteiro transferred to his command.

December 21, 1864. Mosby is shot in the abdomen, he nearly bleeds to death. He hid his gray coat, so the Union wouldn't know his rank. They see how much blood he has lost, and not realizing who he is, they leave him to die. Friends take him to safety. Newspapers start reporting he has died. They were wrong, he was still alive. Doctor Monteiro wasn't yet with us, when he did arrive he was sent to Colonel Mosby's father's house to tend to him. It is said that it took all of his skills as a surgeon to save Mosby.

Christmas, 1864. Once again we're away from home. Praying for family, friends, and especially Colonel Mosby.

1865 comes and we were still carrying out the raids, capturing supplies, burning trains, and taking prisoners.

On reconnaissance one night we were spotted, and riding hard to get away. There were four of us, maybe fifteen of them. I was shot and fell from Logan, I called out to Jeremiah. I was hit on the right side of my lower back. I couldn't get up, it felt like someone had taken a red hot poker and stabbed it into my back. Logan was using his front hoof to paw at my shoulder like a dog, he was trying to get me to get up, the Yankees were closing in fast. Time seemed like it slowed down, I felt like I was watching myself struggle to get up. I remember thinking, if Jeremiah comes back, he will be killed. I hope he don't come back. I also thought to myself, I can't let them take me alive, they would torture me if they discover that I'm a girl. I reach for my revolvers in my boots, I decide that I will fight as long as I am breathing.

Then, I hear Jeremiah yelling, "Charlotte, give me your hand!"

He was shooting at them while he raced toward me. The two other rangers were coming back too. They were all shooting. I raised my left hand as high as I could. I felt Jeremiah's hand grab mine. He yanked me off of the ground onto Jefferson, and yelled, "Come on Logan!"

We all get away. I'm the only one hurt. Jeremiah gets me to Helen's house as one of the others goes for the surgeon.

I wake up. There is Jeremiah, sitting beside the bed. He looks worried, like he may have been crying. I'm scared I'm going to die. I reach my hand out for his.

He quickly says, "Charlotte! Oh thank God."

I ask weakly, "Jeremiah, what happened, why do I hurt so much?" I start to remember as he tells me the story.

I said, "I remember seeing you reach out and pull me up onto Jefferson, it was like I was up and off to the side watching."

He said, "I guess that was your spirit, leaving you. Thank God we got you back!"

"How long have I been asleep?" I asked.

He said, "Three days. Doctor Monteiro performed surgery on you as soon as he arrived that night. He got the bullet out. He said you lost the baby, but you will be alright. With a little luck we might still be able to have children. Charlotte, I was so scared I was going to lose you..." he started to cry.

I started crying too, and asked, "Lost a baby?"

Jeremiah gathered himself and said, "The doctor said you probably didn't know you were with child."

I asked, "I was with child? I didn't know, how could I not know?"

He said, "The doctor said, it was early, and it's common for a woman to be a couple of months along and not know."

I said, "Oh Jeremiah, you must hate me."

He stroked my hair as he said, "Charlotte, I love you. You didn't know, it's not your fault. I just thank God you have survived."

I said, "Thank you for saving me. I love you."

He held me, not tight so as not to hurt me, but he held me for the longest time, while we both cried.

Doctor Monteiro came by the next day to check on me. He had been tending to Colonel Mosby, and me. It was difficult due to Mosby being at his father's home near Lynchburg, and me being in Middleburg. We were about one hundred and fifty miles apart. Both of us wounded too badly to move closer to make it easier for the doctor. He told me he would come and check on me once a week, if I needed him sooner, we could send for him.

He said, "Colonel Mosby had asked me to tell you and Jeremiah, that you have his deepest sympathies.

He was saddened when I told him of you being wounded, and about the baby."

I said, "Thank you doctor. Would you please thank Colonel Mosby for us? How is he?"

The doctor replied, "Well, he's about like you, he's going to be fine, he just needs time. I was worried for both of you, but you've made it through the worst part."

He started to leave when I grabbed his arm and said, "Are you planning to tell anyone about me?"

He patted my hand that was squeezing his arm and said, "No my dear. The day Colonel Mosby asked me to join him, he told me about you. I guess he didn't want any surprises."

I said, "Thank you for everything."

He patted my hand again, turned to leave and said, "You're welcome."

Helen then came in with chicken broth.

I tell Jeremiah, "We have to get a message to Elizabeth, we need to figure out what we're going to tell her. I won't be able to go to Washington for a while."

We decide to tell her I was caught with some runaway slaves, and I was shot by slave catchers. I will have the scars to prove it. This will also get me out of going to the Inaugural Ball. We have to figure out what we are going to do about the runaway slaves that will be arriving here. How are we going to get them to Washington?

Helen says, "I can help with that."

Jeremiah asks, "Do you know somebody we can trust that might be willing to do it?"

Helen replied, "Yes I do. Me."

Jeremiah laughed and said, "Helen you can't think I'm going to let you do this."

Helen looked at Jeremiah and said, "Let me!" She laughed then looked at me and said, "Charlotte, tell me what I need to do."

I said, "Helen... umm, I guess you're right, there is no other way, here's all you need to do."

I gave her the information as to what train to be on. I asked her to speak with Grant and tell him I had been shot by slave catchers. He could relay the information to the Lincolns. I wrote a note for her to give to Elizabeth. When the runaways get here bring them up here to me. They need to meet me. I thought if Elizabeth felt something was wrong, she would feel at ease, if they could describe me.

Then I said, "Helen, only talk to General Grant and Elizabeth. You make sure you are on the return train. Have a newspaper or a Harpers Weekly, something to occupy yourself. The less you say the safer we will all be."

She said, "You young'uns act like I've never been to Washington before. The two of you might be surprised at some of the things I've done. Did you ever hear of the war of 1812?" She was walking out of the room and mumbling, "Hard-headed young'uns act like you're the first people that ever done anything."

Jeremiah and I looked at each other.

He asked, "Do you really think she did this kind of work way back then?"

I said, "With Helen, nothing would surprise me. I bet Mosby would know. Let's ask him when he comes back."

Helen makes her first trip into Washington, she returns saying it was uneventful.

She does say, "General Grant was saddened when I told him you were shot by slave catchers. He asked if there was anything he could do. He said he would relay the news to the Lincoln's. He also asked if he could visit you.

190

I told him you were too bad off for visitors and as soon as you were well enough, we were moving you south until you heal up."

Jeremiah said, "That was good thinking, Helen. I never thought he would offer to visit."

Helen said, "I guess our Charlotte leaves quite the impression on people."

I just smiled and said, "General Grant is a gentleman."

Helen took runaway slaves to Washington every week. She was extremely happy these days.

Late February, 1865. Now having been promoted to a full Colonel, Mosby came to Helen's house to visit. We were in the main parlor. I was in a dressing gown. He walked in smiling.

He walked over to me, took my hand and said, "Ms. Charlotte my dear, my heart was broken when I heard the news. Pauline and my children were with me at my mother and father's home, during my recovery. Many times as I was with my children, my thoughts turned to you, my wounded Ranger, but more importantly my wounded friends. I pray that you will bear children. Holding your children, one knows they are a true gift from God."

He had tears in his eyes. I started to cry. I looked at Jeremiah, there were tears running down his cheeks as he reached for his handkerchief to wipe them away. Nothing in the world broke my heart more than to see Jeremiah cry.

I gathered myself a bit and said, "Thank you, Colonel Mosby."

Jeremiah reached out and shook his hand as he said, "Thank you, Colonel Mosby."

Mosby with Jeremiah's hand still in his, lay his other hand on top of Jeremiah's and said, "You two can call me John, when we're not on duty, and that certain formality is required."

Jeremiah smiled and said, "Thank you, John."

I said, "Thank you, John. I pray that God does bless us with a child, and we get to experience what you're talking about. It means a lot that you would think of us, when you were fighting for your own life. You have been on our minds too. How are you?"

He said, "I'm ready for duty. I've been away much too long. What have you two done, about you not being able to go into Washington?"

We told him. He just nodded his head and smiled.

Jeremiah then asked, "Sir, what do you know of Helen and the war of 1812?"

Mosby replied, "I know, she will tell you what she wants you to know." Then he laughed and said, "She is some woman!"

Spring, 1865. I am better. The armies break winter camps, the fighting picks up.

March 4, 1865. Lincoln is Inaugurated for his second term as President of the United States.

That same day, General Sherman, having left a line of destruction behind him as he went through Georgia and South Carolina, now entered eastern North Carolina.

Greensborough, North Carolina is now involved in a small way. On April 2, 1865, Davis and the Confederate Government retreat from Richmond, they stop in Danville, Virginia for a day or two, then Greensborough for a day or two. For the time they were there, Greensborough was considered the Capital of the Confederacy. North Carolina Governor Vance leaves the Capital in Raleigh, and heads to Greensborough as well.

There were stories of Davis and his men leaving Richmond with a treasure of coins worth about a half of a million dollars in Yankee greenbacks. The train is slow carrying all that weight, so they dump the lesser valued coins off the train somewhere between Richmond and Danville. When the train pulls into the station in Danville the gold and silver are still aboard.

When the train reaches Greensborough, it's all gone.

April 3, 1865. The Union has taken Petersburg. The Union has also taken Richmond, on the same day.

April 9, 1865. Lee surrenders to Grant at Appomattox, Virginia. The war is over. Longstreet is there with Lee.

All Confederates are told to surrender and lay down their arms, then swear an oath to the United States of America, and they will be pardoned.

April 14, 1865. Lincoln is shot in the head at Ford's Theatre, by the famous actor, John Wilkes Booth.

April 15, 1865. Lincoln dies.

April 15, 1865. Andrew Johnson is sworn in as President. Johnson was born in Raleigh, North Carolina, and lived in Tennessee as an adult. In the 1840's and 1850's he served in both Congress and the Senate, representing Tennessee.

April 21, 1865. Our fifth wedding anniversary. Mosby chooses not to surrender, he disbands the Rangers. We gather, and a letter written by him, to the Rangers, was read by his brother William. Many of us take a few minutes to say goodbye to Colonel Mosby.

14 GOING HOME

Jeremiah and I talked that night. There are rumors that some surrenders weren't going as planned and the Confederates weren't being treated according to Grant's orders. With us being rangers, there was a good chance they would be harder on us. Jeremiah suggested we go to Washington, and surrender directly to General Grant.

April 22, 1865. We say goodbye to Helen, she insisted we take half of the money we had been giving her. Jeremiah told her it wasn't necessary, we hadn't had reason to spend much money and we still had plenty of our share of the Yankee greenbacks. Helen gave me the dress I had worn when I first met General Stuart. She thought it best if I looked like a lady while in Washington. I wore men's clothes for the trip.

We left heading to Washington. We got there and checked into a hotel. We both got cleaned up, dressed proper, and set off to meet with General Grant. He was busy, but agreed to see us.

As we entered his office, he glanced up, and upon seeing me, he stood up and said, "Good afternoon, Ms. Charlotte."

I said, "Good afternoon, General Grant."

Jeremiah, dressed in civilian clothes, shook his hand, I held my hand out for him, which he took and slightly bowed to me.

General Grant, being very busy got straight to the point and said, "What can I help you two with today?"

Jeremiah said, "Sir, we have come to surrender to you. I am Major Jeremiah Turner, with the 43rd Battalion, Virginia Cavalry."

Grant stood there for second like he was surprised and said, "Oh, I suppose it was smart on your part to come here, as many of our boys don't care much for you rangers. I think I would have done the same. You are entitled to a pardon, and I will see that you get it. It will be ready shortly. Is there anything else you need? I am very busy and I need to get to North Carolina, as there are a few detail's I need to attend to concerning Johnston's surrender."

I said, "Yes Sir, I also am requesting a pardon. I am 1st Lieutenant Charley Turner, with the 43rd Battalion, Virginia Cavalry."

Grant froze, then looked up at me and asked, "Charlotte, you're one of Mosby's Rangers?"

"Yes Sir." I replied.

He said, "With both of you being officers, I have heard of you. I had no idea Charley Turner was Charlotte Turner. Did Mosby know?"

I felt it best not to say, so I said, "Sir, I can't say what other people know, we, being Jeremiah and myself, told people I was his younger brother. I proved myself as a soldier. That's all I know."

He nodded and said, "We've met a few times."

I smiled as I said, "Yes Sir, numerous times. Please tell Julia, I send my regards."

Grant shook his head from side to side a little and said, "You're Charley Turner? Aren't the two of you from North Carolina?"

Jeremiah said, "Yes Sir, Guilford County."

Grant said, "I am heading down to Raleigh, I would like for you two to accompany me, we can get better acquainted. The war is over and there is no reason we can't be cordial to each other, maybe even friends, as I know Julia and I already consider Charlotte a friend."

Jeremiah said, "We would be happy to accompany you, Sir. Raleigh is on the way home."

Grant said gravely, "There is the matter of turning over your weapons."

Jeremiah opened a carpet bag and pulled out two Union revolvers. I reached in and pulled out two Union revolvers, and we both lay them on his desk.

Grant said, "Nice revolvers you have there, however, I do believe Mosby required his rangers to carry four of them."

Jeremiah reached into the bag and pulled out two more revolvers, he lay them on the desk. I stood there for just a moment, then I raised the hem of my skirts, exposing my tall boots. I reached down and pulled a revolver from each boot, let my skirt fall back into place as I lay the revolvers on the desk. We both had two more guns at the hotel, as we both always carried six.

Grant looked me in the eyes and asked, "Do you always carry guns in your boots?"

"Yes Sir." I replied.

He saw to our pardons, we gathered our things from the hotel, met with him and boarded a special train, the horses were loaded in the back on the stock car. We then headed to Raleigh.

On the train Grant asks, "Charlotte, do you have a revolver in your boots?"

I said, "No Sir."

He looked to Jeremiah and said, "I hope you don't take offense to me asking her to prove it."

Jeremiah laughed and said, "No Sir. I understand. Charlotte, would you be a dear and show the General your boots?"

I lifted the hem of my skirt just high enough for him to see the top of my boots.

Grant said, "Thank you. Charlotte, I do hope you were sincere with Julia, she speaks so highly of you, I would hate to think you were just using her to get to me."

I said, "Julia is such a sweet lady, I have nothing but respect for her. As I had already met you, my friendship with her was an unexpected and pleasant surprise. I didn't use her for anything except friendship."

Grant nodded and said, "That's good to hear. You and I did have many conversations. Tell me about the information you gathered from me."

I said, "My orders were to be on your trains as you traveled to and from Washington. I believe that was a weekly habit of yours. While our conversations were pleasant, there was no way for me to gather information from you, you're much too intelligent for such things. Most of my conversations weren't with you but with the people around you. It is surprising how much talking a man will do if a lady flirts with him a little. It's also surprising how much a lonely wife will talk to someone that is willing to listen. The First Lady is quite lonely.

As for the information I gathered while on your trains, in Washington, and in the White House. I found out about supply trains, supply wagons, troop movement, when railroads and telegraph lines were repaired, and things like that."

Grant then asked, "Did you have revolvers in your boots on those train trips?"

"Yes Sir." I answered.

He asked, "When you visited the White House?"

I said, "Yes Sir."

"I know you have met President Lincoln, why didn't you use your guns?" he asked.

I replied, "Yes Sir, I met President Lincoln, I found him to be a gentleman, he always had a sadness about him. I didn't do anything while at the White House because my orders were to gather information. To try anything there would have been suicide. Julia, Mary, and Elizabeth would have been accused of being spies. I know some have always questioned the loyalties of Julia and Mary, because they are both from slave states."

He nodded as he said, "I appreciate you thinking of them."

We spoke of the evils of slavery. Jeremiah explained to Grant that we had freed the people that work for us, and even helped runaway slaves. He joined up to fight for our home, and for our rights. I joined the fighting to be with him.

Grant understood, as he didn't care to be separated from Julia.

Grant asked, "So were you really helping runaway slaves?"

I said, "Yes Sir. They would stop at our home in North Carolina, my daddy would transport them up close to Virginia, and others would help until they got to me, then I escorted them to Washington, where Elizabeth took over."

He asked, "How many have you helped?"

I replied, "I have no idea Sir, as many as I could."

He asked, "Were you really shot?"

I said, "Yes Sir."

He asked, "Helping runaway slaves?"

I answered, "No Sir, on a raid."

He asked, "What happened to the man that shot you?"

I said, "Jeremiah killed him."

He paused, then he asked, "Charlotte, have you killed men?"

I nodded and said, "Yes Sir."

He asked, "How many?"

I said, "I don't know Sir, as many as I had to, same as you."

He asked, "If Mosby would have ordered you to shoot me, would you?"

I answered, "Yes Sir. Although I'm glad he didn't."

Grant looked at me for a second and said, "I'm curious as to why Mosby chose to not order me killed?"

I said, "Well Sir, we talked about it. Finally he decided you were more valuable to us right where you were. With people in the North starting to hate Grant the Butcher, they were losing their desire to continue fighting. With enough time they may have stopped the war."

He nodded and said, "Charlotte, I'm also glad he didn't. I don't think I'm going to tell Julia about Charley Turner. If we ever meet again, would you mind the three of us keeping this to ourselves?"

We all agreed it would be best to keep quiet. We changed the subject to more pleasant topics.

I asked if he has had a chance to see General Longstreet. He told us of seeing him at Appomattox. He was saddened that Longstreet's right arm was paralyzed, but happy to see his dear friend had survived the war. Grant tells him they must get together, have a cigar and talk of old times.

Later Longstreet asked, "Why do men fight, who were born to be brothers?"

He told us of Longstreet going to the Dent family home with him when he first met Julia.

He said, "When I saw Longstreet. It brought back memories of us in our younger days. I then remembered another friend, Julia's brother Fred. He told me of his sister while we were at West Point. One thing he had said about her, was that she had always said she would marry, "a soldier... a gallant, brave, dashing soldier." I have never been successful at anything except being a soldier. I suppose she always knew that's what I was meant to be." He got quiet for a moment, looking out the window, then said, "I never thought of myself as gallant, brave, and certainly not dashing, but it warms my heart to think she does."

I smiled and said, "Julia is a wonderful lady, I expect she's right."

He just nodded. I think there was a twinkle in his eyes.

He then turned to Jeremiah and said, "Major, what's life at home like with you being married to a 1st Lieutenant?"

Jeremiah laughed and said, "Well, Sir, at home I'm not a Major and she's not a 1st Lieutenant. We are simply Mr. and Mrs. Jeremiah Turner. Although she does have a way of making things happen." Jeremiah told him about giving me the cameo, and a history lesson on Diana the Huntress.

We continued with pleasant conversation. I told him I would send him some of Daddy and Uncle Henry's cigars.

April 24, 1865. We arrived in Raleigh, North Carolina. We say goodbye to General Grant. He now felt like a friend. It would be nice to see him again.

We loaded the horses on the train from Raleigh to Gibsonville, we boarded, and we were on our way home. There hadn't been any fighting to speak of from Raleigh to Gibsonville. When we got off the train, Gibsonville looked about the same as the last time I was there.

We gathered the horses, jumped on and headed home. Home was only eight miles away. We decided we would stop and see my parents first, as it was on the way, spend a few minutes there, go to his parents for a few minutes, then home to sleep, as we hadn't slept much in the last few days. There was lots of hugging and crying when we first saw our families, we promised to visit tomorrow. We then headed home. As we were passing our fields, we could see the tobacco had been planted. We turned onto our driveway, we spurred the horses and raced to the house. It was about the same time of evening as when we first came home on our wedding day.

We got to the front steps, and Jeremiah said, "Stay on Logan for a second," he then got off of Jefferson, walked over to me, smiled that smile that lights up his entire face, took his hat off with a flourish, held it to his chest and asked, "Ms. Charlotte, may I help you off of Logan?"

I smiled and said in my sweetest, southern voice, "Why of course, Mr. Jeremiah."

He reached up and put his big strong hands on my waist and helped me down. He asked me to step up onto the bottom step. I did, as he stood on the brick walkway. This is where we were when he left to join up.

He kissed me and said, "I told you I would come home." He picked me up and carried me to the front door, it was locked, we had to knock and Anderson came to the door.

Anderson said, "We been wondering when y'all was gonna get home. Y'all must be tired and hungry, should I get Sally to get you some food? I'll tend to the horses."

Jeremiah said, "Thank you, Anderson, and you're right, we are tired, we are going to bed, we will worry about food in the morning."

Anderson replied, "Yes sir, good night."

Jeremiah carried me upstairs into our bedroom, just like the day we were married. We were home and in each other's arms. Tomorrow, we will face the world, but for right now, it's just me and Jeremiah in our bedroom.

15 HOME

The next morning was heavenly. We awoke in our bed together. It had been almost four years since we spent the night together, in our home.

I said, "I never thought we would be here together again."

When we came down for breakfast, the room was full of our workers waiting to welcome us home.

Sally was the first to greet us. She took my hand, and in it placed the rings I had left with her. She said, "See, I told you I would take care of them."

I hugged her and said, "I knew you would, thank you."

I gave Jeremiah his grandfather's ring, he smiled and put it on. I took off my wedding ring, and Jeremiah slid my engagement ring onto my finger, and then my wedding ring.

There were lots of hugs. There were also faces we had never seen before. It seemed there were more than a few babies born while we were gone. Everyone wanted the both of us to hold their babies. It was a painful reminder, to us both. There were also new workers. Jessie had hired a few of the runaways. Everyone seemed so happy.

After breakfast we went for a walk with Jessie, as he caught us up on everything with the farm. Houses built for the workers, more barns, more fields cleared, what crops were in the ground, and the seed he had purchased. The farm had prospered while we were away, thanks to the hard work of everyone there.

Jeremiah hugged his cousin Jessie and said, "I am indebted to you. I hope you are planning to stay here."

Jessie said, "I reckon I could stay on a while longer, I've got nothin' better to do. Besides, I do enjoy kickin' back on the porch with a fine cigar and sippin' a bit of whiskey. Jeremiah, that's somethin' we ain't done together."

Jeremiah patted him on the shoulder and said, "Sir, we shall remedy that this evening."

Later at dinner, Jeremiah asked, "Ms. Charlotte, would you care to go for a walk with me along the river?"

I smiled as I tried to hold back tears and said, "I would love to."

He held my hand as we walked to the spot where we had picnics so long ago when we were courtin'. He spread out a blanket. We sat there, I cried. I didn't think we would ever see this spot together again.

Jeremiah took my hand, wiped away my tears, and asked, "Do you remember Aunt Polly's prediction about the Northern Lights?"

I answered, "Remember? I felt like I've carried it with me all these years. I was convinced you weren't going to survive the war."

He said, "Did the thought ever cross your mind that it could have been a sign about you?"

I replied, "No, it didn't. We saw them on your birthday, so I thought it was a sign about your death, not mine."

He said, "Maybe it was a sign about our child's death."

I looked down and said, "Maybe it was."

He said, "Charlotte, we need to put the fears of death, the Northern Lights, all of that behind us."

I said, "You're right, I feel like that too, but I will always feel a loss. I'm so sorry."

We held each other for a long time, as we cried. He took out his handkerchief and wiped my tears away, then he said, "We will have children, I just know it. Deep down I can feel it."

I said, "I'm so sorry."

He continued to wipe my tears, he also had to wipe away a few of his own. Then he said, "You didn't know, I don't want to hear you blame yourself, anymore."

I just nodded.

We sat there quiet for a few minutes, then he said, "I guess we have a nephew we need to go see. How old is Sara and George's son now?"

While I was gathering myself I answered, "I guess he's getting close to two years old."

Jeremiah asked, "Are you up to going to see him?"

I sat there for a minute, took a deep breath and said, "Yes, I have to. We can't get upset every time we are around a baby. Besides, he has to meet his Aunt Charlotte and Uncle Jeremiah."

Jeremiah laughed and said, "I imagine with three grandma's he's pretty spoiled. Of course the two grandpa's are probably just as bad." He paused, then asked, "Are you ready?"

I replied, "Like a wise man once told me, there's no time like the present."

We got up, Jeremiah picked up the blanket, shook off the sandy loam soil, we folded it and walked to the house.

He said, "I'll meet you out front in a few minutes." He left to get the horses.

He pulled up riding in the vis-à-vis carriage we had rode home on the day we were married. Anderson was driving.

Jeremiah jumped out of the carriage, took his hat off and bowed to me, stood there with his hat held against his chest and said, "I haven't had the pleasure of seeing my beautiful wife in a carriage in years. Would you indulge me?"

I smiled as I said in my most charming, southern way, "Why of course Mr. Jeremiah, I do so love a carriage ride with a handsome gentleman."

He asked, "Just how many handsome gentlemen have you rode in a carriage with?"

I, still talking in my sweet, southern voice answered, "Well, as of late, I have rode with General Grant, I've heard some refer to him as dashing."

Jeremiah smiled as he said, "That old man? I bet he couldn't even help you into the carriage." He then he put his hands around my waist and lifted me into the carriage. He sat down beside me and kissed me.

I informed him, "The next time I see him, I'm going to tell him you said he was an old man that couldn't even help a lady into a carriage."

Jeremiah smiled and asked, "When will we ever see him again?"

I smiled as I said, "Why Mr. Jeremiah, you may recall I have been invited to one inaugural ball. When I am invited to another, and I'm dancing with General Grant, I am going to tell him."

Jeremiah laughing said, "When we go to that ball, I will tell him myself! As a matter-of-fact, I will tell him the very next time we see him!"

We laughed and he kissed me again.

Then he said, "Pardon us Anderson, I apologize, we will try to conduct ourselves as a proper lady and gentleman.

We are ready when you are."

Anderson laughed and said, "Mr. Jeremiah, no need to apologize, these are happy days."

As we were going down the driveway, Jeremiah asked me, "Do you smell the jasmine?"

I answered, "Yes I do."

He said, "I always think of you when I smell jasmine."

I snuggled against his chest and said, "Everything around here reminds me of you." I sat quietly for a minute, and then I asked, "Do you think we will see General Grant, Colonel Mosby, or any of them again?"

He hugged me tight as he said, "I doubt it, they are so far away. Although it is nice to think we might see them in peaceful times."

I replied quietly, "I hope we do."

We arrived at Sara and George's house. Jeremiah helped me out of the carriage. Sara came running out of the house. She was with child again. She grabbed me and held on for what seemed like a long time. We were both crying. George came over and shook Jeremiah's hand, took off his hat and slightly bowed to me.

George picked up a little boy and said, "Willie, this is your Aunt Charlotte and Uncle Jeremiah."

I reached for him, he pulled away, acting a little shy.

He reached for Jeremiah. Jeremiah smiled as he took Willie into his arms, and started quietly talking to him. They both started laughing.

Sara said, "Please come in the house for some coffee, and let's catch up. Anderson, you come on in too."

We all went inside. A lady brought the coffee in and I introduced myself.

She said, "Ms. Charlotte, I know you and Mr. Jeremiah. I'm Mae, George's mama."

I hadn't even recognized her. She was beautiful. Sara had made her nice dresses, helped her learn to take care of her hair, taught her how to talk proper, and taught her to read and write.

I got up and hugged her as I said, "Mae, you are a beautiful lady."

She smiled a huge smile, she was so proud, as she should have been. She then took Willie upstairs for a nap.

We visited for the rest of the afternoon. George asked us to stay for supper, but we knew Sally was cooking for us and our parents. We said our goodbyes and headed home.

A few minutes after we got home, Daddy John and Mom Peggy arrived. About fifteen minutes later Mama, Daddy, Aunt Polly, and Uncle Henry got there. We all sat out on the west veranda enjoying the warmth of the late afternoon sun. Sally came out to tell us supper was ready. We all went inside, sat down, joined hands, and Jeremiah asked the blessing...

"Dear Lord, we come to you as humble servants. We thank you for ending the war. We give thanks for reuniting our families. We ask that you guide us to do what is right, to help us to do unto others as we would have them do unto us. We pray you forgive us of our sins. We pray you will bless our families as well as the others throughout this country, as we know a lot soldiers are with you now, and can never go home to their families. We also pray you will heal the wounds of the broken bodies, and this broken country. Amen."

He had said a lot in those few words. I don't believe there was a dry eye in the room. We started eating and catching up with everybody.

Daddy asked, "Charlotte, now that slavery has been abolished, and there are no runaways to help, what are you going to do with yourself?"

I almost choked on my food, I couldn't believe he had said that in front of Mama, Jeremiah's parents, and everyone for that matter. I asked, "Daddy, what do you mean?"

He said, "Everybody here knows, they all helped."

Jeremiah looked at his daddy and asked, "You helped runaway slaves?"

Daddy John smiled and nodded his head as he said, "After Charlotte ran off to be with you, William came and had a talk with me. He told me what Charlotte had said to him, "do unto others as we would have them do unto us". He told me how well things were going after he freed the people at his place. Every one of them stayed on when he made them the offer to stay and work as free people, or take the manumission papers and leave, with his blessing. I made the same offer to the workers at our place, and they all stayed. I have found that a man will work harder for himself and his family, than if he's being forced to work. I regret a lot of things in my life, but none more than holding my fellow man in bondage. I pray the good Lord will see fit to forgive me. I hope by helping runaway slaves, I might be redeemed a little." He took out his handkerchief and wiped away his tears. "Jeremiah, it does my heart good to know I raised you to be a better man than I have been."

I got up and walked to him, he stood up and I hugged him, I then kissed him on the cheek and said, "You're a good man, Daddy John."

Jeremiah walked over and hugged his daddy and said, "I love you Daddy, you are a good man."

Aunt Polly then asked, "Charlotte, did you fight in the war?"

"What?" I asked, shocked.

She said, "Now don't you lie. Some of us here know you fought in the war, and some think you didn't. Who's right?"

I looked at Jeremiah, petrified. He nodded, I said, "Yes, Aunt Polly, I did."

She looked at Mama and said, "See, I told you what she was doing."

Mama replied, "I don't care if she did or didn't, I'm glad they are both home."

Daddy, trying to change the subject, said, "Jeremiah, it should be a good year for tobacco. I hope you are ready to be a farmer again."

Jeremiah replied, "Yes sir. I am."

After supper we all went out on the front veranda. The evening was cool, the men all lit cigars, and had a glass of whiskey to sip on. The ladies had tea.

Uncle Henry sat down beside me, leaned back in his chair, and said, "Welcome home darlin'."

I smiled and said, "Thank you Uncle Henry. You should know there were more than a few army officers that really enjoyed your cigars. Oh, by the way, General Grant would like for me to send him a few."

He looked at me and asked, "General Grant? How do you know him, what side was you and Jeremiah fightin' for?"

Jeremiah took a long sip of his whiskey and said, "Henry, that's a fine question. I suppose we were fighting for the South, but fighting to end slavery at the same time. If that makes any sense... it's a long story."

Uncle Henry looked confused, but he smiled and said, "I would like to hear about it sometime. Being how Charlotte was there, I bet it was confusing, she has a tendency to stir things up."

Daddy leaned back in his chair, took a deep breath, and said, "She does do that. I thank God y'all are home safe. These are the times in life to cherish, being with family, the people you love and care about. Takin' a few minutes to just enjoy being together."

We sat around talking, laughing, and enjoying the evening. I smelled oak wood burning, I guess Anderson thought the house was getting chilly and had built a fire. The smell of the oak mingling with the cigars, the light scents of jasmine, honeysuckle, and of the whiskey. It smelled like home.

16 A HIGH PRICE

Johnston and Sherman finally worked out the terms of surrender in Durham, North Carolina.

When Sherman left, the state was under Military Rule, he had put General John M. Schofield in charge.

White people gave up their slaves. Some still felt the former slaves could never be equal to white people. They called them stupid niggers. All of the former slaves we knew were far from stupid. They had managed to survive this far. They were ignorant, only because of those few whites that had refused to let them learn.

A couple of years back, Daddy had built a church on his farm for the workers. I heard that Daddy enjoyed attending the services once in a while. He said Zeb was a man of God, a fine preacher. After the church was built, Daddy asked Zeb to use the church as a school too, and start teaching all of the people that worked for him to read and write. Zeb was happy to do it.

Sometimes Mama and Sara would help teach. Daddy said Mama had found her true calling. The workers from our farm, as well as Daddy John's farm, had been going over there in the evenings to learn. These people were far from stupid. They were eager to learn.

Daddy said, "They learned quick, because they wanted it so much. I've only had to tell one person how important it is to learn, everybody else hungers for it."

I asked, quizzically, "Really, who was the one?"

He smiled as he said, "You."

I said, "I wasn't that bad, you taught me a lot."

He said, "I know I did, but you fought your mama tooth and nail about learning from a book. I reckon you and me never appreciated it. Nobody ever told us we were too stupid to learn to read and write. If they had, I reckon that would have lit a fire under our tails and we would have picked up a book just to prove them wrong."

I said, "You're right. I never really thought all the things Mama wanted me to learn was important. You know, the things I learned from her served me well during the war, and of course the things I learned from you and Jeremiah helped me too."

Daddy quietly asked, "What did you do in the war?"

I told him of being one of Mosby's Rangers, of being a spy, and how I got the runaway slaves to safety.

Daddy asked, "Wasn't that awful dangerous?"

I said, "Yes sir, it was."

He looked at me as he asked, "Were either of you ever hurt?"

I answered, "Yes sir." I told him everything. He just pulled me to him, hugged me tight, and we cried.

After a few minutes he asked, "Does the doctor think you will ever have children?"

I answered, "He said maybe, if we're lucky."

Daddy said, "That's a mighty high price to pay."

I said, "Yes sir it is. I didn't know about the baby. Also, I have to keep remembering how many people we saved. I saved Jeremiah's life, so would he have died if I wasn't there? Would somebody else have saved him? Would somebody else have found a way to get all of the runaways into Washington? The countryside up there is crawling with slave catchers. How many would they have caught and tortured, or killed? Maybe to me and Jeremiah, the life of our unborn child was the most important one, but to all those people we helped, their babies are just as dear to them. How many babies, how many people did we save Daddy?"

He looked down, tears falling from his face, he shook his head from side to side as he said, "I don't know Charlotte, there were too many to count, and not enough time to worry about numbers."

I asked, "Would you have done anything different?"

He said, "Offer freedom right off, like you and Jeremiah did. What would you have done different?"

I looked him in the eyes and said, "I would like to say not go on that raid when I was shot but... I know it's hard to hear, but nothing, I would have done nothing different. We didn't pick and choose our raids. Mosby sent the rangers that had the skills that were needed. He picked me, I went. Had I known about the baby, I wouldn't have went on anymore raids. It happened, now I have to live with it."

He just nodded his head. We just stood there for a few minutes, then Daddy said, "Well, the people around here sure do like learning. Maybe one Sunday you and Jeremiah ought to go to Zeb's Church service. I think y'all would like it. It's just good old-fashioned preaching from the Bible. I enjoy hearing him preach."

I smiled and said, "I think we are going to Friedens Church this Sunday, maybe next Sunday we will go hear Zeb. Jeremiah has been looking forward to going to our church for four years now."

Being at church and in town was an eye opening experience. It seemed like a few white people that didn't like the idea of a black person having freedom is up there yelling and hollering about uppity niggers, and how we need to put them in their place. I guess they think if they yell loud enough, people will be afraid to stand up for themselves, or for what's right.

That night as Jeremiah and I lay in bed talking, I said, "This has to stop. It's not safe for a black person to leave our farm, and go any further than our daddies places. It's dangerous for them to go to town. This is not the South we fought for. I'm ashamed of these people. The worst part is the black people have no protection, when they were slaves, they had some protection. People couldn't go around messing with another man's slave. It was illegal, and nobody would have put up with it."

Jeremiah said, "You're right. You know as well as I do, most of the people around here are good people. It's just a few trying to stir up trouble. If people stood up to those few, it would stop. They need to know we are not going to allow them to scare us and the people we care about. I think tomorrow, I'm going to ask George to go into town with me, just to let people see he's my friend. Maybe some people just need a good example to follow."

I said, "Maybe you're right. I would still carry a couple of them Yankee revolvers if I were you."

He laughed a little and said, "I had already planned to."

The next day, Jeremiah goes to ask George if he is willing to ride into town, just to let people know he is Jeremiah's friend. George says he will. They get into town and all is fine, they go into the store general store and buy a couple of things.

Everybody is nice, everything is pleasant, and Jeremiah was beginning to think someone was just having a bad day. He and George were standing around talking to a neighbor, they all laugh at the story the neighbor had just told, some silly story about his old coon dog.

A man then walks up to George and pushes him as he asks, "What's so funny, nigger?"

Jeremiah steps in between George and the man, puts the barrel of a revolver to the man's neck and asks, "Why are you bothering my friend?"

The man says loudly, "Who the hell are you to come into town with a nigger, claiming him to be your friend?"

Jeremiah smiled what he called, a Mosby smile, as he said, "I am Major Jeremiah Turner, of Mosby's Rangers. Born and raised just down the road. I was best man at my friend here's wedding," he used his head to motion toward George, "and he at mine. Once again sir, I ask, why are you bothering my friend?"

The man stood there for a minute then said, "Beggin' your pardon Major Turner, I didn't know who you were, I didn't know he was a friend of yours."

Jeremiah then asked, "Does it matter that he's my friend? He was just standing here enjoying a nice conversation with our neighbor, he wasn't bothering you. What has he done to deserve such harsh treatment?"

The man replied, "Well Sir, some of the niggers around here need to know their place."

Jeremiah said, "George is not a nigger, and what place would that be?"

The man said, "You know Sir, some of these darkies think they are just like us now."

Jeremiah said, "Oh, I guess you're right. I'm not like George, I can't shoe a horse to save my ass. I hope you can. You see, George is the local blacksmith, a very talented man. If I were George and you showed up at my shop, I wouldn't shoe your horse. Now do you want to keep talking with this gun at your neck or do you want to be a good boy and run along?"

The man said, "I reckon I'll be runnin' along Major Turner."

Jeremiah told me the man was an older man that he had never seen before.

On the way home, George said, "That man had been around town for the last couple of months, just stirring up trouble."

That night we all met at Daddy's house. George told everybody what happened.

Anderson asked, "What if they come here, looking to lynch one of us, to scare people into being quiet and not standing up to them?"

I said, "Kill them, then come find one of us white people, we will fetch the Sheriff, and say we killed them." Everybody except Jeremiah and Daddy, turned to look at me. I continued, "We will do everything we can to protect y'all, but you have to help protect yourselves and your families. Don't go anywhere alone. Keep a gun with you. Let's just try to get by until the state has a government put in place, then maybe things will calm down. Don't worry, remember, me and Jeremiah were Mosby's Rangers, we know a thing or two about staying a step ahead of the enemy."

May 29, 1865. President Johnson issues two proclamations. The first one being The Amnesty Proclamation: To all Southerners, if you swear an oath of loyalty to the United States Constitution, you are pardoned, and can keep your property, except for slaves. Pardon exceptions include the very wealthy, and leaders.

The second Proclamation appoints William W. Holden as Governor of North Carolina. Johnson tells Holden to restore North Carolina to the Union, by calling a State Convention to repeal the Ordinance of Secession, ratify the 13th Amendment, and cancel Confederate war debt.

The 13th Amendment abolishes slavery and involuntary servitude.

The convention is to meet on October 2, 1865. They are to set a date for elections of Governor, State Legislators, and U.S. Congressmen.

Meanwhile, some former slaves held a convention in Raleigh, North Carolina. They called it the Convention of the Freedmen. They decided they were going to ask the State Convention for three things: Admission of black people's testimony in court. The right to be on a jury. Races to be treated equally.

The Freedmen Bureau is established by Congress, it is to last for one year. The purpose is to help people transition from slavery to free people. They plan to rent abandoned or confiscated land to former slaves, provide food, clothes, medical attention, and an education. Some say the concept is based on an organization Elizabeth Keckley had started in Washington. Their help is desperately needed as thousands of people are now in refugee camps. These camps are full of poor people, both black and white. The Freedmen's Bureau helps both races.

We have newly freed people coming to our farm almost every day looking for work, needing food, water, and shelter. We hire as many as we can. When we can't hire anymore, we let them stay on the farm and help out in trade for a safe place to stay and food. It's the best we can offer right now.

One day Jeremiah said to me, "We have to figure out a way to bring more money in."

I replied, "I have been thinking the same thing. You know something I noticed while in Washington during the war? There seemed to be plenty of money there. Everybody loves Daddy and Uncle Henry's cigars, wine, and whiskey. Sara makes the prettiest dresses I've ever seen. Maybe you and I need to take the train to Washington, give General Grant a bunch of cigars, wine, whiskey, maybe a dress or two for Julia, and ask them to spread the word that we are producing these things here. We can make more money there in a few weeks, than we could here in a year."

Jeremiah said, "That's a good idea." Then he laughed and said, "Do you really think we can make money there, or do you just want to tell General Grant what I said?"

I smiled and said, "I know we can make money there, but I might as well enjoy knowing you'll have to tell him."

We talked to our parents and they agreed with us. Two days later we are on the train headed for Washington.

We go see General Grant at the War Department. Like before, he is very busy. He agrees to see us and is walking around his desk to greet us as we enter his office.

He takes my hand and bows his head slightly, as he says, "Charlotte my dear, what a pleasure, I feared we would never see each other again."

I said, "As I did too, Sir."

He shook Jeremiah's hand and asked, "What do I owe the pleasure of your visit?"

Jeremiah said, "Sir, we would like to talk a little business with you, if you have the time, or we can make an appointment and come back. We know you are busy."

Grant said, "Yes I am busy, but I can always find a few minutes for a couple of old friends.

Have you eaten? If not, let's go have dinner."

I said, "Oh General, that would be just wonderful," I found myself talking in my most sweet, southern, charming way. "but before we go, I do believe Jeremiah has something to confess to you."

Jeremiah said, "She's teasing."

"No Sir, I am not... Jeremiah Turner, you said if we ever saw the General again you would tell him... if you don't, I will." I said with a smile.

"Alright, alright," Jeremiah said, "you see General, the day after we arrived home, Charlotte was teasing me about riding in a carriage with the dashing General Grant. I didn't like the idea of her riding in a carriage with another man and I said you were an old man that probably couldn't even help a lady into a carriage."

General Grant looked at me and asked, "Did he really say that?"

I replied, "Yes Sir, he most certainly did."

Grant sternly looked at Jeremiah and said, "Major Turner, I believe that was harmless teasing by your wife. I find it funny, and I am not in the least offended by it."

Jeremiah, looking relieved, said, "Thank you Sir."

Grant then held out his arm to escort me, then casually asked Jeremiah, "Do you mind if I escort Ms. Charlotte outside, and help her into the carriage?"

Jeremiah put on a weak smile as he said, "No Sir."

We got to the carriage and General Grant picked me up at my waist and placed me in the carriage. He looked at Jeremiah, raised his eyebrows a bit, and asked, "Old man?"

He patted Jeremiah on the back, and they got into the carriage.

General Grant then looked at me and asked, "Charlotte, do you have guns in your boots today?"

I answered, "No Sir, I'd be happy to prove it."

He replied, "That will not be necessary, we're friends now, and we can trust one another."

We talked as we ate. We told him of our ideas and what was happening in North Carolina, and in our part of Guilford County. Grant said he was hopeful that come fall, when there is a state government in place, things will get better. He also says he would love to share a few cigars, a sip of whiskey, or a glass of wine, and tell people where to get them. I tell him of the store that has agreed to sale our products. We are leaving a small supply with them today, but will return in a couple of weeks with more. Hopefully sales will be good and we will be coming to Washington every month. He says on our next visit we must come to supper and visit with Julia. I tell him we are planning to visit her today and leave two dresses that Sara had made for her. He says Julia is visiting family, and she will be back next week. We left the dresses with him, he promised to give them to her. We catch the evening train and are home that night.

Rumors began getting worse, spread by interlopers that are just here to cause problems. Now white people are afraid of the black people they have known their entire lives. Black people are afraid to be around the white people that have never caused them any harm. Carpetbaggers, (the name people have given to wealthy northerners that have come down here to manipulate the situation to their advantage) seem to be the biggest source of the rumors and lies. They are using fear to get people to sale their farms at a fraction of its worth, then using fear, lies, and fraud to control the poor people, black and white, that work on these farms. Scalawags, (the southerners that help the carpetbaggers) are doing the dirty work and spreading the rumors, causing the fear in both black and white people.

The carpetbaggers have figured out it is to their advantage to keep the races at odds with each other. If blacks and whites become friends, they will have no power over them, and they can't steal the farms away, force people to work for little money, and charge such high prices for necessary items like food, seed, and clothes.

We were very fortunate as we grew or made most of what we needed. There were very few things we needed to buy, and we also had the privilege to go to any store we wanted to buy these things. Most poor people could only go to the closest store. The carpetbaggers were trying to buy up the stores so they could control the price of goods. They were making money off of the backs of the poor, and neediest groups of people.

On our farms, Daddy's, Daddy John's, and Jeremiah's, we grew tobacco, food for us, food for the animals, animals for meat, made cigars, whiskey, wine, brick, soap, and cloth. We also had a saw mill, cabinet makers, a harness maker, a blacksmith, a dressmaker, a school, and a church.

A lot of people came to our farms for some of the things they needed. Daddy, Daddy John, and Jeremiah let it be known that if anyone came to our farms in need of goods or services, they would get the best products around, at a fair price, but they had to treat all the workers with the same respect that they would show them. We had taken our stand, now all we could do was wait.

Life on the farm was good. Then one day, Sara rode into town with me. Nobody had bothered me in the past, and even if they did, I could take care of myself. We went into the store and bought some sugar, and as we came out two men I had never seen before, came up to us. One grabbed Sara, ripping the shoulder of her dress as he said, "Well ain't you the prettiest nigger I've ever seen."

I grabbed Sara's arm, pulled her away from him, with my other hand I grabbed my knife and sliced his throat. It was over in seconds. His friend was surprised and slow to reach for his gun, and I got my knife to his throat first.

I said, "If you so much as flinch, I'll kill you. We are going to wait right here for the Sheriff."

We didn't have to wait long, as a crowd grew quickly. The Sheriff came over and asked, "What happened?"

The man said, "We was just having a little fun with this here nigger, when this white woman came over and killed him."

I calmly replied, "I was walking with my friend when we were attacked, for no reason, and I killed him."

The Sheriff asked in a nasty tone, "Missy, did you kill him over a nigger?"

Before I could answer, I heard a man say, "These men attacked the women."

I looked up, and it was one of my neighbors. Then a couple of other people started saying the same thing.

The Sheriff told the friend of the dead man, "You had best leave town." Then the Sheriff looked at me and said, "Missy, maybe it'd best if you and your... friend don't come back into town."

I was shocked! I said loudly, "Missy? I'll have you know I am Mrs. Jeremiah Turner! Best if I don't come into town? This is my town!" I looked around at my friends and neighbors and said, "Our town. It's your job to protect us. If you were doing your job I wouldn't have had to kill him. You're letting these people come in and destroy this town. I have a right to come into town and not be attacked. I also have friends with the power to remove you from your position as Sheriff."

Sara put her hand on my shoulder and said, "Come on Ms. Charlotte, let's go home."

I looked at Sara, there were tears running down her face. I said, "You're right Sara, let's go home."

On the ride home, Sara was crying and she said, "Thank you Charlotte. I'm afraid to think what they would have done to me if you hadn't stopped them."

I said, "We both know what they would have done to you. We need a Sheriff that will enforce the law."

She asked, "How do we get a new Sheriff?"

I smiled and said, "I'm going to Washington in three days. I'm going to ask General Grant to do something about this."

When we got home and George saw Sara, before we could say anything, he asked, "Who did this?" Then exclaimed, "I'm going to kill him!"

Sara calmly touched his arm and said, "Ms. Charlotte has already killed him."

George looked at me and asked, "You did?"

"Yes, George, I'm not going to stand by and let anyone hurt Sara. Listen, we need to get everybody together, let them know what happened, and we should be expecting trouble."

Jeremiah wanted to go into town to pay the Sheriff a visit. I told him of my plan to ask General Grant for help. He agreed that was a better way to handle the situation. That night, we all gathered at Daddy's house. Everyone went home expecting trouble. We didn't have to wait long.

Around two in the morning we were awakened by the sound of breaking glass as a rock was thrown through our bedroom window. Jeremiah and I both grabbed our guns, went out of the french doors of the bedroom, and stepped out onto the loggia.

We heard cousin Jessie on the veranda below us ask, "Y'all alright?"

Jeremiah replied, "Yes. You?"

Jessie answered, "I'm fine."

We saw six men on horses with torches, one said, "Mr. Jeremiah Turner, we advise you to get your women, both black and white, under control. We felt the gentlemanly thing to do was to let you know, they are causing trouble."

I raised my guns, Jeremiah put his hand on my arm and slowly lowered my arms. He whispered, "Not now."

Jeremiah yelled to the men, "I heard what you had to say! You can leave now!"

They turned to leave, and as we watched them go down the driveway, six more men joined them, they had been waiting down by the stables.

We went inside and Jeremiah said, "I saw the men by the stables, I didn't know how many there were. That's why I didn't want you to start shooting. We need to get a group together and start keeping watch at night. Like you've said, we were Mosby's Rangers, we know a thing or two about staying a step ahead of the enemy."

The men left our place and stopped by Daddy John's. They pulled a black boy out of bed, hauled him outside and nearly beat him to death. I guess they wanted Mr. John Turner to get his son under control.

The boy's daddy, Hiram, told us the next morning, he tried to stop the men, and one of them said, "Come one more step, and I'll cut his head off, then I'll cut your head off too."

Jeremiah looked at me and asked, "Do you think it's a coincidence, or could it be one of the men that murdered some of the rangers and that boy in Front Royal? Isn't that the exact words one of Custer's men told that boy's mama, before they shot and killed him?"

"Yes, that's what he said." I answered. "Do you really think ex-union soldiers are down here, stirring up trouble?"

Jeremiah said, "It appears so. We had better get to Washington to see General Grant right away."

Jessie said he could handle things at home, we left a day early so we would have plenty of time to conduct our business, and then see General Grant.

General Grant was mortified at what we told him. He excused himself, and left the room. When he came back he said, "I just sent a wire to your Governor Holden informing him of the events you described. I also told him to send someone to Gibsonville, today, to remove the Sheriff and restore order. Ms. Charlotte, I am glad you have been keeping your guns in your boots. It might take a while for things to get better, if there are people down there taking advantage of the situation, and people making easy money. They must be making a lot of money, and they won't walk away without a fight."

Jeremiah said, "We're ready for a fight, we can take care of ourselves, we have to get others ready for that fight." He then asked, "General, you've led lots of scared men into battles, how do we get these people to overcome their fears, and fight for themselves?"

General Grant paused, then answered, "Well, there is a good deal of difference, but lead by example. If you two don't show fear, it will give the others confidence. When Charlotte killed the man attacking Sara, she gave the people of the town enough confidence to stand up for her. Feed that confidence. Slowly, more and more will come around and see that they have to be willing to help themselves. I wish you luck."

We said our goodbyes and boarded the train for home.

The next morning Jeremiah and I rode into town. There was a new Sheriff. We talked to a few neighbors on the way home and told them our ideas about patrolling the area at night. We also told them that we needed help.

We needed men to patrol and some men to stay home, and be ready for a fight. We had six white men volunteer to help. Everybody else said they thought it best to stay put and protect their own home. Every black man we asked, volunteered.

Jeremiah told them, "If there's no one at your own house left to protect your family, stay home. If there is someone there that is willing to kill to protect your family, then come with us."

We had twenty men. Jeremiah explained we were to break up into two groups, half go with him, the other half with me. He said, "Charlotte was one of Mosby's Rangers, she knows what to do. Listen to her."

One white man said, "I ain't gonna have no woman tellin' me how to fight."

Another one agreed, saying, "Yea, me either."

Jeremiah looked at the two and said, "Are you willing to listen to me?"

"Yea." they both answered.

Jeremiah turned to his group and asked, "Any of you men willing to trust that Charlotte knows what she's doing?"

A couple of men rode over to my group.

Jeremiah looked at me and said, "We rendezvous here in two hours."

"Yes Sir." I answered.

We departed, I have four revolvers, and most of the men had hunting guns. I thought they might as well have swords. I giggled to myself as I remembered Colonel Mosby once said, "Someone coming at his rangers with a sword, might as well be coming at them with a cornstalk." Maybe not his exact words, but still, I pictured cavalry coming at me with cornstalks raised like swords.

I talked quietly as we rode. Telling them what we were doing. We are watching and learning. We want to know where they are, how many, and try to find out what they are planning to do.

We came to an old barn, there were ten horses tied outside.

George asked, "Ms. Charlotte, why don't we just ride in there and kill them?"

I quietly said, "That's murder, George. There is a difference in defending your family and home, and just killing someone. We all know they are in there planning to do something to one of us, or our families, but think for a minute, what if they're not? They could be in there planning a dance. If we bust up in there and kill them just for gathering together, then we're no better than they are. We then become what we hate, and set out to destroy, but in the end we destroy ourselves. We are better than that. We gather our information and return to rendezvous with the others, like we were ordered to do."

We met up with Jeremiah and exchanged information.

Jeremiah said, "We saw four men leave their homes, and head east of our farms. We don't know them, but they work for the people that have been buying up the farms."

I said, "We saw ten men gathering at the old Johnson farm." (Mr. Johnson had sold the farm for about nothing and left).

We decided we should all ride out to the old Johnson farm. We stay just inside the edge of the woods and wait. Finally they came out. We can see them, we know who two of them are, one is the friend of the man I killed in town, and the other is the former Sheriff. None of us knew the other eight, but we knew where four of them lived. They get on their horses and head out. They quickly spilt up, like they are going home. Jeremiah orders two men to follow each man.

Jeremiah said, "Just follow, don't let them see you, and don't do anything unless you have to. We meet at the rendezvous point in one hour."

One hour later we all meet. All the men had went home.

Anderson asked, "So what do we do now?"

Jeremiah said, "We'll meet back here tomorrow night and do the same thing. Go home and get some sleep, we should be able to rest easy knowing they all went home."

We did this for eight nights. Every night, a few more neighbors came. We now had four groups, Jeremiah had George, and Anderson, each over a group. They both had five white men in their group. Our neighbors were beginning to come around, and willing to stand up for themselves, just like General Grant had said they would.

Night nine, after we had watched the men leaving their homes, we all met up and went to the old Johnson farm. Tonight the meeting was breaking up early. Eighteen men came out of the barn, they all got on their horses and head out together. Tonight is the night. We quietly followed. They were heading toward Daddy's farm.

We were close enough to hear them laughing, and one man said, "Yea, tonight we gonna lynch us a uppity nigger preacher." More laughing. I believe they were passing around a bottle of whiskey. That same man said, "What's gonna be more fun? Hanging the nigger, or getting over to Jeremiah Turner's place and teaching his women a few lessons?"

One man shouted, "I'm looking forward to putting that nigger-loving Turner bitch in her place!"

Now that we knew where they were going, we split into two groups. Jeremiah ordered my group to follow. His group was going to circle around. Jeremiah and his men left. We got close to Daddy's preachers house. I knew Jeremiah and his men should be in place. The men we were following suddenly spurred their horses and started hollering. I told my men to wait and give them time to get closer to Jeremiah and the others. I direct my men to spread out and close in on my signal. We wait.

Then someone up ahead fires a shot and we race in, all hell is breaking loose. Jeremiah had gotten there in time to warn everybody. They waited until the former Sheriff lit and threw a torch at the church. Jeremiah shot the former Sheriff and we all closed in. When it was over, all eighteen lay dead or dying. The church didn't catch on fire and we were all fine.

Hiram, the daddy of the boy that had been beaten at Daddy John's place said, "I killed the man that beat my boy. That man said, "I knew I should have cut your head off the other night." Then I shot him right between the eyes, just like killing hogs... Ms. Charlotte, he was the one, said them awful nasty things about you."

I patted him on the back and said, "You did good, Hiram."

Daddy, Uncle Henry, and everybody was there now. Jeremiah sent somebody to get the Sheriff.

I was leading Logan, walking over to Jeremiah and Jefferson, when I heard Daddy say, "Thank you Major Turner."

Jeremiah smiled as he said, "You're welcome."

I was in my mens clothes, guns on both sides of my belt, guns in my boots, and of course, my knife on my side. I stepped up beside Daddy, he turned to me smiled and said, "Thank you 1st Lieutenant Turner. You're one hell of a soldier."

I kissed him on the cheek and said, "Thank you Daddy."

Daddy walked over to thank the others. I stood beside Jeremiah, I leaned my head on his chest and said, "I miss being a ranger, just a little bit."

He replied, "Yes, I know what you mean. I wonder how Colonel Mosby is adjusting?"

I said, "Maybe we can find him and go visit. I wonder if he would want to see us? Maybe he has put the war behind him and returned to being a lawyer and don't want reminders of the rangers."

Jeremiah said, "Maybe General Grant knows where we could find him."

The new Sheriff arrived and questioned everybody. He was satisfied we were telling the truth, as he knew trouble was coming. He had brought wagons for hauling off the dead. We all went home.

17 OLD FRIENDS

The next week, Jeremiah and I go to Washington. We are told our cigars, whiskey, wine, and dresses were selling well. We are going to need to start making two trips a month. We will need to hire about ten more workers. This is wonderful news! We have supper with General Grant and Julia. It was nice to see her wearing one of the dresses Sara had made.

At supper Jeremiah asked, "General Grant, do you know where we could find Colonel Mosby?"

General Grant said, "Jeremiah, we have been friends for some time now, don't you think it's about time you started calling me Sam? You too, Charlotte."

Jeremiah said, "Yes Sir, uh Sam, do you know where we could find Colonel Mosby?"

Grant replied, "As a matter-of-fact I do. He has opened a law practice in Warrenton."

I asked, "In North Carolina?"

Grant said, "Oh no, Warrenton, Virginia. It's only about fifty miles from here."

Jeremiah added, "It's between Culpepper and Middleburg."

Grant said, "Yes. Do you plan on stopping by there before going home?"

I looked at Jeremiah, and he looked at me and said, "Well, there's no time like the present."

Julia then piped in and said, "Maybe you could finish eating first."

We all laughed, agreed, and had a nice supper.

We left for Warrenton the next morning. Once we arrived, it was easy to locate Mosby's office. We went inside, there was a gentleman at a desk and he asked if he could help us.

Jeremiah said, "We are Mr. and Mrs. Jeremiah Turner. We wonder if Colonel Mosby has a moment for a personal visit?"

Before the man could answer, Colonel Mosby was coming out of his office with his hand out to shake Jeremiah's hand. He kissed my hand and slightly bowed as he asked, "My dear Charlotte, how are you?"

I replied, "I'm well, and yourself?"

He said, "I'm well. Please come in, sit, and let's visit for a while."

We all sat down and he asked, "What brings you two so far north?"

I said, "We were in Washington and asked General Grant about you. He told us you were here. We have been thinking about you lately and just wanted to see you."

He said, "I've also thought of you two quite often these months since we disbanded. How's everything back home?"

Jeremiah told him everything that had been going on. About me killing the man in town. The community banding together and killing the eighteen men that attacked the church. How General Grant had helped us with the problems around home, and also with sharing the cigars.

Mosby asked, "Did it make you miss the life we led up here?"

We both answered, "Yes Sir."

I then said, "Maybe it's not the life we led here, maybe it's the people. That's why we came to see you. We miss you, we care about you."

He nodded and smiled, then said, "I know what you mean. I miss the two of you also, and the others. I did come to think of some of the men as friends, excuse me, think of some of the rangers as friends." He paused for a bit, then asked, "So you have remained friends with General Grant? Does he know you were one of my rangers, or does he just know you as Charlotte?"

I said, "Yes Sir, he knows I was a ranger, as I also surrendered to him, when Jeremiah surrendered." I then told him about us surrendering to Grant, turning in our guns, Grant asking me if Mosby would have ordered me to kill him would I, and me answering yes. I then said, "Grant's a good man, I like him, and I respect him."

Mosby said, "I've heard a lot of people say he is a good man. Fair, honest, a man of his word. I remember that's what Longstreet had always said about him."

Mosby told us about there being a bounty on him, President Johnson not giving him a pardon. Grant said he was entitled to it, as of yet, he has not received it, only parole.

He continued, "I was down at my father's home, but I needed to earn a living, so I came here and opened my practice. I keep getting arrested, even though I'm on parole and have done nothing to violate the terms."

We asked how Pauline and the children were. He said they are well. We invited him to come visit us. We said our goodbyes and started home.

Things at home were quiet and going well. We were hiring more people all of the time. The more we hired, the more money we made, and therefore could help more people in need.

I think we helped two families for every one that worked for us. So there were a lot of people on the farm. When we hired people, they were from the families that we had been helping.

All of these people were going to Daddy's school to learn, so as to better themselves.

In the warmer months, school was held outside because there were so many people wanting to learn. Daddy had expressed concern about the coming winter. He worried, how were all the people going to be able to go to school.

September 2, 1865. We celebrate Jeremiah's twenty-fifth birthday at home. It is the first time he has been home for his birthday since 1860.

October came. The State Convention ignored all three requests of the Convention of the Freedmen. They did approve the 13th Amendment, abolishing slavery. They also set an election date for November 9, 1865. Johnathan Worth, a man that didn't agree with canceling war debt, announced he planned to run for governor. Holden tried to explain that President Johnson wouldn't allow the state back into the Union without canceling the war debt. Holden also announced he planned to run for governor.

Worth won.

The U.S. Congress comes back into session, and says the President doesn't have the power to decide how and when a state is allowed back into the Union.

With all the bickering that was going on in the government, nothing was really getting done. We knew we still had to look out for ourselves. We will continue to patrol our local area.

October 12, 1865. Sara has a daughter. They name her Charlotte Diana Smith. She is a beautiful, bright-eyed girl. I walk out of the bedroom carrying her to see her daddy for the first time.

George carefully takes her, and quietly says, "My baby girl." He looks at me and asks, "How's Sara?"

I smiled and said, "Sara is fine. Aunt Polly says to give her a few minutes, and then you can go in."

George walks over to Jeremiah and asked, "You want to hold her?"

Jeremiah smiling, says, "Yes, George, I would like that very much."

Jeremiah took the baby, and held her close, smiling and whispering quietly to her.

I heard Jeremiah telling Willie, "As a big brother, it's your job to look out for your little sister."

Willie replied, "Yes sir, Uncle Jeremiah."

Jeremiah turns to George and said, "George, you're a fortunate man."

George answered proudly, "Yes sir, I am."

Aunt Polly came to the door and said, "George, you can come in now."

Jeremiah looked at the baby one more time and gave her back to her daddy. George took the baby and went in to see Sara.

Aunt Polly said, "Sara and the baby are just fine, I'll look after Willie. It's late, y'all should go on home."

I said, "Yes ma'am, we will stop by tomorrow." I kissed Aunt Polly on the cheek and we went home.

We got home and went to bed. We lay there with my head on his chest, his arm around me. There was nothing to say that we hadn't said before, just tears.

The tobacco crop was good that year. We were raising more for cigars, but we still had plenty to take to Danville. The Confederacy had built a railroad from Greensborough to Danville. This was the first year we would take our tobacco to market by train. We loaded the tobacco onto wagons and drove to Gibsonville, where it was loaded onto the train. Jeremiah, Daddy, and Daddy John all board the train to take the tobacco to market.

They were back the next day. Later in the month, there was a harvest dance in town. Oh, to go to the dance, it had been so long. I love the feel of Jeremiah's strong hands leading me in a dance. He is a wonderful dancer.

As we were dancing a waltz I said, "Don't forget, one of these days I will be dancing with the dashing General Grant."

He smiled that smile that lights up his face and said, "Of course you will my dear, and I will be dancing with the lovely Julia Grant."

This was the first dance that black people were allowed to come to. Uncle Henry is a fine dancer. It is a bright, moon-lit night, one that I will always remember fondly.

After the incident at Daddy's church, the carpetbaggers around here left. They just abandoned the properties and the people. Jeremiah thought we should go visit Mosby and see what we could do to legally acquire those properties, and put the people to work.

It turned out we just needed to pay the taxes. The taxes are more than a few years behind. Jeremiah, Daddy, and Daddy John came up with the money to pay the taxes on eleven farms. This added to our farms twenty-five hundred acres, numerous houses, barns, and lots of timber. We also had the people on these farms that were counting on us to help them. Now our three farms, together, have right at six thousand acres.

Jeremiah, Daddy, and Daddy John had decided to split up the duties of the farm, right now it is up to Daddy to clear the land for crops, get the logs to the sawmill, and get houses built. There were a lot of people that needed a warm place to live. Every person on the property that didn't have a job, offered to help him. Daddy chose a good many of the men to help him, and a bunch of the boys to cut firewood. The rest of the men and boys he sent to Uncle Henry. The women and girls he sent to Aunt Polly, she could always find work that needed to be done.

Daddy had the boys cutting wood working behind him and his men. The boys were to cut the limbs off of the felled trees, cut it up for firewood, load it onto wagons, then take it to the houses, and neatly stack it. They were to cut firewood for every house, tobacco barn, and smoke-house on the property.

Uncle Henry is in charge of killing hogs. He can use all the help he can get. They killed two hundred hogs. After killing the hogs, he planned to start killing the steers.

None of us were tanners, but it turned out there were more than a few living amongst us. The leather will help us a lot.

Aunt Polly and a bunch of the women are rendering down the fat from the butchered animals to make soap.

She said, "It takes a lot of soap to keep this many people clean."

At the sawmill, someone was to gather the oak bark. They were to soak the bark for a few days and then the water is to be used to tan the hides. The bark will then be dried and burned to heat the tanning vats. The oak ashes would be mixed with water, soaked for a few days, and then the water drained off. The water was acidic, it was then mixed with the lard that Aunt Polly was rendering out of the fat, cooked down, and lye soap was made.

We won't have to buy leather for the harnesses, saddles, bridles, and such anymore. More importantly, we can make the shoes that are so desperately needed. Once again, there were a few people that knew how to make shoes, they started making them as soon as the first hide was tanned.

Uncle Henry and Daddy both were keeping a close eye on the cigars, whiskey, and wine being made.

There were also a group of women making sausage. Daddy and his helpers had to build a few more smoke-houses for all of the meat.

Daddy John went into Greensborough and got a contract for brick. "The city is growing and they just can't get enough brick."

He put more people to work and is expanding the kiln. He also plans to sell all of the lumber that we don't use on our properties.

Some of his bricks are going to be used to build the new church for the workers. It had bothered Daddy when those scalawags tried to burn his church, so he asked Daddy John for brick to build a good solid church building, we also needed the space for teaching. This church would be built in about the center of all the properties. It wound up being a little bit north of my and Jeremiah's house.

Anderson was overseer of the building of that church, he had proven his skills as a brick mason when he built our stables.

Jeremiah and George were building a gristmill, right across the river from the sawmill. Jeremiah knew how to build it and make it work, George would make the metal parts. Anderson sent over a few men he had taught to lay brick. They will build the building. We will then be able to grind our own wheat into flour and corn into meal. It will also bring in money, as we will grind the wheat and corn for our neighbors. Some will pay with money, and some will pay with a percentage of wheat or corn that is ground.

Jeremiah also wants to build a large ice house, right beside the river so we can harvest the ice in the winter, and keep meat and vegetables cold during the summer.

Mama and Mom Peggy are teaching the children. Mae and Sally are overseeing the cooking for the large groups.

Sara is in charge of the making of the dresses. She has a large group of women sewing with her. She draws a picture of the dresses on paper, and they start sewing them. The younger girls are taught to make lace and buttons.

I am making weekly trips into Washington, carrying our goods.

Sara starts going with me so she can do final fittings of the dresses. When we return home, the final alterations are done, and the dresses are delivered the next week.

When winter came, we had enough houses for everybody. There were some houses that weren't big enough for the family living in them, but we were all warm, dry, and had food. We would start building more houses next spring.

Work and learning continued, carding of the wool and the little bit of cotton we grew, braking the flax, spinning the fibers into yarn, and weaving the fabrics. We weren't making a profit, as the money we did bring in went to pay people and provide for everybody. All of these people had brought their skills to our place, and we were pulling together to get through these rough times. This was how I had ran the farm after Jeremiah left to join the cavalry. There were black and white people working together. Daddy, Daddy John, and Jeremiah, all let it be known that they wouldn't put up with any fighting and arguing. The people they put in charge of tasks were chosen because they had the best skills and were the best person for the job. The color of their skin had no bearing on their decisions.

One time I remember Daddy John said, "This morning a white man told me he wouldn't take orders from a nigger." He shook his head, then said, "I told him to pack up his family and move on. It's a shame that he's willing to let his children go hungry because he thinks he's better than a man who's skin happens to be darker than his own."

I put my hand on his arm and said, "You're right, Daddy John. You had no choice, he couldn't stay here and cause problems. I know you feel bad, but that was his decision, not yours."

One morning we woke up and there was about a foot of snow on the ground.

Jeremiah asked, "Do you remember how we used to love days like this? When we would spend the day upstairs. Lingering in bed, enjoying each other. Maybe go in the library to play chess, read, and talk?"

I said, "I remember, it seems like a long time ago."

He took me in his arms and kissed me. He smiled that smile I love so much, and whispered, "Ms. Charley, would you consider spending the day in bed with me?"

In my sweet, southern, charming way, I said, "Why Mr. Jeremiah, I declare that sounds down-right scandalous. However, I do believe I'd love to."

We never went downstairs that day. It was wonderful. I still smile when I wake up to see there has been a big snow during the night.

Christmas was festive, everybody gathering and celebrating. For many of the people here, this was their first Christmas as a free person. It was our first Christmas home together in years. We decorated with running cedar, mistletoe, and a huge tree. We didn't need a bunch of gifts. We were happy to celebrate the birth of our Savior, Jesus Christ.

As we were getting dressed for Christmas supper, Jeremiah said, "Whenever I think of Christmas, I picture you the Christmas before the war. You wore that red and white velvet dress, and your hair smelled of jasmine. Those thoughts carried me through the loneliest times of my life. Would you mind wearing that dress this evening?"

His words made me want to cry, I couldn't speak, I just nodded.

18 WE WERE RANGERS

February 13, 1866. A bank is robbed in broad daylight in Liberty, Missouri. Men from the group, that during the war called themselves Quantrill's raiders, are suspected.

Some people think Quantrill and his raiders were with the Confederate Army. They were not. They went about killing, robbing, doing whatever they pleased, to both sides, North and South. It appears their loyalties were only to themselves. The claim of them to be confederate raiders, led people to believe that Mosby's Rangers, were raiders. We were not raiders, we were the 43rd Battalion, Virginia Cavalry. We had a chain of military command, we had rules and regulations we followed. We were part of the Confederacy.

February 24, 1866. We celebrated my twenty-third birthday. This was my first birthday at home in three years.

In June we were visiting Colonel Mosby for the first time in months.

He laughs and says, "I must show you this." He removed a piece of paper from his breast pocket, and handed it to Jeremiah.

Jeremiah reads it aloud,

John S. Mosby, lately of the Southern Army, will, hereafter, be exempt from arrest by military authorities, except for the violation of his parole, unless directed by the President of the United States, Secretary of War, or from those headquarters.

His parole will authorize him to travel freely within the state of Virginia, and as no obstacle has been thrown in the way of paroled officers and men from pursuing their civic pursuits, or traveling out of their States, the same privilege will be extended to J.S. Mosby, unless otherwise directed by competent authority. (Signed)

US Grant

Lieutenant General

Mosby said, "Pauline was in Washington and she acquired this for me from General Grant, after President Johnson wouldn't help her. President Johnson was more than rude to her. That man was at my wedding, he has known Pauline her entire life. There was no need for him to be rude to her. She then went to see General Grant. He wrote this out and it has helped me tremendously. I have seen what you two meant about him being a fair and honest man. I have more news to share, Pauline is with child again." he said as he smiled.

We congratulated him on both the baby and the letter.

ANGEL MATTHEWS

His smile faded as he said, "I forgot myself there for a moment. I apologize. In my happiness, I have overlooked your sorrows."

I said, "Thank you, John. You are supposed to be happy about a baby. No need to apologize."

Jeremiah said, "She's right." He shook Mosby's hand and said, "Congratulations! We are most happy for you and Pauline."

Mosby took my hand and said, "Charlotte, I may have forgotten for a moment, but please know that you and Jeremiah are in my thoughts often. I do hope you will be blessed with a child."

I smiled and said, "Thank you. That means a lot to us."

We then spent a while catching up, and we left some cigars with him. He took the cigars, smiled and said, "A good cigar always makes me think of Jeb."

Jeremiah said, "We think of him often as well. He was a fine man. His dying was a great loss to all of us."

I nodded in agreement.

We returned home. Trying not to think about babies. That night as we lay in bed, with my head on his chest, his arm around me.

I asked, "What if we never have a child? Can you be happy knowing we aren't?"

He replied, "Charlotte." He raised my chin up to look me in the eyes. "What's this talk?"

I started crying and said, "I know how much a child means to you, and I can't give you one. How long has it been, and still no child?"

He said, "To answer your questions, it's been one year and six months since you were shot. Maybe, you still need more time. The other question, yes, I can be happy without us having children. I love you!"

244

I said, "I think about you telling me how you passed time at camp by daydreaming of me holding your son. It breaks my heart, that because of me, you will never have a son."

He, wiping away my tears said, "Things were different back then. Now, I figure like the doctor said, if we are lucky, but I haven't given up hope. If God intends for us to have children it will happen. If it doesn't, I take it to be God's will as well. You need to think that too."

I said, "I haven't thought of it that way, I guess you're right. It still makes me sad."

He held me tight as I cried.

Some things changed in this year. The State of North Carolina changed the black codes. Now the State refers to black people as "persons of color".

The persons of color are now entitled to the same rights in court as a white person.

If an apprentice, the person of color's master must provide an apprentice diet, clothes, and lodging. The master must teach the apprentice how to read, write, and do basic arithmetic. At the end of the apprenticeship, the master must pay the apprentice six dollars and give them a Bible.

Marriages of persons of color are recognized.

A person of color convicted by due process of the law for attempting to rape, or rape of a white woman, shall suffer death.

It appeared to me that the State of North Carolina's laws hadn't change much at all. The rape of a black woman isn't mentioned. Why not, did the State of North Carolina think raping black women was acceptable? All this time the State had been deciding what rights they were willing to give freedmen, what about freedwomen, and white women. Women did not have any rights.

The United States passes the 14th Amendment to the Constitution. It grants full citizenship to black people, and tasks the Federal Government with protecting these equal rights. The rebellion states must ratify this Amendment before being readmitted to the Union.

There were groups asking that women be included in the 14th Amendment. We were left out.

I started reading about some of our history and found, that before the American Revolutionary War, women had more rights than we do now. Women having rights was left out of the United States Constitution. Maybe Susan B. Anthony was right when she said women shouldn't put aside the struggle for rights during the Civil War.

After all the fighting, everyone was still under the control of wealthy white men. The State of North Carolina was trying to appease white women by saying that they will hang a black man that tries to or does rape us. There was no mention of the punishment of a white man convicted of the same crimes, or of any kind of punishment for the rape of a black woman.

The best way to protect women is to let us make decisions that concern us, by giving us the right to vote. We should have equal rights.

July, 1866. Tennessee is readmitted to the Union.

The groups of ruffian's were joining together. They now called themselves the Ku Klux Klan, or the KKK. They are a bunch of cowards that dress in white robes with hoods, so people can't see their faces. They spread hate and fear. They kill black people, and any white's they deemed as nigger-lovers. They burn homes, and rape women. We don't have a problem around here, but it is close by. The KKK is spreading throughout the South. We continue our patrols. It still isn't safe for a black person to venture from the farm without the protection of a white man.

September 2, 1866. We celebrate Jeremiah's twenty-sixth birthday with the Grants while in Washington. We have a lovely supper, with a birthday cake.

General Grant asks, "How old are you Jeremiah?"

Jeremiah replied, "Twenty-six."

General Grant said, "You're still a child."

Jeremiah grinned and said, "Yes Sir, I am."

In late September, we got a letter from Colonel Mosby, he and Pauline had another daughter. They name her Victoria Stuart Mosby. They plan to call her Stuart, after Jeb Stuart. I quickly wrote a letter of congratulations, saying we can't wait to see the baby.

The year passed much as the last. The crops were good. Always working, but now we were producing and selling enough goods that everybody was working for pay. The families we had taken care of, were now able to work and take care of themselves.

February 24, 1867. We celebrate my twenty-fourth birthday.

The South is divided into five districts and put under Military Rule once again.

From March until August, North Carolina is Under Major General Daniel Sickles.

He studied law, then got into politics. In 1859, he shot and killed his wife's lover. That man was Francis Barton Key, the son of Francis Scott Key, who back during the war of 1812, wrote the Star Spangled Banner. Sickles defense in court was "temporary insanity", he was the first man to use that defense successfully. He was rumored to be a drinking man that spent a good deal of time visiting bordellos. He had joined the army when the Civil War started. He began his career as a Colonel with the 17th New York Infantry.

By July of 1863, when he got to Gettysburg, he had been promoted to the rank of Major General. There were some that said he disobeyed orders and his decisions cost the Union many men's lives, plus his own right leg.

Brigadier General Edward R. S. Canby, takes over in September.

He was born in Kentucky, graduated from West Point in 1839. He fought in the second Seminole war in Florida, the war with Mexico, served out west before the Civil War, and during it. In 1863 he served in New York as General of the draft. He was then sent to the deep south. General Grant didn't care for his skills as a fighting general. From what General Grant told me, I gathered he was too kind-hearted, although a stickler for following the rules. Once during the war, a friend that had sided with the South was a Northern prisoner. The man's father wrote Canby a letter asking for his help in getting parole for his son. He wouldn't intervene. Also while Military Governor he declined to help relatives who he thought of as carpetbaggers.

September 2, 1867. We celebrate Jeremiah's twenty-seventh birthday.

The crops were good this year, and tobacco prices were up. Around the middle of October, Jeremiah said, "I miss the State Fair. I wonder if we'll ever have another."

I said, "I wonder too."

November 25, 1867. Congress looks into the impeachment of President Johnson.

Christmas, 1867. We decorate the house with the running cedar, mistletoe, and a huge tree. Our third Christmas home, the decorations are starting to feel like a tradition. I like that feeling.

February 24, 1868. My twenty-fifth birthday. Also Congress votes 126 to 47, to impeach President Johnson.

March 5, 1868. The U.S. Senate organizes, to decide charges against President Johnson.

General Grant told us people had been talking to him about running for President, but he was reluctant. He was a soldier, not a politician. Jeremiah and I both agreed, he was the best man for the job.

I said, "You already do so much trying to bring the country together, you're fighting with President Johnson trying to get him to do the right things. If you're the President, you won't have to fight him. You can do what you are good at, getting things done."

April, 1868. A new North Carolina Constitution is adopted. It gives more power to the people and the Governor. The Governor will now hold office for four years instead of two.

State and County officials are to be elected by popular vote. All men are eligible to vote and hold office. Representation in the State Senate would now be divided by population, not wealth.

Capital crimes were reduced to four: murder, rape, arson, and burglary.

Free schools for people between the ages of six to twenty-one.

The state was to build a penitentiary.

Allows for state charities.

May 20, 1868. The National Convention of the Republican Party was held in Chicago. General Grant was nominated as the Republican Candidate.

His letter of acceptance ended with, "Let us have peace."

General Longstreet, and numerous former Confederates, campaigned for Grant.

The Civil War had been over for more than three years now, as soon as it ended, the people of the South started fighting a new war. A war of politics and carpetbaggers, scalawags, ruffian's, and the Ku Klux Klan. Black people were hanged simply because they were black, people both black and white were living in fear.

We had put a stop to these things in our part of the county, but it was rampant elsewhere. The country had to unite and move forward. All the political bickering and mollycoddling had to stop. General Grant was the man to take a stand and fix the stalled effects of reconstruction. We knew he would do whatever it took to end the lawlessness. We also campaigned for Grant.

May 26, 1868. President Johnson avoids impeachment by the Senate by one vote.

More states are readmitted to the Union:

In June. Arkansas, Louisiana, Florida.

In July. North Carolina, South Carolina, Alabama and Georgia, although Georgia did get kicked out in the fall.

September 2, 1868. We celebrate Jeremiah's twenty-eighth birthday.

November 3, 1868. General Grant won the election, it was called a landslide. Three states weren't allowed to vote because they hadn't been readmitted to the Union. They were Mississippi, Texas, and Virginia. He was to be inaugurated March 4, 1869.

19 THE REEDY FORK

The next Sunday morning, I am in the kitchen and Sally comes in to tell me Jeremiah wants me to come to the front steps. I walked onto the front veranda, Jeremiah was standing there on the walkway, holding the reins of Jefferson and Logan. Both horses were saddled, Logan with the sidesaddle. Jeremiah took his hat off with that boyish flourish, bowed to me, held his hat to his chest, smiled that smile that lights up his face and asked, "Ms. Charlotte, would you be so kind as to as to take a ride with me?"

I tilted my head to the side a bit, and in my sweet, southern, charming way, said, "Why Mr. Jeremiah Turner, I would be delighted. Please allow me a moment to change into a riding habit."

He, still smiling, said, "Of course my dear, I shall await you here."

I calmly turned and walked into the house, as soon as I closed the door, I ran upstairs and changed. I put on the riding habit that I had worn on our first picnic. I ran downstairs, calmly opened the door, walked outside, and down the steps to Logan.

Jeremiah asked, "May I assist you?"

I smiled and said, "Yes sir, you most certainly may."

He put his hands on my waist, picked me up and placed me on Logan.

He walked over to Jefferson and jumped on without using the stirrup. I loved seeing him do that. We rode off.

I then asked, "Where do you plan to take me, without an escort?"

He said, "I thought we would ride on the north bank of the Reedy Fork. We haven't done that together for some time now."

I replied, "No sir, I can't recall the last time."

We arrived at our spot. The spot of our first picnic, and where he asked me to marry him, and he said, "Let's stop here for a while."

He helped me off of Logan, he went to Jefferson and got the picnic blanket that was tied to the saddle. He spread it out, and we sat down beside the river. We could hear the water rushing over the rocks.

He said, "I do believe you are more beautiful than the first time we came here."

I blushed, lowered my head a little, tilted my head to the side, and looked up with my eyes and said, "You get more handsome. I guess we were just children then."

He said, "I guess we were. Do you remember when you offered to meet me in the barn?"

I said, "Don't tease me about that."

He said, "I'm not. Would you have met me in the barn that night?"

I said, "Yes."

He kissed me and asked, "Would you be opposed to being with me, right here at our spot?"

I shook my head from side to side as he was kissing me, then I whispered, "No sir, I wouldn't be opposed to it at all." We made love there on the bank of the Reedy Fork, at our spot.

December 14, 1868. The New York Tribune reports, Custer and his 7th Cavalry attack a group of friendly Indians heading to the reservation. They kill men, women, and children. The newspaper calls it a massacre. Some newspapers report it as the Battle of Washita River, and hail Custer as a hero. From what I know of Custer, I'm inclined to believe the New York Tribune. I plan to speak with President-Elect Grant about it the next time I see him.

Christmas comes and we decorate the house in what was now our traditional manner. It was wonderful. Things were getting better, and with Grant being elected, we thought we would be seeing change quickly.

General Grant invites us to the Inauguration Ceremony and the Ball.

Jeremiah reads the invitation, looks at me and says, "I guess you really are going to dance with General Grant at an inaugural ball."

I smiled, tiled my head and said, "Why, of course I am."

Jeremiah said, "The ball should prove to be interesting, General Grant doesn't dance. He claims to only know two songs, one is Yankee Doodle, and the other isn't. You, my dear, should have a wonderful time dancing with an old man that can't dance. I on the other hand, will have an enjoyable evening, as Julia loves to dance."

Smiling I said, "He is not an old man, isn't he the youngest man to be elected President? He's only forty-six."

He said, "Yes, my dear, he is, but he still can't dance." He put his arms around my waist, and we danced a few steps as we laughed.

We accepted the invitation. Sara sets to work, making me a dress.

January, 1869. While in Washington, I go visit President-Elect Grant. He doesn't seem excited about the idea of being President.

I said, "I read the New York Tribune's article concerning Custer in Oklahoma."

He said, "Yes, I read it. I also read the reports from General Sheridan."

I said, "I'm sure the reports called it a battle. You are aware of Custer and the murder of Mosby's Rangers that had been taken prisoner, and the boy they accused of being a ranger. They threatened to cut his, and his mother's head off, then murdered him in front of his mother. The man that made the threats is dead now, but he wasn't acting alone. They were following Custer's orders."

Grant said, "I am aware of all of that. I am aware he was court-marshalled and was suspended for the last year, then he does this."

I asked, "Do you intend to do anything about it?"

He said, "Yes, Charlotte, I plan to appoint Ely Parker as Commissioner of Indian Affairs. I know he will provide me with information that is true. He has the best interest of his people. I, mine. Together, we should be able to work it out peacefully."

I smiled and said, "That's wonderful. What do you plan to do about women's rights?"

He replied, "Nothing. I fear if I push the southern states harder, the country will never come together. We have to get all of the states back in the Union, end Military Rule down there, stop the KKK, and stop the fighting out west. Then we can look to other things. I'm sorry Charlotte. We will get there, but we need time."

I then asked, "Do you see women as less than a man?"

He replied, "No Charlotte, I do not."

I sat silent for a minute. That's the thing about Grant, he gives you his honest opinion, even when he knows you aren't going to like the answer. I took a deep breath and said, "I don't like it, but I do understand."

He said, "I knew you would, you're a smart lady." He paused for a moment, "Are you and Jeremiah coming to the Inauguration?"

I smiled and said, "Yes Sir. We plan to come to it, and the Ball. We wouldn't miss it."

Ely Parker is an Iroquois Indian, an educated man. He had been friends with Grant for years. He had been on Grants personal staff since about the middle of 1864. It was Parker that drafted the Articles of Surrender, for Lee to sign at Appomattox. Grant was best man at Parker's wedding, Christmas of 1867. He was a large man, a gentleman. Some people referred to him as Grant's Indian, I don't think either of them cared for the term.

Mid-February, 1869. Colonel Mosby tells us Pauline is with child again.

February 24, 1869. We celebrate my twenty-sixth birthday.

March 3, 1869. We take the train to Washington and check into the Willard Hotel. We figure the Grants are busy and it may be a bother for them to worry about guests. Jeremiah writes a note informing them we are in Washington and look forward to seeing them tomorrow.

March 4, 1869. It's raining. We attended the Inauguration. Grant's speech was short and to the point as he was aware that people were in the cold rain. We returned to the hotel and started preparing for the Ball. My hair was wet and I will need a lot of time to get ready.

When it was about time for us to leave, Jeremiah walked into my dressing room. He was wearing a black tailcoat, black trousers, white shirt, white tie, and a black top hat.

He looked as handsome as the day we were married, almost nine years ago. I had just finished dressing.

My dress was pearl white, with lavender and black trim, an off-the-shoulder bodice, that fit very tight at the waist, as was the fashion. The bodice came to a point in the front and back, laced up the back and had hook and eye closures in the front. It had bell sleeves. The skirt had a train as was the fashion during these times. It is similar to the dress I had worn when I first met General Stuart.

Jeremiah took his hat off with a flourish, held it to his chest, as he said, "May I offer you my assistance, my dear."

I smiled as I said, "Why Mr. Jeremiah, you may. Would you help me with my cloak?" I got up from the dressing table, as I pinned Jeremiah's cameo to my bodice.

He said, "Let me take a moment to look at you." He smiled. "You are going to be the most beautiful girl at the Ball. I hope Julia doesn't hold it against you."

I said, "Thank you. It's fitting as I am being accompanied by the most handsome gentleman at the Ball. I hope that old man, President Grant, don't hold it against you."

He laughed and said, "I'm sure he forgave me for that years ago." He helped me with my cloak and we left for the Ball.

We arrived just minutes before the Grants.

We saw them enter, speaking to people as they made their way over to us. When they did get to us, there was a gentleman with the President.

Grant said, "Pete, may I present Mr. Jeremiah Turner and his lovely wife, Charlotte."

The man with him was reaching for Jeremiah's hand. Grant said, "Jeremiah, this is General Longstreet."

Longstreet asked, "Would that be Major Jeremiah Turner of Colonel Mosby's Rangers?"

Jeremiah said, "Yes Sir. It is an honor to meet you."

Longstreet said, "The honor is mine, sir." He then reached for my hand, kissed it lightly, bowed his head and said, "It is also my honor to meet your lovely wife."

I said, "Thank you Sir. I am very pleased to meet you."

Longstreet, still holding my hand, turned to Jeremiah and asked, "Is your brother, 1st Lieutenant Charley Turner, here? I would like to meet him as well. I received many reports praising the two of you."

President Grant cleared his throat, as he looked to see that Julia was far enough away as not to hear, then he said, "Pete... you are holding the hand of 1st Lieutenant Charley Turner."

I smiled.

Longstreet looked a bit surprised and said, "Did Colonel Mosby know? He had to know. It would be an insult to the Colonel's intelligence for one to think, he could look at a lady as beautiful as you, and think for a second you were a boy."

I replied in my sweet, southern voice, "Why thank you General Longstreet, but I haven't the faintest idea as to what Colonel Mosby knows."

He grinned and said, "It's an honor to meet you, 1st Lieutenant Charley Turner."

I said, "It's an honor to meet you as well, Sir."

President Grant said, "Be careful Pete, charm is her strongest weapon, followed by the Yankee revolvers she is still inclined to carry in her boots."

General Longstreet smiled as he said, "I will be on guard against these weapons, Sir."

President Grant shook Jeremiah's hand and said, "I'm pleased the two of you could be here tonight. I am President due to the hard work of you two, Pete here, and many others just like you."

He then took my hand and bowed his head just a bit and said, "I will dance the first dance with my dear Julia, will you be my second dance, and I hope my last, as I have never cared much for music, nor dancing?"

I smiled and in my sweet, southern, most charming way, said, "Why yes, Mr. President, I do believe I would enjoy dancing with you." I looked at Jeremiah and smiled.

Grant said, "Ms. Charlotte, that look and smile leads me to think you are aware that I cannot dance."

Jeremiah, laughed and said, "No Sir, that look and smile was about the day a long time ago when I told her you were an old man that couldn't help a lady into a carriage. She told me she would tell you what I said, when she danced with you at an inaugural ball."

Grant asked, "So you thought way back then, that we would remain friends and dance at an inaugural ball?"

I said, "Yes Sir, I knew you are as loyal to your friends as we are to ours. The ball was just a girl's fantasy."

Grant nodded and said, "Yes, you can never have too many friends."

General Longstreet leaned over and asked only loud enough for me and Jeremiah to hear, "Ms. Charlotte, may I have the dance after the President, as I have never danced with a 1st Lieutenant?"

I said, "Yes General, I believe dancing with my husband, a Major with Mosby's Rangers, a President, and a General, should round out the evening quite well."

President Grant and Julia danced the first dance. A waltz. They were beautiful, he in his black tailcoat, she in her lovely jeweled gown.

Jeremiah held his hand out and whispered in my ear, "Ms. Charley, may I have this dance?"

I smiled as I said, "Why Mr. Jeremiah, I'd love to, as I know how all the girls just swoon over you rangers, it would certainly be my pleasure."

He took me in his strong arms and we danced. I love being in his arms. Never do I feel more like a lady than when he is holding me. The night felt magical.

When the dance ended, President Grant came over, held out his hand and asked, "Ms. Charlotte, may I have this dance?"

I smiled and said, "Why yes, Mr. President, I'd be delighted."

He took me in his arms as we started to dance a waltz. Jeremiah asked Julia to dance. They were right beside us.

Grant said, "Charlotte, you look lovely."

I said, "Thank you Mr. President. You look quite dashing." I think I saw a slight twinkle in his blue eyes.

He said, "There's something different about you. You are exceptionally beautiful tonight."

I blushed as I said, "Why Mr. President, I think it's just the magic of the evening, but I do thank you for the compliment."

He stopped dancing and said, "I know what's different."

Jeremiah and Julia also stopped dancing, as they thought something was wrong. President Grant held my hands and stepped back, as to look at me. He smiled and said, "I have been blessed to see my beautiful Julia with this same radiance, four separate times in our lives."

Jeremiah grabbed my hands from the President and asked, "Charlotte are you really?""

I said, "Why yes, Mr. Jeremiah, I do believe I am!"

Bibliography

State Library of North Carolina.
Governor's Letter Book: reply by Governor Ellis to request by the United States Secretary of War for troops from North Carolina, April 14, 1861.

The Gray Ghost
Memoirs of Colonel John S. Mosby.
Little, Brown, and Company. 1917

Personal Memoirs of U.S. Grant.
New York: Charles L. Webster & Company, 1885-1886
ISBN 0-914427-67-9

University Library at the University of North Carolina at Chapel Hill.
Documenting the South.
DocSouth.unc.edu

University of North Carolina at Greensboro.
UNCG Digital Collections
The Greensborough Patriot
libcdm1uncgedu

Friedens Lutheran Church
Gibsonville, North Carolina.
www.lutheransonline.com

Angel Matthews has spent most of her life in rural Guilford County. She is married, and has two sons. She has always had a love of learning, history, and telling a good story.

Charlotte Confederate Cavalry Soldier

39565740R00164

Made in the USA
Charleston, SC
10 March 2015